Chasing Beverly

by

ASHLYNN CUBBISON

Ashlynn Cubbison

FROM THE TINY ACORN...
GROWS THE MIGHTY OAK

This is a work of fiction. References to real people, events, establishments, organizations, or locales are intended only to provide a sense of authenticity and are used fictitiously. All other characters, and all incidents and dialogue are drawn from the author's imagination and are not to be construed as real.

Cover design by Damonza
Interior design by Debra Cranfield Kennedy

ISBN-13: 978-1-947392-54-0 (hardcover)
ISBN-13: 978-1-947392-53-3 (paperback)

For the girls and women
who don't feel smart enough,
struggle with self-doubt,
and battle negative self-talk.
You're my people, my tribe,
and I believe in you.

— 1 —

Three Years Ago

Beverly

I slide sweaty palms down the sides of my track shorts as I size up each of my competitors. Mere months ago, they were my heroes. To avoid the cameramen, I study my legs. They look inadequate compared to the long, sturdy machines attached to the bodies of Danielle Felix in lane three and Sammy Jenkins in lane five.

I'm four days shy of my eighteenth birthday, sandwiched between two Olympic gold medalists, and preparing to race for a spot in the 2016 Summer Olympics for the 400-meter event.

How did I even make it to the finals?

Hot bile floods my throat. As sweat drips from my brow, I hear a crazy woman shouting over the crowd.

"Breathe, baby! Breathe!"

Peeking over at the gate to the right of me, our eyes connect. I realize she's *my* crazy woman. With her huge smile and eyes blazing with pride, my mom always brings me comfort. My gaze slides from her encouraging face and lands on that of my boyfriend. Patrick's crooked smile has been the same since we were kids.

Just the sight of them, here by my side, reassures me. I gulp in a deep, cleansing breath and bow my head. This silences the deafening noise, and it helps me to forget my shortcomings.

"On your marks!" a stern voice—the voice I've been listening for—bellows over the loudspeaker.

I step in front of my tightly spaced starting blocks, jumping one last time into the air to activate my muscles. Then I crawl backwards into the blocks, my left foot positioned in the back. As I slide my feet in, a smirk creeps across my lips. I picture Coach Schwarz in the stands, scolding me like he does before every race.

"Morgan, switch your damn feet, and space out your blocks more!"

My left knee digs into the rubbery Tartan Track. I focus on the connection of my damp skin against the hot track below. I say a silent prayer, thanking it for supporting my feet and body race after race.

Then, one last breath. I position my fingers behind the white line and await my next command.

"Set!" booms the Starter's robotic voice over the loudspeaker.

My hips shoot straight up. Fire replaces my blood, surging through my veins.

BANG!

The starting gun reverberates through me.

I push out of the blocks, careful not to go out too hard in the first 200 meters. Keeping my eyes glued straight ahead, I don't allow my opponents to bait me. Instead, I wait for my time. I stick close to the pack until I see my sweet spot ahead.

"Kick. Kick. Kick." The words play like a mantra in my head as I round the second curve of the track. My body is weightless. My brain needs no prompting as it propels my legs forward.

My feet become lighter, and my spikes barely touch the track before shooting forward for my next stride.

My arms pump harder as I enter my part of the race. The part in which I shine, the part I relish. The finish line is just ahead. Movement on my right enters my peripheral vision. I feel Sammy closing in. She's right on my tail.

My lungs burn, yet I continue to push harder, determination shooting me forward. With a quick forward lean of my body, I cross the white finish line. Cheering engulfs the stadium and pierces my ears. But with my burning lungs and shaking legs, I only make it a few yards past the finish line before I collapse onto the track.

Did I do it?

Most of my opponents have toppled over. Two approach me, pat my back and congratulate me as chaotic cheering ensues around the track.

Then I hear it.

The announcer shouts over the loudspeaker, "Seventeen-year-old Beverly Morgan just broke the world record in the 400! Can you believe it? She's number one in the world! What a performance the young Miss Morgan showed us here today! She just rewrote history!"

I can't believe I've done it. We've done it. Together, Mom and I are going to the Olympics!

A combination of sweat and tears drench my face. I'm unsure where to go or what to say. But I peel myself off the track and make my way toward the stands. A small crowd of reporters closes in on me. Their proximity makes me feel hot, and I start gasping for air. My heart pulses in my ears as they hurl questions at me from every direction.

Then before I see her, I hear her.

"Excuse me! Excuse me! Move, people. That's my daughter!"

Delirious laughter bursts out of me as my beautiful mom emerges from the crowd, chestnut curls bouncing and tears glistening in her warm brown eyes. She wraps loving arms around me. With one hand stroking my hair, she repeats in my ear, "You did it, baby. You're going to the Olympics!"

—

"BEVERLY, SLOW DOWN," my boyfriend Patrick moans from the back seat of my reliable blue Jetta as we head into the harsh glare of the setting sun toward our hotel.

I arch my left eyebrow, then glare at Patrick's worried green eyes in my rearview mirror. "I'm going the speed limit." I press more firmly on the accelerator.

"Honey, are you sure you don't want Patrick or me to drive?" Mom starts in.

I change lanes, weaving through traffic to dart around an elderly driver, who shouldn't be allowed on the freeway. My adrenaline, still charging from the race, is morphing into panic.

Did my running career just peak at seventeen?

"There're a lot of extra cars on the road for the holiday weekend," Mom says.

My back straightens, and I pinch my lips together as my boyfriend and mother continue to negotiate with me like I'm a child who needs a nap. One panicked outburst in the middle of my burrito at dinner, and they're acting as if I've lost all reason.

As I prepare to school them on how I'm a teenage girl and it's socially acceptable for my emotions to be unstable from time to time, tires screech.

Cars in front of me swerve in different directions. Mom's primal scream assaults my ears.

"Beverly, look out!" Patrick shouts.

My muscles seize. I grip the steering wheel tighter at the sight of a red pickup truck heading directly at us.

I jerk the steering wheel to the left. I hear a loud cracking sound, then feel a violent jolt from my car clipping someone in the next lane.

I try to correct my wheel, but I pull too hard. My car is out of control. We're skidding sideways on the four-lane freeway. No matter how hard I slam on the brakes, our momentum keeps us screeching forward.

My mom's arm shoots across the car and covers my chest. All at once, Patrick and Mom scream. The pickup truck plows into the passenger side of my car.

My head slams into the driver-side window. Glass crunches into my skull. Two detonations, louder than bombs, sound as the airbags explode.

The pain shooting through my head, the metallic taste of blood on my tongue, and the stinging on my arms where the airbag hit, is nothing compared to the burning fear that's racing through my body. I try to shout for help, but my ears are ringing and I can't hear. With shaking, sticky hands, I shove at the airbag, streaking it with blood.

After pushing aside the deflating airbag, I see my mom. She's covered in fragments of glass and talcum powder, her hair matted with blood. It covers her face.

"Mom!" I pant, my entire body rigid, even the hairs on my arms are erect. "Mom, are you okay?"

No movement. No sound. Nothing.

"Mom?" I reach for her, but my seat belt locks tight against my chest, caging me in. My legs tremble. I gasp for air. My nose burns hot with the smell of rubber and gasoline.

Is this real?

I hear a moan from somewhere behind me.

Oh my God, Patrick!

"Patrick?" My boyfriend since freshman year, the person who freezes Dixie cups full of water at his house for me to ice my shins after practice, and the only boy I've ever loved, doesn't respond.

"Patrick, are you okay?"

I recall his concerned emerald green eyes from just moments ago. The way he always knows the right thing to say when I've fought with my dad. His caring hands, and the way they cradled mine earlier at dinner when I felt overwhelmed.

I struggle to unbuckle my seatbelt. It's jammed into my body. I can't break free.

I need to see him!

"Please!" I sob. "Talk to me!"

"Help!" I scream in desperation. My eyelids start to feel heavy and little black spots dance in front of me. Through my sobs, I hear sirens wailing just as all of my muscles go slack.

Help is coming.

— 2 —

Beverly

Steel-gray clouds stack in the shadowed morning sky. I hug myself for warmth as the damp air causes chill bumps on my arms. The gathering storm above reflects my inner turmoil. I have a potentially career-changing meeting in two hours, and this has already been one of the roughest mornings since that fateful day more than three years ago.

My eyes sting from lack of sleep. I've lost count of how many hours I've stood on my hotel balcony and stared out at the Pacific Ocean. My throat is so tight, I'm barely able to force down a few sips of coffee.

My friend and Chief Procurement Officer, Aubrey, received terrible news last night. Her dad suffered a stroke and was hospitalized. Seeing my level-headed friend frantic and in tears triggered anxieties in me I thought long buried. Understanding her need to bolt home to Portland and be with her family, I booked a flight for her and our assistant, Melonie, and rushed them to San Diego International Airport. Until I return to the office next week, Melonie needs to run things for Aubrey.

Now they're gone, and I have to take over the only meeting

· 11 ·

I've ever wanted to avoid. Aubrey is the one who was prepared for today; she knows how to pitch our company and us. Now, it's up to me. How will I convince Gavin Reed, owner of the number-one Hybrid Sports Management and PR company on the West Coast, to take a chance on my Sports Modeling Agency? Though, that's the least of my problems. It goes so much deeper than that.

I've admired Gavin Reed from afar for the past year. When I meet him, I'll need to pretend I haven't been tracking his career like a twelve-year-old fan-girl follows her favorite boy band.

Gavin and I work in the sports promotion industry. My fascination with him started last summer after a night out with the girls. They gushed about the young and successful business-man's undeniable good looks and kind heart. After they dropped me off at home, I Googled him for hours.

I read article after article, mostly boring, but one stood out about his mentorship of children without fathers. I stared at dozens—okay, maybe hundreds—of photos of him. He's twenty-seven years old. Probably around six feet tall. His dark wavy hair, square jawline, and deep blue eyes make him nearly irresistible.

Gavin Reed, owner of Reed Management, Inc., was commissioned to head a massive advertising campaign for Nike, which focuses on empowering women to fight for equal rights in the sports world. That's where I come in. Reed Management only represents a handful of female athletes, so he needs fitness models. From what I've heard, if he does well, they'll use his services for part of their Olympic campaigns, as well.

My scalp prickles and chest tightens at the thought of taking on a project related to my biggest failure. I'm also secretly terrified of working closely with a guy I can't get out of my head. If Gavin

Reed's as good as I've built him up to be, I'll need to reinforce the barriers around my damaged heart. If I fail, I'm positive love will be my downfall.

The people I love the hardest die. It sounds crazy, but it's true. The only way to protect myself and anyone special is to freeze them out.

But this job could advance my company and position us to help more women, so here I am. I must ignore my trepidation. Mom would want this. This is her dream, and securing this contract will help me fulfill it. My mother is worth the risk.

— 3 —

Beverly

My phone pings from the bohemian-style cushioned chair on the hotel balcony, jolting my already ragged nerves.

Get a grip, Beverly.

Snatching up my phone, Aubrey's name runs across the screen. I fumble to unlock it. The lump in my throat grows, making it difficult to swallow.

> Aubrey: I'm at the hospital. No new info yet.
> Just wanted to tell you, don't stress over the
> meeting. Remember Gavin has a great
> reputation. His company sought you out. Just
> breathe and remember why you're doing this.

My throat relaxes slightly. I slump down onto the comfy chair, relieved not to read bad news about her dad. I'll never be able to understand how she always does that, how she's able to still have room in her heart to worry about me.

I reread her text. It's enough to push me forward. I step

inside the oversized suite Aubrey insisted on booking for me, and I head for the shower.

—

OUTSIDE OF REED Management, Inc. the sky rumbles above me. As I tilt my head up to take in the high-rise, a chill shoots down my spine. Today's the day I find out if everything I've heard about Gavin Reed is true, and if he's as handsome as the pictures I've seen.

I shake my head, hoping to boot his image from my mind's eye. When the clouds start opening up and a few drops of rain fall on my face, I dart into the building. As much as I love rain, I prefer not to look like a drowned rat at our meeting.

Yanking open the door, a burst of dry, heated air assaults my face. Once inside, an older gentleman with salt and pepper hair and dark brown skin behind a large circular desk stands to greet me.

"Good morning, Miss. Do you have an appointment this morning?" he asks with a bright smile that reaches his deep brown eyes.

"Morning. Beverly Morgan for a 9 a.m. with Gavin Reed." I tug off my peacoat, thankful I'm wearing a loose-fitting blouse underneath.

"You don't need that coat, do you?"

I glance at the gentleman's name tag. "No, I don't, Mr. Sosa. I probably shouldn't be surprised the heat is cranked up so high. If it dips below sixty-five degrees in Southern California, everyone is in Ugg boots and has their parka zipped up to their eyeballs."

He chuckles. "Sometimes I wait by the door just so I can open it for visitors and get a fresh gust of that cool San Diego

air." He shakes his head. "Now, let's get you where you need to be, Miss."

He walks out from behind his desk and points down the hall to a second set of elevators. "Press the button closest to the wall. The elevator on the right will open. Once inside, press 'R' and it'll take you to Mr. Reed's assistant, Miss Jennifer Nash. Have a good day, Miss . . ."

"Beverly. Just Beverly." I smile at the man whose kindness manages to help me forget to feel nervous. Then, I march to the elevator, which may lead me to one of the biggest moments of my career.

Once inside I discover the only floor listed is "R". I press the button. The doors immediately shut, whisking me upward. When the doors glide open, I'm welcomed by Jenny's bright blue eyes and a smile that showcases each shiny white tooth in her mouth.

"Good morning, Miss Morgan!"

"Morning, Jenny. And how many times do I need to tell you, please call me Beverly."

Jennifer Nash and I know each other. Close friends with Aubrey since childhood, she flies to Portland a few times a year to visit her family and Aubrey. We've gone out to dinner, had drinks at multiple pubs, even gone fishing together. She and Aubrey have urged me to work with Gavin Reed for over a year now.

"Right. Sorry, Beverly. Mr. Reed isn't ready for you just yet, but please let me show you to the waiting room." She pivots on her pointed black heels.

I follow her, admiring her shiny golden hair.

She guides me into a spacious room. Jenny pauses beside a large, glass table. "Please help yourself. You'll find donuts, bagels,

and fruit in the fridge and fresh coffee in the pot." She points to the coffeemaker atop the counter in the kitchenette.

"Thank you." My mouth waters at the earthy coffee aroma filling the room.

"Of course. Mr. Reed had a few unexpected things pop up, and he's running a little behind schedule. I'll come for you as soon as he's ready."

Strike one. He's running late on our first meeting.

"Thanks, Jenny."

She turns, leaving me in this cold, sterile room.

A loud grumble sounds deep in my stomach. I answer its demand, slip a glazed donut out of the box and pour myself a cup of steaming coffee. Treats in hand, I settle onto the hard, black couch, which faces large plate glass windows. I am grateful my throat has loosened enough to eat.

I watch the swirling rain outside, and I realize not even the blasting heater could make this room warm. The only warmth is the coffee I'm clutching in my right hand. I regret not cancelling this meeting and going home with Aubrey.

Everyone would understand. They'd assume the possibility of working closely with the Olympics would be too painful for me. Everyone except Aubrey. She alone knows why I started this company, and she'd probe for more details. I would never admit I'm afraid of meeting Gavin, because if he isn't as amazing as everyone's said, and as I've imagined, then in some unhealthy way it feels like losing someone again.

I close my eyes, and emerald green eyes— the same eyes that have haunted me since that day— flash in my head. I sit up straighter, uncomfortable with where my mind wandered.

Call Stan! the sensible voice in my head yells.

I place my half-eaten donut and coffee on the sleek glass coffee

table in front of me. I pull my phone from my purse, adding a note to call Stan, my therapist, to schedule an appointment.

I reclaim my coffee, downing the last of the energizing liquid. As the wait drags on, my right leg starts bouncing to an erratic rhythm. I try to focus on the storm outside to calm my nerves, which are quickly morphing from anxiety into annoyance. I hate when people are late.

After another fifteen minutes, Jenny steps into the room. "Miss Morgan, we're ready for you."

This time I don't bother correcting her. If she wants to keep our relationship strictly professional, so be it. I gather my things and join her, expecting to follow her to Mr. Reed's office.

Instead, she pauses and bites her bottom lip. "I feel obligated to warn you. Mr. Reed is a bit out of sorts today." She clears her throat. "I've actually never seen him so disagreeable."

"Okay, thanks for the heads-up."

He's about to be a hell of a lot more disagreeable after making me wait thirty minutes beyond our scheduled appointment time.

— 4 —

Gavin

I slam my phone down on my desk, satisfied by the loud crack sounding on the wood. Cupping my throbbing head in my hands, I try to figure out how things got so bad.

Last night was a real-life nightmare. My stalker ex-girlfriend broke into my garage and took a baseball bat to my prized 1967 Ford Mustang Fastback Shelby GT500 Tribute. That car was everything to me. My grandfather, who helped my mom to raise me, spent his final years fixing it up with me.

I rake my fingers through my hair, thinking about the options the police officer on the phone provided. As uncomfortable as it would be to file charges against Peyton, because I know it will affect her career and it's likely the media will get hold of the story, consequences are necessary this time. Between her frequent phone calls to my mom, her constant threats to sell stories about me to the media, and now this, she must be stopped before her violence increases.

Why now? Unfortunately, I have no time to figure this out. Instead, I have to pretend to be the put-together CEO and interview some small modeling agency I know little about. I'm

lucky I even made it into the office. Though, I am unshaved and starving. I didn't even have time to sneak into the waiting room to grab breakfast. The CEO of Hope Modeling Agency is already in there. Clenching my jaw, I stand, pour a glass of water, and pop the lid off an ibuprofen bottle.

"Mr. Reed . . ."

Shit. I jump at the sound of Jenny's voice behind me. Pills scatter across the flat-polished concrete floor, which makes my office look part jail cell.

Is she training to be a ninja? What happened to knocking first?

"I'm so sorry. Here let me help." Jenny rushes to my side, prepared to crawl on the floor in her perfectly pressed, gray pants suit.

I toss the empty bottle into the trash. "Just leave it, Jenny." I ram my fingers through my overgrown wavy hair, fully aware I must resemble an alpaca in need of a haircut.

"Are you sure, sir?"

I pinch my eyes closed and remind myself that Jenny's done nothing wrong. "I'm sure," I push out through clenched teeth.

"Okay." Her voice is level, but her furrowed brows display her confusion at my foul mood. She straightens and squares her shoulders. I imagine her calling me an asshole in her head.

"Mr. Reed, this is Beverly Morgan." She turns and gestures to a petite woman with dark brown hair piled neatly in a bun atop her head. I'm drawn into her beautiful honey brown eyes. Beverly Morgan scans my appearance, her gaze finally resting on my ruffled hair. Judgment flashes across her features, her delicate left eyebrow twitching her disapproval.

I ignore her displeasure. Instead, I step forward and take a closer look at her. She's impeccable, not even an eyelash out of

place. A stark contrast to my current state. Her pink blouse is tucked neatly into her fitted black slacks. I don't trust people who look perfect.

What secrets are you hiding, Beverly?

I assess her a bit longer, ticking off all of the reasons I shouldn't be attracted to her. She isn't tall, blonde, or light eyed. She is nothing like the women I usually find attractive. And yet, she's beautiful.

I thrust out my hand, forcing my gaze to remain on her face even though I want to closely inspect the rest of her. "Nice to meet you, Miss Morgan." My voice sounds lower than usual. I clear my throat.

"Nice to meet you, too." She grips my hand.

As our palms meet, my lips part. I draw in a deep breath. My body fills with an odd tension I've never felt before.

Her eyes fall to my mouth. When she struggles to hide a smile, my excitement evaporates. I yank my hand free and straighten my tie. I doubt this young woman has a single worry in her life.

"Jenny, bring in the clothes rack," I command, eager to conclude this meeting.

Jenny shoots me a look, but she says nothing. She stalks out of my office to retrieve the clothes, no doubt annoyed with my lack of manners.

Where is Beverly's model? I step back to my desk, shuffling through a stack of folders as I search for my meeting notes. Then I remember they're still sitting atop my kitchen island. *Looks like I'm winging it today.*

I glance at Beverly. Her left eyebrow is still twitching. Other than that, nothing is different in her perfect professional presentation. Why do I feel inadequate in my own office?

I'm certain Beverly's already concluded I'm a jerk, and the last thing I need to do today is to find her attractive. Her standoff personality works for my purposes. Otherwise, I would probably do something stupid.

I bite the inside of my cheek. Miss Morgan and I remain frozen in a staring contest for a long moment. But I lose when my gaze dips down to her plump lips.

Damn that one condition, which requires me to use athletic models in all of the ads for this project. Today would've been much easier if I could've used our regular agency, Santoro Models. But Evelyn, my COO, insists Hope Modeling Agency is the next big thing for fitness models since retired Olympians are flocking into their office.

Evelyn's exact words when I agreed to collaborate with Hope Modeling were, "It's about damn time. You'll wind up with quality advertising that features healthy women, not starving sticks with big tits!"

I glance at my watch. "Have a seat." I gesture to the chair in front of my desk as I settle into the chair behind my desk.

Beverly hovers near the chair across from me. Her expression remains blank, not a speck of emotion evident. I can't tell if she's refusing to sit or if she's lost in thought. Reading people is normally in my wheelhouse, but I don't have a clue about what this woman is feeling or thinking. It doesn't help that she's practically mute.

I rub the back of my neck with one hand and open my mouth to speak just as Jenny pushes through the door. She drags the rolling rack of clothes, overflowing with red, white and blue sports uniforms, after her.

Beverly stiffens at the sight of Jenny and the clothes. She clenches her hands at her side. Jenny offers her a concerned look.

I'm missing something important, but what?

Beverly looks away. She slides back into professional mode, attempting to hide whatever transpired seconds ago.

"Do you need anything else, Mr. Reed?" Jenny asks.

"No, Jenny."

I look at the rack of clothes and choose the outfit placed at the front. "We can start with the track uniform." I sound irritated.

Beverly slowly turns to look at me. Her perfect eyebrows bunch and her lips press together.

"Is there a problem?" I ask.

"What exactly do you expect me to do with it?"

My eyes narrow. "Are your models here yet?" With one quick swoop, I scan the length of her body. She looks like an athlete, maybe a little short, but she could pull it off. Too bad she's not today's model.

When my gaze returns to her face, I regret my visual inspection. She looks arrogant again, so I brace myself for whatever's coming my way.

"The meeting instructions provided to me and my staff only requested my portfolio. Which was sent to you over three weeks ago, Mr. Reed. We weren't advised to bring any models. The detailed email your team provided stated we'd review terms today."

If last night had unfolded differently, I'd have reviewed the meeting outline my staff creates for every appointment. I shove papers around on my desk until I locate my monthly calendar. My office might be a train wreck this morning, but I find exactly what I'm looking for. "Then why do I have *two* people noted on my schedule for our meeting?"

She narrows her eyes at me. "I spoke with Jenny this morning. I explained that Aubrey, my CPO, had a family emergency, she

was going to be accompanied by our assistant. Fortunately, I was already in town and able to handle her appointment with you."Wait a minute. Who the hell set up this meeting? Why wasn't Beverly Morgan's presence a given? I fold my hands atop my desk, steadying myself so as not to sound harsh.

"Why wasn't *this* appointment important enough for you to show up? *Do you even want to do this project?*" All right, I failed to keep my irritation in check, but this campaign is the biggest of my career. I don't want or need a weak partner on my team.

Her eyes widen and she shifts her feet ever so slightly. I'm satisfied knowing I've hit a nerve and made her squirm.

"I had scheduling conflicts."

Lame, I think. "Yet, here you are. So, how do you expect to negotiate without showing me what I'm hiring?" I ask.

"If the instructions provided to me from your company were wrong, who's to blame for that?" She glares at me as she finishes speaking.

— 5 —

Beverly

I stare into Gavin Reed's deep blue eyes, which appear unaffected by my attitude to his annoying questions. The donut from earlier churns in my belly.

This handsome, passive-aggressive prick knows about me. He knows about my past, and just like every other jerk, he's baiting me. I shouldn't be surprised he knows, but I expected him to be different.

Even so, dialing down the attitude right now is a smart decision. I'm the little company in this room, and he's the one holding the power and my future. He can help me fulfill *her* dream and attain the redemption I've needed for so long. The redemption I need for Mom, Patrick, and myself.

Gavin pushes away from his desk, his chair scraping against the ugly concrete floor. He stalks toward me and positions himself in front of me, his six-foot, three-inch frame towering over me.

At first, I think he's trying to intimidate me. I experience the primitive urge to kick him in his shins. I hesitate, though. His eyes are soft, and the tension in my shoulders loosens.

"Look, Miss Morgan, I'm very interested in working with your agency on this project. We've heard great things about your company, and we believe your business is the positive change to an industry that's quickly cheapening itself. Our goal is to appeal and relate to women worldwide. We want more women watching the Olympics, more little girls dreaming about being a professional athlete, and our top priority is to get more girls and women active in sports. The long-term vision is for there to be demand and acceptance for professional women athletes making a living doing what they love and what they're great at, the same as male athletes.

"I don't know where this meeting went wrong. But I think it's best if we take a look at the uniforms, costumes, whatever you want to call them, and then let's regroup and meet for dinner tonight. It'll give us both time to gather our thoughts and negotiate in a clear-headed manner."

—

MY HEAD IS SPINNING, my stomach is doing some stupid bubbly thing, and my legs feel unsteady. Once I'm in the refuge of my rental car, I rest my head on the headrest, close my eyes, and try to figure out how the heck to feel.

At the beginning of the meeting, Gavin Reed was a complete jerk. He was late, disheveled and rude. Not to mention he checked me out more than once.

But then he became professional, polite, and even complimented my business. He seemed like the person Aubrey and Jenny bragged about, and more like the man who fascinated me. I thought my infatuation with him was just a game. A safe way for me to feel something akin to romance without actually allowing myself to be loved.

My body is rebelling against common sense. I feel an attraction so strong, it makes me want to pack my bags and head home to Portland. I worked to create a protective shield after what happened *that* day over three years ago. Every breath I take reminds me that love can disappear in the blink of an eye, and if you let a man in deep, love will bury you. Even more importantly, I know after what I did, I don't deserve love again.

I take a few steadying breaths, my legs stop trembling and I regain some of my composure. I can't drive yet, so I check my phone to kill some time. I tell myself I'm just exhausted. I should know better than to lie to myself. After all, I'm my father's daughter, and checking out from reality is nowhere in our DNA.

I'm not ready to interpret that meeting, yet. So, I go over my messages. The first text is from Aubrey.

> Aubrey: Still at the hospital. Dad isn't looking good. The doctor said the prognosis is good, but it'll take time to heal and a lot of physical therapy to walk again. How was the meeting?

I type out a quick response, not because I'm rushed or don't care that she's been through hell today, but because that's who I am. At least, it's who I've become—no longer a person to offer hope, no longer a person to promise things I can't guarantee, and no longer a person loaded with false optimism. Thankfully, this is the woman Aubrey met. Somehow, she likes and accepts me.

> Me: Thanks for the update, Bre. As soon as I get home, I'll come and visit. Meeting was fine.

There's also a text message from my dad, asking me to come

by today before one. I grew up in San Diego. Visiting Dad is a great distraction. It will snap me back into reality, back into the detached and collected Beverly who's gotten me through life since the accident.

My dad lives in Carlsbad, a forty-minute drive north of downtown San Diego. I send him a quick text, letting him know I'm on my way. But before I turn the key in the ignition, my phone rings with an incoming call. Aubrey. I let her go to voicemail. I need to get my friend, Nell, on the phone and schedule her to join us for dinner tonight before I end up dining alone with Gavin Reed.

Nell answers on the second ring. Thanks to her exotic good looks—a unique multiracial mix of African American, Irish and Spanish—I was able to hire her as one of my models a few years earlier. I can picture her pretty face, smiling from ear to ear, and her long black hair swaying as she glides around her downtown living room and talks to me. "How'd it go?" Excitement flows from each word.

"Hey. It went well. I hope you're free for dinner tonight. We're meeting Gavin Reed at Aura restaurant at six." I'm relieved to hear my voice has regained that monotone indifference I usually carry off so well.

"Hell yeah, I'm free! He's so hot, and I can't wait to meet him." Her excitement almost makes me feel guilty for using her as a human shield—a beautiful, sexy, and flirtatious human shield. "Did he ask to meet a model? Oh my gosh, did he ask for me?"

"Not exactly. He wants to meet so we can go over the particulars. He's going to bring the draft contract for me to review. He didn't seem prepared for our meeting, and he expected a model this morning. He made a fuss, so I think

it's best if you join us. Plus, I don't want him to finalize the contract without meeting you. I doubt he even reviewed our portfolio."

All of that was true. Besides, he should meet a model before signing on with us. Poor judgment on my part. Nell is a former competitive volleyball player. She's perfect for this project. And the ideal woman to keep Gavin Reed's attention off me.

I can hear Nell's breathy excitement as she exhales. "Good thinking, sis, and you know I'll slay it. I gotta go clothes shopping. Do you want me to meet you in your hotel lobby or at the restaurant?" She sounds like a giddy teenager preparing for prom.

"Five-fifteen at my hotel. Enjoy shopping. I'll see you later." Growing up we would often fantasize about living downtown together someday. Dreams change, people change. Although in our case, Nell is almost the same. I'm the one who did all the changing.

Closing my eyes, I hang my head. A pit expands in my belly. I grip the steering wheel. Is this a new low for me, dragging Nell to dinner, knowing she's interested in Gavin Reed, knowing that I'm using her to deflect his attention? I've done this before. Many times. Why do I need backup and a distraction?

Because you're attracted to him, a rogue voice whispers in my head as it nudges me to act on my feelings. I push aside the thought. I so wish I could dispatch an army of women into my head, to locate that stray voice and imprison it for speaking out of turn.

God, I hope this works. No, it will work. Nell's caramel colored skin and mesmerizing hazel eyes draw attention everywhere we go. To top off her looks, she's a fun, lovable, and friendly extrovert. Most men instantly fall in love with her.

The thought of Reed and Nell in love might drive me to drink and to consume an unhealthy amount of chocolate—the best alternative for all parties. I feel steady enough to ease out of my parking space and drive forty minutes up the coast to Carlsbad. I don't make it out to the main road before my phone rings again. My office.

"This is Beverly," I say over the rental car's Bluetooth. I check my mirrors and grip the steering wheel tighter.

"Hi, Miss Morgan, it's Andrew."

He's the temporary assistant subbing for Melonie, who is taking over Aubrey's current duties. "Hey, Andrew, what's going on?"

"A woman named Peyton Hollis has called the office several times this morning. She says it's urgent that she speaks with you."

I roll my eyes. Melonie would never bother me with something like this. I ask Andrew a few questions, then instruct him to email me the woman's contact information and a brief description of her needs. I end the call and try to enjoy the drive up the coast.

I can't get the mystery woman out of my head, though. Why would she repeatedly call my office? Did one of our models piss her off?

— 6 —

Beverly

It's the typical scene when I pull into Dad's long driveway. I see him puttering around in his perfectly maintained garage, his dirty-blonde hair combed neatly.

Remembering Aubrey's voicemail, I check my phone before climbing out of the car.

She wants additional details on the meeting with Reed. I toss my iPhone into my Kate Spade purse. Aubrey can wait. I don't need her scrutiny right now.

Looking up, I see Dad standing beside my car. I step out, and he draws me into a bear hug and kisses my forehead. "Sweetie, you look beautiful."

"Hi, Dad," I respond as I hug him back, inhaling the comforting scent of his spiced cologne. It's one of the few things I can still enjoy without sadness tainting it.

Since I moved to Portland shortly after the accident, I don't see Dad very often. He travels all over the country as a private investigator, and I've thrown myself into my work. Neither one of us comes up for air very often. Staying busy is the coping mechanism we share.

"Afraid I've got some bad news. I have to be gone this weekend. I got a lead today on that fourteen-year-old girl who went missing five months ago." He pauses, which is one of the investigator things he does. Slow-talking and long awkward pauses allow him to observe other people's reactions.

I stay quiet and maintain eye contact, so he continues. "I have to hop on a plane tonight for Arizona. I know we had plans for Saturday, but I don't think I'll be back in time. I'm sorry, sweetie." His unwavering stare usually is enough to make people squirm, but I mastered standing my ground with him as a teenager when I lied about dating Patrick.

"It's okay, Dad. I understand, and I hope you find her. I wish I could take you to the airport, but I've got a six o'clock meeting tonight."

Internally I breathe a sigh of relief. I love him. I really do. But whenever I see him, he brings up the past, and that's not something I want to delve into. Especially not right now.

"Not a problem. Your brother's driving me. You two should still spend some time together. He misses you a lot, kid. You have your mom's heart, you know. I think it brings him comfort."

My chest constricts at his mention of Mom. It takes extreme concentration to remain impassive. I know he's watching my reaction. He continuously observes, his way of gauging the amount of screwed up I am.

Over the years I've gotten better at fooling him. Still, I hate that he's trained to read people. Give him a few more minutes, and he'll ask if I'm still in therapy.

"Of course, we'll see each other. I'll call him later today." I avoid responding to his other comment and try to throw him off course. "Can you spare a few minutes to grab some ice cream with your daughter?"

Distraction and avoidance are what keeps me sane when I'm around anyone who knew Beverly 2.0, the old me. My life went into a ditch, and I was demoted in software. And it didn't go unnoticed by the users—aka my friends and family.

"I was afraid you'd never ask." His aging face lights up, and I welcome the warmth of his reassuring smile. "I would say let's take the bikes, but I don't think you can ride in those things." He points to my high heels.

"I have a change of clothes in the car. I'll grab them."

"That's my girl, always prepared." He flashes an adoring smile at me. There are three ways to Dad's heart. The first is ice cream, the second is always being prepared—as in having fire escape routes, carrying a pocketknife, keeping water in your trunk kind of prepared—and the third is baseball. Lucky for me, I'm proficient at two of the three. I'm working to redeem myself for number two, but it's impossible to repent for such a massive failure.

I head into Dad's unfamiliar house to change. He bought this place right around the time I moved away, and it still feels foreign to me. He and my brother didn't want to stay in the house where I grew up, the home with happy memories lurking in every corner, reminding us daily of the hole in our hearts and our family.

It no longer felt like a home to them without her there, and I understood their need to leave. At the same time, I was upset at Dad for selling it so quickly. It felt like all of my happiest memories—in essence, all of me—remained trapped inside those walls.

Nobody knows I visit the house every now and again. I sit outside in my car and let the memories wash over me like an incoming tide. And for just a few moments, I go back in time to the place where I once felt whole.

— 7 —

Beverly

Our bike ride to the local ice cream shop is refreshing. The rain clears. It's cool, but not Portland cool, and sunny. There aren't many things that give me a genuine smile anymore. So, I feel thankful my dad and I still enjoy this adventure together whenever I'm in town.

As we walk into the cool shop, the smell of sugar and waffle cones beckons me to the glass windows, which feature dozens of colorful flavors. Dad orders—Cookies-n-Cream for me and Rocky Road for him. After he pays, we head outside. I feel his eyes on me as I quickly devour my melting ice cream. He probes for any sign I'm still not well.

"What?" I demand. I can feel my eyebrows lift. The left one embarks on a twitching rampage. Anyone who knows me recognizes it as a sign of my annoyance.

"There's something different about you, kid."

Huh?

His response throws me. Not an easy thing to do. I'm normally prepared for every possible moment, question, or insult someone might throw at me. It involves reading people and

reading them well. My brother says it's an exhausting way to live. Maybe he's right, but over the years I've made a game out of it. And each time I'm right about a person or situation, I feel a little more secure in this volatile life.

"What do you mean?" I struggle to conceal my perplexity.

Dad scans my face for what feels like forever, then he shrugs his shoulders. "I can't put my finger on it, but something's different. Whatever you're doing, keep it up. You almost look like Beverly again."

A cold breeze kicks up. My hair, no longer secured in a bun, slaps me in the face. "That's good, since I am Beverly," I snap with more bite than I really feel.

"I'm not trying to upset you. I mean it in a good way. You've made yourself suffer for too long, so it's nice to see you looking a little less burdened. I love you and want you to be happy. She would want that too, you know."

The most frustrating thing is, he's right. I actually do feel different today. Even though I haven't slept in over twenty-four hours, my best friend's dad, whom I adore, is in the hospital, and my meeting this morning was a disaster, I've felt energized all day. No repetitive replays of the past in my head. I even feel a competitive thirst that used to course through me like blood in my veins.

My dad's still on me like a hawk, observing me, and I realize I haven't responded yet. "Love you, too, Dad." He smiles at me, then he shakes his head.

"What?" I ask, smiling back at him.

"Something really is different. You didn't even try to argue with me."

"Maybe I'm tired of arguing."

He chuckles. "If that's true, we better get you to the

doctor. You came out a fighter, my little wolf."

"Ha. Ha. Very funny." I wipe ice cream from the corners of my mouth in an attempt to hide the stupid grin still plastered across my face. It feels strange, yet so good to hear him call me by my old nickname. He used to tell me I'm like my spirit animal, clever, loyal, and a fierce protector.

I lick the last few layers of ice cream before crunching into the sugar cone. For the first time in years, our conversation flows without awkward pauses.

The clouds roll in from the ocean as we return to Dad's house. We ride single file in silence. I reflect upon my day as I follow him. A small piece of me feels repaired. Our conversation signals a turning point in our relationship, or in my "healing," as Stan, my therapist, would say. For the first time in years, I'm disappointed we won't be able to spend more time together this weekend.

Perhaps we can rebuild the relationship I destroyed. I know it's what Dad wants. He misses me. I realize I haven't only been punishing myself, I've punished him, too—this man who has already lost his everything, this father who has been nothing short of amazing to my brother and me.

My thoughts shift to Aubrey and her father. I need to check in with her again. I know he means the world to her, and she is frightened he'll take a turn for the worse and won't be able to walk her down the aisle in May.

With nothing left to focus on, I lose my willpower. My thoughts wander to Reed, whom I've tried to ignore. For some reason, I prefer to call him by his last name. Could be it suits him better. The more likely reason is it helps me to remain detached from him. Or maybe it's because we're both in the sports world and it comes naturally to me. No matter the

reason, I feel let down by the man I envisioned versus the real Gavin Reed.

His manners were sparse, his ego inflated, and his appearance despicable, yet—and I curse myself for admitting this—he's the sexiest man I've ever seen. Not even his crooked tie stained with toothpaste, wild hair, or half tucked shirt could hide his strong jawline, perfectly sculpted lips, and stunning blue eyes.

"Kid, you okay?"

Dad's voice cuts through my thoughts, the sensation like a bucket of Arctic ocean water being dumped on me. I realize I rode the last half of the way back to Dad's house on autopilot. I don't remember watching for cars when I crossed the street, or bumps in the road, or even pacing myself at a safe distance behind Dad. I think again of my therapist Stan. He would call my preoccupation living too much in my "mind's eye," not being present.

I need to make an appointment to see Stan.

Dad wastes no time hanging the bikes back on their racks; God forbid they spend any additional time out of their proper place. "So, I was thinking about coming up to Portland soon."

He nervously shuffles his feet. I didn't know anything or anyone could make him feel uneasy. Have I damaged our relationship so much, he thinks he wouldn't be welcome?

"I'd like that."

"Really?" He sounds surprised.

"Of course, Dad. You're always welcome to visit." I've secretly wished he would visit me more, but it's difficult for him to step foot in Portland, so I've never pushed the issue.

He engulfs me in a hug. "Today was nice, kid," he says as he kisses my forehead.

"It was." I chew on the inside of my cheek, savoring the sweet

yet unusual visit. "I better get going. Be safe in Arizona." I hug him once more before I head down the driveway to my car.

— 8 —

Gavin

Three hours ago Beverly left my office, left my head dizzy with thoughts and doubts, and left an odd ache in my gut. How can one hour with someone make me question my entire life's goals?

I am deflated yet energized, opposing emotions that make no sense when paired together. I'm a walking contradiction. My brain is exhausted, trying to process the shit show I caused this morning. My body tingles with an electricity I haven't ever felt before. I ache for a woman I shouldn't want.

I need to get my head on straight before our meeting tonight. I want her company to do this campaign with us, but I'm worried I might've screwed it up. Then again, maybe I didn't. Why would she agree to meet for dinner if she wasn't contemplating the job offer?

Rolling out my shoulders, I start in on the draft contract I need to fine-tune for Beverly. I usually leave this stuff for my staff, but not this time. Everything from here on out needs to be perfect.

I scowl when I hear a loud knock on my door. Before I can

get up, the door swings open. Evelyn, more of a second mom than a Chief Operations Officer, marches into my office. Her salt and pepper, springy corkscrew curls bounce with each step. Her cocoa-colored skin displays not a single laugh line or crow's-foot, despite being the same age as my mother.

"Boy, some mess you got yourself into this time." The ever-direct Evelyn jumps right into the issue at hand.

"How did you hear?" I haven't left my office since my appointment with Beverly. How could she know it was a disaster?

"I don't know what you're talking about, hun, but we'll circle back to it. I'm here to deal with the mess better known as your stalker ex-girlfriend. Peyton."

Of course, that's why she's here. She's ready to set me straight and lay down the law. "Right," is all I manage to say. That's fine, because Evelyn isn't someone I need to fish information out of when she has something to say.

"After Peyton left last night, did she contact you again?"

"Yes, she texted me. I ignored her."

"Damn. I thought I got through to her last night. I didn't want to play the bad guy, because sometimes that will only fuel someone's crazy." She huffs. "Sounds like the whole caring mother act didn't work, in any case. She's a lost young woman, Gavin, and she takes your rejection personally. Kinda like her parents rejecting her all over again."

"Then she needs therapy."

"I don't disagree, but I'm worried about what a woman with her kind of platform and ambition could do to you and your reputation."

My ex is a relatively successful TV actress, who got noticed through her booming Instagram account. She was an influencer.

I'm still kind of shocked people were influenced by a ditz who couldn't hold her own in any conversation. Although, I did ask her out when I first met her at that art gallery opening in La Jolla.

"You said she made threats. What did she say?"

"When I opened the door, she had a red mark on her face and said you hit her. She also claims you took the bat to your own car to frame her and keep her from going to the police."

"What?" I shoot straight out of my office chair. This is a low blow, even for Peyton. I don't hide my past, my father ended up in jail for beating my mom when I was a kid. "I only dated that psycho for three months. How could she become so attached?"

Evelyn raises her hand, and I realize I learned that gesture from her. Evelyn's been best friends with my mother since before I was born.

"Let me finish." Gracefully, she lowers herself into the chair across from me as I flop back down and try to collect myself.

"I invited her in and sat her down on my couch, placed my hand on hers, and gently told her I'm sorry her heart is hurting, but that simply wasn't true."

Peyton probably didn't anticipate that I tell Evelyn almost everything. Not only is she like a second mom to me, since Evelyn never had children, she thinks of me as her only son.

"The most devious smile spread across her pretty little face." Evelyn shivers. "And she said, 'But the media won't know that.'"

I rub my head, craving more Ibuprofen. "How did I miss this? She seemed so normal, and I'm usually really good at reading people." *Were there signs I missed?*

"Hun, I'm not trying to kick you when you're already

Chasing Beverly

down, but what you mean is that you *think* you're good at reading people. Truthfully, you should attribute your success in life to your work ethic and honesty, not to reading people."

The more I think about Peyton's threats, hot firecrackers burst under my skin, leaving a sharp sting in their wake. Once the heat dissolves, I'm left with extreme exhaustion. I feel like throwing my arms up in surrender.

Evelyn reads my body language and immediately begins to speak.

Although I'm hardly listening, my brain is in preservation mode. Too much more information, and I'll be heading to a breakdown. I run my fingers through my hair and pull slightly. If Peyton spreads these lies, it could taint my brand and negatively impact the huge deals in the offing. Even worse, what if Beverly hears?

By the time my brain refocuses, all I hear is the last part of Evelyn's plan. "Backup all the correspondence you have from her. Block her number and block her from any social media accounts. I've already spoken to security, and she's no longer permitted in this building. And try not to worry."

I'm not sure how much time has passed since Evelyn departed my office, leaving me dazed and on edge. I never would've expected Peyton's maliciousness. When I first met her, she seemed to be a peppy, sweet girl, who was candid about her feelings for me.

She turned clingy—fast. Some of the reasons I started to pull away should've been red flags. She used her charisma and beauty to manipulate people. If we didn't do what she wanted, she pouted. Still, does immature behavior translate into a raging lunatic who wants to destroy my character?

Now, what concerns me—not completely sure why—is

· 42 ·

Beverly. Will she believe Peyton's lies? My appearance and questionable behavior this morning, combined with the lie of a power-hungry CEO smacking around his ex-girlfriend, isn't an impression one can easily amend.

I take several deep breaths, and I acknowledge and accept I can't control what others do. I shift my focus back to the draft contract and work on what I can control. Only one paragraph in and my damn office line rings.

"Reed," I answer.

"Hey, man, it's Trevor."

My irritation evaporates when I hear my cousin's voice. Trevor is the closest thing I have to a sibling. He's also a client.

"Did Evelyn call?" I ask.

"Yeah, but that's not the only reason I'm calling. Not sure if you already know, but I'll be in San Diego this weekend. You free to grab a drink?"

"You better make it a strong one. What time should I have Logan pick you up from the airport?"

Trevor crashes with me when he's in town. With our respective schedules, it's practically the only chance we get to catch up with each other. Ever since he moved to Boston to play for the Red Sox, we don't see each other much. I savor our few weekends a year together.

"Already have a ride, and I'm staying at a hotel in Carlsbad."

"Why? You know I don't mind you staying with me."

"I know. It's just easier this time to be farther north where the ad will be filmed."

Knowing Trevor, he probably intends to meet up with some woman. Although staying at my place hasn't ever stopped him from bringing dates back to my house. I rub the back of

my neck. "All right. If you change your mind, the door is always open and downtown's only a forty-minute drive. You're doing the domestic violence ad campaign, right?" Disappointment drips from my voice. I'm not one to hide my feelings.

I have a feeling Trevor is doing this commercial because of my mother and me. I appreciate that he cares. He's always donating his time and money to domestic violence charities.

"Yeah, I just got off the phone with your marketing director. He told me to behave myself. Beverly Morgan is going to be there, and he's trying to land me a shoot with her company."

The skin on my face turns hot. Tension tightens my shoulders, and jealousy, an emotion I rarely experience, lodges deep in my gut. "He's worried you'll hit on her and screw up your chance to work with her?"

"Nah, I think he's more concerned I'll hit on Shelby Lane, the producer. Beverly's cute, but not my type. She's way too uptight."

My pulse quickens. "You've met her before?"

"Yeah, about a year ago. In Boston. I thought I told you this already. She was working with Jeremy on a project, and I ran into her at his office."

Hearing Jeremy's name causes puzzle pieces to snap together inside my brain. The jerk makes my blood boil.

My cousin continues to ramble as my brain struggles for traction. I recall Jeremy's words. "Beverly's the perfect challenge, and I'm gonna get a taste of that tight body."

At the time, I didn't know who he was talking about, and I didn't much care.

Anger isn't my go-to emotion. I'm generally mellow, a difficult-to-rile-up man. But one meeting with Beverly Morgan has roused emotions in me I didn't know I could feel. I've only

spent an hour with this woman, and I'm ready to defend her honor and protect her like I'm a character from some chick flick.

Jeremy's too comfortable sharing his personal life with guys in our industry, ones that he considers his pals. Since I never respond to his lame comments, he probably believes we share similar interests. That couldn't be further from the truth.

But business is seldom about real friendships. It can involve working with people you hate as you attempt to further your company's interests. You need to separate feelings from facts and weigh all of the risks. I didn't become one of the wealthiest men in this industry by passing up on million-dollar deals because a CEO was a jerk.

Jeremy is a sociopath. He gets off on destroying relationships, making a game of sleeping with an endless string of married women. He doesn't stop with married women. Any woman who gains the attention of the industry becomes his next target, his mission to conquer her. To make things worse, he breaks them down, deliberately encouraging the women to feel insecure and jealous. His ultimate goal: make them fall in love with him, then dump them.

Most of this I know courtesy of Trevor. He likes to make himself feel better about sleeping around with every girl he meets, saying, "Well, at least I'm not a dick like Jeremy."

The fire in my stomach burns into every inch of my body at the thought of that pig getting anywhere near Beverly.

"Hellooo? Gavin? You still there, bro?"

Crap. "Yeah. Sorry, I was distracted by an email."

I lie to him. I can't tell him I'm imagining breaking Jeremy's fingers, toes, legs, arms, and neck, if he ever touches the woman I met for the first time today.

I clear my throat. "So, I actually met Beverly Morgan today. Looks like we'll be partnering up for at least one gig."

"Oh, cool, man. She'll get the job done, that's for sure. She's all Miss Business."

"That's if she accepts my offer. I didn't make a very good impression. Last night's fiasco really screwed me up."

"Dude, I still can't believe what Peyton did. That car was everything to you."

"I don't even want to talk about it anymore. I need to focus on making a thoroughly professional impression on Beverly. She and I are meeting tonight to negotiate."

"Gavin, you gotta be careful with Beverly. I've heard she straight up walks away from contracts if anyone hits on her. She has a zero flirt and dating policy. Why don't you come with me to the filming tomorrow? She'll be there and you can try to win her over."

"Do you know her well?" It sounds like he has a ton of info on her.

"N-no, I've just heard she's uptight and controlling, and, you know, when I met her, she wasn't all warm and fuzzy. That's all," he stutters.

"If nothing else, I'll keep you in check, so you don't ruin your career. I don't need the wrath of Aunt Tammy because I didn't protect my baby cousin from messing up," I say.

"For God sake, you're one month older than me. One. Month. And you're as dramatic as ever. I'm curious, how'd you just meet her today? She's single-handedly changing the modeling and sports industries. Her company is the hottest commodity in our sports bubble for like the past year. Women relate to her, and little girls want to grow up to be her. She—"

I cut him off. "Sounds like you know too much about Miss

Morgan. Should I get you into a stalking support group?"

"Hey, bro, I'm just giving you the full scoop to prep you for tonight. She's cute, young and successful, I'm sure men are interested in her, but there are like *zero* rumors of her ever dating someone in her industry, in your industry or in professional sports. So, just in case your stupid gene kicks in and you get the hots for her, it ain't gonna happen. Trust me on that. She's damaged—"

I cut him off, unwilling to hear anyone speak poorly of her. *Maybe she just has standards and keeps work separate,* I think.

"Your workload is too light if you have this much time to gossip like a middle school girl. Shift your focus to baseball and any additional marketing I find for you. Gotta run, cousin. See you this weekend." I cut short our conversation, because the last thing I need is Trevor digging any deeper into my curiosity about Beverly Morgan.

"Later, asshat!" my cousin says, ever the charmer.

Two appointments left, then I can prepare for tonight's dinner. I know the owner of Aura Restaurant, and I've never had to wait before, but in the past twenty-four hours karma has been moving against me.

I dial Jenny's extension; I haven't had an opportunity to talk to her since Beverly's departure earlier.

She answers with her usual pleasant tone. "Mr. Reed, how may I help you?"

"Jenny, would you please book my normal table at Aura Restaurant for six tonight?"

"Of course."

"Oh, and Jenny?"

"Yes, sir?"

"I apologize for this morning."

"We're all entitled to a bad day, sir. I hope the meeting went well with Miss Morgan."

"I'll know tonight. If she agrees to the draft contract, this morning didn't go as poorly as I feared."

"You're meeting with her tonight?" she asks, surprise in her voice.

"Yes, I'm working on everything now. I want to get a definitive answer before the weekend."

"Will it be just the two of you?"

She sounds bewildered, which isn't her normal. Jenny is reserved and rarely voices her curiosity about my plans.

"As far as I know." *Who else would join us?*

"Be prepared for anything with Beverly. She's a sharp cookie. Would you like me to prepare a detailed profile about her for your meeting? My friend Aubrey works for her."

Learning Jenny knows Beverly and one of her employees bothers me. Was Trevor right? Have I been living in a cave this whole time? Everyone seems to know about Beverly, except me. Of course, I know about her company, but it sounds as though she's all the buzz.

"Thanks, Jenny, but I'm not comfortable delving that deeply into her life. I think it's best I learn whatever information she's willing to give me for the time being. I didn't make a stellar impression this morning."

"I was afraid of that. Whatever you do, Mr. Reed, don't hit on her. She hates when businessmen flirt with her during a meeting. Aubrey said she's backed out of deals because of it. Some men make the mistake of presuming she needs them and their projects, but she's the one in demand. She has exclusive contracts with the best models. You don't sign with her, you don't get the model. It gives her the edge. Just know that she

won't tolerate nonsense from anyone."

I hear admiration underscoring Jenny's words as she speaks about Beverly.

Before I can reply, she says, "Sir, your one o'clock is here. Shall I send in lunch?"

"Please."

"Are you ready for Mr. Palmer?"

"Give me five minutes."

Throwing down the phone, I pull up Gabe Palmer's file on my computer and hastily print out his paperwork. A professional football player, he recently fired his agent. This is an enormous deal, and I am rushed and unorganized, because I'm preoccupied with thoughts of a brown-eyed woman.

— 9 —

Gavin

The next three hours of work fly by. I sign Gabe, and I negotiate an advertising gig with *Juice for Health* for another client. Thankfully, my day and my mood continue to improve.

Sitting down at my desk, I retrieve my cell phone to check messages. I discover three phone calls and four texts from a number I don't recognize. My first thought jumps to Beverly. I slide my finger across the screen and pull up the messages. Peyton. My gut clenches.

> I'm sorry. I made a poor choice. Xo – P
> Let's talk about this. – P
> Please don't ignore me. – P
> Haven't you learned yet not to ignore me? – P

This is past the point of ridiculous, and I need to handle this. I block her new number. Day by day, she gets worse. The tension I felt this morning is trying to creep back up my neck. I force it down and roll out my shoulders. I need to remain focused.

As I organize my desk and prepare to leave, a knock at my door interrupts me. "Come in!"

Jenny stalks into the room, clearly on a mission. She carries a notepad and pen in one hand, iPad in the other.

"Mr. Reed, I know you didn't want me to compile a detailed profile on Miss Morgan and I didn't. However, I should give you a couple of tips before you go." She looks at me, waiting for my permission.

"All right, let's hear it, Jenny." I drop into my chair, curious what has her so determined.

"Well, I already told you that she doesn't like to be hit on, but Beverly also needs personal space. Aubrey has mentioned several times that since some men are attracted to her or just plain sleazy—I'm not sure which—they try to touch her. They think they're being subtle, but it infuriates her. Don't order for her or speak for her. She expects to be treated as an equal. She views it as degrading when a man, specifically, a businessman, orders food for her." Jenny glances up from her notebook to confirm I'm listening.

I frown. "Why would I order for her? I don't have a clue what she likes to eat," I manage to mutter, but my thoughts are on this morning and how my arm brushed against hers. She didn't seem uncomfortable, but if it happens too often, she might be good at masking her distaste. I make a mental note to keep my hands to myself.

Jenny chuckles. "You'd be shocked at the stories Aubrey has told me. I think you'll do great, sir. You're a professional, and not like some of the old-timers out there in the business world. She'll see that."

"All right, thanks for the info, Jenny. I should head out now."

"Of course, sir. See you tomorrow."

———

IN AN ATTEMPT TO quiet my nerves, I spend ten minutes cruising the coast highway before I head home. Windows are down and the breeze rushes in as Jack Johnson's soothing voice floats through the speakers of my Tacoma.

I love this old dependable pick-up truck and its remarkable ability to uncover pretentious women. I never pick up women on first dates in my Mercedes-Maybach. Mostly only my driver, Logan, drives that car to pick up out-of-state clients at the airport. Like every thought of mine today, I inject Beverly into the middle of this one. I wonder what she'll think of my vehicle choices. Would she even care? Although composed and a little uptight, I didn't notice any flashy jewelry or clothing that would hint to her being obsessed with expensive things. Then again, I could hardly peel my eyes away from her face.

No matter what Evelyn thinks, understanding people and figuring out what makes them tick is what I do best. So I try to persuade myself that this is all that's bothering me. Beverly is a complex puzzle, and I will need to spend enough time figuring out her unique algorithm.

Maybe if we'd met on a different day or if Peyton had not destroyed a cherished piece of memorabilia, I would've paid closer attention to Beverly's body language and energy. I wonder how today would have gone if I'd been in a better place?

I pull into my custom paver-stone driveway in old Del Mar, the exclusive seaside town I dreamed of living in while growing up in a modest two-bedroom home with my mom in small-town Ohio. Owning my dream home should make me happy.

Instead, I feel the ache of isolation as the turbulence inside me builds with every passing moment.

Hustling upstairs, I snatch a pair of swim trunks, eager for the water to engulf me and purge all worries from my mind. Lap after lap I swim in my rectangular, midnight blue, Pebble Tec Bottom pool, to liberate my mind of the images of the past twenty-four hours. My mind strays from the stress of dealing with Peyton and the police, to beautiful, yet, judgmental honey eyes, supple olive skin, and a prim pink blouse. The more I think about Beverly, the calmer I feel. Strange.

After fifteen laps, a cramp, and shaking legs, I haul myself out of the cool blue water. Miss Morgan is affecting me more than any other woman ever has, and I sense that her appearance in my world on the worst day of my life is no accident.

Concentrate, Gavin. Enough bullshit. It's time to finish the draft contract.

Sitting in my den, carefully curated bookshelves and sports memorabilia surrounding me, I realize all I needed was a diversion not forced upon me. Concentrating on business, my brain hasn't deviated too much into my unresolved problems or into the ever-expanding Beverly region. If that part of my mind isn't regulated soon, I fear it will attain control over the entire temporal lobe.

- Three weeks of commitment. *Check.*
- Reed Management, Inc. to make travel arrangements. *Check.*
- Reed Management, Inc. will choose the location(s). *Check.*
- Reed Management, Inc. will select the hotel(s) for all parties signatory to the campaign. *Check.*
- Compensation will be 2.5 million to Hope Modeling Agency. *Check.*

While dressing, I wonder if I should look up Beverly online?

Jenny did attempt to give me a history on her. God, why does it still feel contemptible to search for information on this woman? Maybe if my staff would've given me a rundown on her before our meeting, I wouldn't feel connected to her in some way. Now, researching her feels like an invasion of her privacy.

Instead of continuing with this torture, I decide to leave early for our dinner meeting. First, I text my driver, requesting that he put himself on standby tonight, just in case Beverly or I need a lift from the restaurant.

—

PULLING INTO THE parking lot of Aura, I feel less overwhelmed with whizzing thoughts, and more like the level-headed man I am.

The second I step foot into the restaurant, the vulture known as Kayla descends and sinks her talons into me before another hostess greets me. She licks her overly glossed pink lips and flips her dyed ruby hair over her shoulder. Convinced that her number-one goal in life is to end up in my bed, I always exercise caution around her.

Kayla and me? Never going to happen. With long, shapely legs and full breasts, she may be built like a woman, but I doubt she's even out of high school. Jailbait.

"Hey, Mr. Reed. I have your table all ready. I was so excited to see you on the reservations list for tonight!" Her blue eyes dance over my body, as though she's been at sea without fresh water for days.

"Good evening, Kayla." I keep my distance to avoid having her hands anywhere near my body. The last thing I need is for Beverly to witness an exchange like that and assume the worst.

Following the exaggerated swaying of her hips, I smother a

laugh as I imagine the force of her hip swing causing her to lose her balance and go sprawling.

"How's your day going so far?" Kayla places my menu in front of me and stands too close. She's more confident than most models I've met.

"Fine, thanks."

She quickly strokes my shoulder. All husky voice and fluttering eyelashes, she says, "Just call me over if you need anything."

As she walks away, hips swaying, I hope she knocks herself into next month so that she isn't around when Beverly arrives.

A few minutes later, Kayla returns with Beverly and another beautiful woman. I don't know the other woman, but she looks familiar. When I stand to greet them, the green-eyed friend shamelessly scans my body, oblivious to the daggers Kayla shoots her way. Two vultures circling for the same meal.

"Good to see you again, Miss Morgan. Any problem finding the place?"

I reach out to shake Beverly's hand. I notice her friend observing us. As our palms meet, something I can't place flashes in Beverly's eyes. Her hand lingers in mine longer than the average business handshake. Not knowing what she's feeling or thinking is pure agony.

"None at all. Gavin Reed, this is Nell, one of my models. Since you were disappointed I wasn't accompanied by a model this morning, I thought it beneficial for you both to meet."

Her tone is terse, but her faint smile is mischievous. I think she's teasing me.

Forcibly peeling my eyes away from Beverly, I turn to Nell. She looks the part of a typical model; tall, beautiful, slim, but not rail thin. She has an athletic shape that's put on full display with her skin-tight, white dress.

"Nice to meet you, Nell."

"Gavin, the pleasure's all mine. I can't wait to work closely with you." She bites down on her lip, and I quell the impulse to roll my eyes. I suspect Beverly wouldn't appreciate that.

Before responding to Nell, my eyes shift back to Beverly. "Yes, I hope Miss Morgan and I can work out an agreement tonight. Please, let's make ourselves comfortable."

I note Beverly chooses the seat farthest from me, while her model sits directly across from me. Before Nell lowers herself into her chair, she pulls her dress down even more than it already is. If she goes any farther, I fear her breasts might pop right out onto the table.

The way Nell eyes me like I'm what's for dessert tonight makes me feel jittery. My leg starts to bounce under the table. Another thing Trevor always jokes about with me is my aversion to any woman who throws herself at me. My year as a professional baseball player scarred me. I learned overly aggressive, gorgeous women were either too much work or they considered me just another rung on the dating ladder to fame and fortune.

In the beginning, I got off on the attention. I had a few one-night stands, but always felt used when a selfie would get snapped or a woman would pitch herself. Women were into being with a baseball player, not me.

Glancing over at Beverly, she gives me a weak smile, which confuses me. Wasn't this her plan? I don't buy her excuse that she wanted me to meet a model before signing her company. I think she wanted my attention anywhere but on her.

I wonder if she does this with all her meetings. Create a buffer. A distraction. And, if so, does Nell know that's what she is? The thought is disheartening. Is Beverly propositioned so much that even a business dinner is a threat to her?

Nell's flawless caramel skin, exotic eyes, and stunning figure would make it easy for most men to be distracted around her. Unfortunately for Beverly, all my fervor and electricity is coursing to the woman sitting at the end of the table. The woman whose eyes have taunted me in every thought since this morning, and whose attitude has, for some reason unclear to me, only made me more intrigued about what Beverly has gone through to get this far.

If this were even six months ago, maybe I wouldn't have noticed Beverly. I have a type, and Nell is much closer to the kind of woman I used to want on my arm. But after being burned over and over again, and now the mess with Peyton, I'm maturing. I'm much less attracted to flashy women. Depth of character suddenly appeals much more.

Within moments of settling in our chairs, our waiter with the man-bun appears. He's unenthusiastically going through his spiel when his eyes land on Nell. I practically hear his throat constrict. He stands taller, and the words he's supposed to be speaking cease. He recovers, then manages to ask us what we'd like to drink.

Beverly orders an Arnold Palmer as the douchebag waiter stares at Nell's chest before shifting his gaze to Beverly. She doesn't seem to notice. And if she does, she doesn't show it. Her expression remains neutral, her body relaxed.

"Sure thing." He flashes her a smile, eager to turn his attention back to Nell.

"I'll have a glass of your Pinot Noir," Nell says, not really acknowledging his presence.

"And for you, sir?"

He's talking to me, but ogling Nell. When I clear my throat, waiter boy sets his attention on me.

"Iced Tea." My tone is clipped.

"Of course, sir," he says before scurrying away.

I hoped for a nice glass of wine tonight, but since Beverly didn't order one, it's best to follow her lead. After all, this is a business meeting. Before anything else, I need to professionally win her over. Then, I'll gain her trust on a more personal level.

At least, I hope I will. I see secrets hidden behind those beautiful golden-brown eyes of hers. *Stop staring at her, Gavin.* I barely manage to drag my gaze away from her plump lips and focus on my menu.

After a few minutes of silent menu inspection, Nell's the first to speak. "I'm going to try the Acorn Squash dish. How about you, Bev?"

Bev? Are they more than boss and employee? Beverly's composed and hardened appearance doesn't strike me as someone who would allow just anyone to call her by a nickname.

Beverly continues to scan her menu. "I can't decide between the salmon or halibut."

Disappointment rushes through me when she doesn't look up, depriving me of another chance to get a glimpse at those big eyes.

"And what about you?" Nell stretches her hand across the table to touch mine.

I flinch and pull away. *What in the hell is the matter with me?*

I glance at Beverly to see if she notices Nell flirting with me. If she does, she gives nothing away. At this moment, I wish Nell had stayed home.

I feel compelled to connect with Beverly and to get to know her. I want to ask her questions like: Why did you choose this industry? Where are you from? Is there a guy in your life?

Beverly peers up from her menu, her eyes gliding back and forth between Nell and me, a faint half-smile on her face. I look over at Nell. She arches her eyebrows like she's expecting something. Oh, right, she's waiting for my response.

"The Seabass. The green curry-coconut sauce is delicious. I've begged my friend for the recipe, but he won't relent," I manage, splitting my attention between the two women. My gaze lingers a bit longer on Beverly. Her lips purse to one side as she concentrates on the menu. She looks adorable, and much more relaxed than during this morning's meeting.

"Oh, you know the owner?" Nell asks.

Beverly ignores us. Doubts fill my head. Was I the only one to feel energy between us this morning? Sure, it was a little bumpy at first, but I felt some attraction, at least I thought I did.

"Yeah, my friend Danny owns this place. Most of the recipes came from his family, but he's added some twists to them."

This comment actually draws Beverly's attention from her menu. Before she can speak, the damn waiter returns with our drinks.

— 10 —

Gavin

Our sleazeball waiter, Carson, now extends his creeper ways to Beverly. While placing her Arnold Palmer in front of her, he leans in so close his arm grazes her.

She looks uncomfortable, but she doesn't say anything. I press my lips together and remind myself she can take care of herself. She doesn't want a knight in shining armor to save her. As he moves away from her and down the table, she releases a sigh of relief.

When the weasel makes his way to Nell, he gets even closer to her. I wonder how he even has a job with this kind of behavior. After lingering a beat longer near Nell, he sets down my Iced Tea, then proceeds to take our orders. He avoids eye contact with me and more than a few times peers down the front of Nell's dress.

Danny needs to hear about this guy.

With nothing left to distract us, our conversation shifts to the contract. As I expected, the first thing Beverly mentions is the three weeks term.

"Earlier, you mentioned a term of three weeks for this project.

After giving it more thought, I realize we won't need that much time. I am willing to fly all of my models to Hawaii if you need them, to make the shoot quicker. They are professional and efficient. Let's compromise and start with ten days. We can go from there. I don't want your company overpaying for work that can be completed in a week."

I let her talk and consider her points. Although my mind is made up, and I won't budge on the amount of time I want for the shoot. Anything shorter would mean we'd be rushed and constantly working. It would leave zero time for me to crack the shell in which Beverly seems to live.

"You make good points, and I'm sure you and your team would be capable of finishing sooner. For the sake of my health and sanity, I want the three weeks. I created a draft contract for your review."

I hand the folder to her and continue my pitch, making certain she knows I'm flexible and ready to compromise on some items.

"If you have any 'must-haves', let's discuss those now," I suggest. "Please take the contract with you, review it tonight, then either call me tonight or tomorrow with any change requests. I'll make any necessary revisions, and have the final draft completed tomorrow. Once completed, I can either courier it to your hotel, or you're welcome to swing by my office to sign."

Eager to jump in and lay down her laws, Beverly dons her business face. She is clearly ready to make sure I know she's a professional woman to be taken seriously.

"My must-haves are: I must have final say on which model represents which sport, and I will be involved in the casting of any commercials. Lastly, my approval is required on all messages of any pictures, videos, commercials, etcetera." Confidence

radiates from her every pore. Not once does she break eye contact, and I savor each moment I get to stare into those gorgeous honey eyes.

Victory washes over me as I smile at her in affirmation. "Great. Those items are already listed in the proposed contract. I know you're passionate about the message your company sends, and I'll always make sure you're happy working with me."

Her mouth pops open, then turns up into a genuine smile. It's the biggest smile I've seen from her. My breath catches, forcing me to gulp in air.

She slides her fingers in her hair and tucks it behind her ear. "All right, then. I'll review the rest of the contract, and we'll go from there." She brings her drink up to her mouth.

When her lips wrap around the straw, I have to look away and readjust myself beneath the table like an easily excited teenager.

"Thank goodness I'm a model, because this meeting is *so* boring," Nell whines.

Her comment helps my adult brain return to the body it vacated a few moments ago. Honestly, I forgot she was here. And by the way Beverly jumps, I think she did, too. Beverly narrows her eyes at Nell.

"Oh, don't look at me like that! You didn't need me for this, Bev. Why am I even here?" Nell rolls her eyes, then tips back the rest of her second glass of wine. She's either tipsy, or she enjoys a significant personal relationship with Beverly.

Before Beverly has a chance to respond to Nell's question, our waiter arrives with our food. Shocker, he serves Nell first. He inhales deeply, taking his creepiness to a new level.

Nell shifts her arm to move away from him, rolling her eyes again. How can Danny employ this loser?

Beverly's voice peels me from the plan I'm concocting in my head to get Carson fired. "You're here to meet Mr. Reed, who can help your career. This campaign is huge, and I want you to take on more responsibilities, but you need to prove yourself first. Complaining about accompanying me to an important business dinner isn't an effective business tactic." Beverly's voice is soft and kind, but her message is clear. Stop bitching.

Eventually, Nell ends the pouting. At the beginning of the night, I thought I'd have to fight her off the entire meal. What I wasn't expecting was feeling freaked out by the knowing little looks she keeps throwing my way, all lifted eyebrows, small smile that hides her teeth like she's giggling inside, and a damn sparkle of knowledge glinting in her eyes. It's clear she's picked up on my interest in Beverly. Surprisingly, I think she's rooting for me.

"How long have you worked for Beverly?" I ask Nell since I haven't made much of an effort to talk to her tonight. If she and Beverly are as close as they appear, I need Nell on my side. Besides, she gives up information much more freely than her boss.

"Since she started the company, I was her first model." She beams affectionately at Beverly, confirming my suspicion they are good friends.

"So you've known each other for a while. Loyal employees are a gift," I continue, fishing for more information. I glance at Beverly, trying to gauge if she's on to me.

Nell sets down her fork and wipes her mouth with her napkin. "Yeah, but we go *way* back. We've been besties since we were kids."

Life-long friends, huh. This creates a new challenge for me.

It's necessary to ensure Nell likes me enough to approve of me with Beverly, but not too much to make me off limits to Beverly.

Beverly's eyebrows pull together, and she looks lost for a moment. "Nell is as loyal as they come," she says with a soft smile that doesn't reach her eyes.

"Thank you, Gavin, for the meal and the contract. I'll review it tonight, and let you know if I have any revisions." Beverly effectively shuts down any further questioning on my part. And with her last bite of veggies, she places her fork on top of her plate and gently pushes it away.

"I look forward to it." I want Beverly to repeat my name. I love the way it sounds coming from her mouth.

"It was nice meeting you," I say, turning toward Nell.

"You, too. Thanks for dinner. If you'll excuse me, I need to use the ladies room before we leave." Nell winks at me as she walks away. Oh, yeah. Points for Gavin, the best friend approves. Though I can't help but wonder why she is encouraging me. She barely knows me.

Beverly and I sit for a moment in awkward silence. Crossing her arms over her chest, she says, "I'm surprised you haven't asked me yet."

Odd statement. Her defensive tone throws me. *What the hell does she mean?*

"Asked you what?" I tilt my head in question. Does she want me to ask her out? Does she get asked out so often, she expects it now?

"About the Olympics." For the first time since meeting her, she avoids eye contact and looks down at the table as she speaks. Without being able to see her eyes, I have no clue what's running through that head of hers.

I drag my hand through my hair. "I'm lost, Beverly. I don't

know what I should've asked you about the Olympics."

Her eyes jump to my face when I say her name. Her brow furrows, and her eyes dart from me to the table and back again. She searches my face for several moments until she seems satisfied. With an obvious exhale and a shake of her head, she relaxes.

Right when I'm about to press her further, Nell returns from the bathroom. Since Beverly privately brought this up, I drop the subject for the time being.

— 11 —

Beverly

The moment our car doors shut, Nell is on me like white on rice. She patiently waits for me to make a mistake.

"You could've at least told me he was into you. I would've come and protected you, either way, ya know?" She crosses her arms.

I brace for a new Nell-pouting session.

I consider how best to respond. "He isn't into me. He's just trying to land this deal." Yeah, he checked me out a little this morning, but he was also a rude jerk, so I'm not sure if his looks were of interest or distaste.

Nell shifts her body to face mine. Her suspicious eyes prowl over my face, sniffing out the truth. I keep my emotions neatly tucked under my mask, but Nell has years of practice reading this face I've adopted. She's a pro at finding the smallest clues buried in my features.

She claps her hands together, causing me to jump back in my seat. "Oh, my gosh!" she yells, bouncing in her seat like a child whose mom just gave her a lollipop. "You like him, Bev! That's why you wanted me there. Yaaasss! I never thought I'd see the day!"

Without thinking, I shake my head back and forth so hard, I risk whiplash. "Whoa, whoa, whoa. He's cute, but I never said I liked him. And don't get excited, because nothing is *ever* going to happen. It can't. You know my rules about dating someone I work with. Hell, you know my rules on dating period."

There's no point in trying to lie to Nell about my attraction to Gavin Reed. She knows me better than anyone—well, almost. In recent years, I've opened up more to Aubrey. Nell worries about me too much, regularly checking in to make sure I'm okay. Sometimes it's just easier to keep certain things from her. But this situation is impossible. Gavin is attractive to anyone with functioning eyeballs.

"Bullcrap. You think he's more than *cute.* That's why you went out of your way to sit away from him, why I caught you on more than one occasion staring at him when he wasn't paying attention, and why you didn't want to come alone tonight." She rubs her hands together as she plots. "Beverly, this needs to happen. You haven't been with anyone in forever, and it's time to stop torturing yourself." Pausing, she gives me a pointed look, then continues her pitch. "And, I mean, come on. He is *so* hot, I bet he's amazing in the sack. Live a little, and just have some fun. Don't you miss having contact with guys?"

Her question startles me. I haven't told anyone, not even Stan, that I feel an intense yearning lately for some emotion I can feel, other than regret and shame, for a connection with someone I can trust, for intimacy with a man. For a kiss, to be held by a man, or even just for a steady hand to hold. I tug on the edge of my sleeve with nervous tension. This secret needs to remain deep inside me. I can't risk the temptation to break free

from the prison I've sealed around my broken heart. I don't deserve redemption.

I roll my eyes. "He probably sucks in bed. *'The hot guys never have to try.'* Isn't that what you're always telling me? Besides, we're business partners, Nell. If I want to make a more substantial impact in the world, I need this contract. I can't risk losing this project over a meaningless physical attraction, and I have to remain professional. This needs to stay between us. Tonight cannot become the latest model gossip. Am I clear?"

"Ouch." She pinches her eyes shut.

I immediately regret sounding so harsh.

"You know me better than that. I've never spilled the tea on any of your secrets or your past."

Her injured tone causes a knot to form in my belly. She's right to be hurt. She's always been here for me, even when I haven't deserved it. Her friendship has always remained a constant.

"Nell, I'm sorry. Of course, I don't doubt your loyalty. It's been an exhausting and confusing day for me. Let's head back to the hotel; I have a contract to review."

As I put the car in reverse, she reaches out and squeezes my hand. I know that I've been forgiven.

— 12 —

Beverly

As we pull into the hotel parking lot, Nell announces she's tired and plans to head home for a hot bubble bath. When she clears her throat for the third time, I know she's really leaving to lick her wounds because I hurt her feelings. Maybe if I were a better friend, I'd stop her, talk about it, reassure her of my appreciation for her. Instead, I let her go.

The moment my hotel door clicks shut behind me, I begin to strip off the constricting black blazer and clothes I opt to wear, hoping my internal mess remains hidden by the perfect façade of my exterior. I climb into the shower, eager to erase the dozens of emotions that have bubbled up in my body today. Under a surge of steaming hot water, I scrub my eyes for the third time, hoping the image of Gavin Reed will be washed away with my mascara. His deep blue eyes remain seared into my memory and will probably plague my dreams.

How could I have been foolish enough to think that my attraction for him wouldn't get in the way of this transaction? And the possibility of working closely with the Olympics is already stirring up painful memories. I'm also afraid I'll break

my promise to never open my heart again. I feel untethered and lonely, and I wish I'd invited Nell to stay.

"Snap out of it, Beverly!" I yell.

My plea bounces off the shower walls. I instantly experience chills as the image of a small seven-year-old girl I met in Kenya last year fills my head. I traveled to the Horn of Africa with one of my favorite charities, *A Splash of Life,* to help dig a well for a community in Southeastern Kenya that suffers from a lack of clean water. I also went there as a reality check.

Kioni had a fiery spirit that refused to be broken. I tried my best not to show her pity, only kindness and encouragement. But witnessing that tiny warrior walk nearly four miles with her mother and siblings each and every day just to collect water for their family crushed my already damaged soul.

My memories of her sweet, frail, yet determined face as she carried her containers of water is the reality check I need right now. Slamming my hands against the faucet, I shut off the shower and scold myself for allowing my own trivial problems to consume me. This isn't me, I remind myself. I didn't go through all that pain to turn back into some self-absorbed creature.

After calming myself and climbing out of the shower, I throw on my black sweats and a plain white T-shirt, clamber onto the king-sized bed, and prop myself up with a few pillows in order to focus on work.

I analyze each line. The contract is rather impressive. Every detail is outlined, organized with thoughtful precision, and includes incredibly generous terms for my company. However, a peculiar requirement catches my attention. Stated under paragraph six of the contract, it requires all employees to stay in a separate hotel from Gavin and me.

Even though it's almost eleven o'clock and Reed might already

be asleep, I decide to text him. I input his contact information into my phone. He urged me to reach out with any questions.

As I type Reed as his name, I realize there are some things about my sports days I'll never be rid of. There's also something about his last name that just suits him better.

> Me: I read the contract. Looks good. One question, why separate hotels for the models/athletes and us? Thanks again for dinner. – Beverly

I reread the text I just sent and cringe at the word "us." I should've worded that differently. It doesn't take long for my phone to ping. When I see "Reed" across the screen, my pulse quickens. I pretend not to notice.

> Reed: That was fast. Glad you're satisfied with the contract, and again, you're welcome. It was the best business dinner I've had in a long time. As for your question, I like to give my employees space and privacy. After shooting all day with them, I need to get away, too. It's a win-win, I suppose. – Gavin

Taking a moment to really consider his reply, I agree with him, especially when I look back on projects that lasted more than five days. Exhausted, I simply wanted to get away. I'm sure their comfort level increases when I'm not around 24/7.

> Me: Makes sense. Ditto on the dinner. Looking forward to working with you. I'll stop by your

office tomorrow to sign the final contract. If
it's easier, you can leave it up front with
Jenny.—Beverly

Reed: Text me when you're on your way to the
office, and I'll meet with you.

I chew on the inside of my cheek, aware that seeing him
again so soon is not a good idea. I need to squash this and
quickly. Because even a woman with a dead heart has basic
needs, and I'm a woman who hasn't been touched in years, not
to mention a woman who is insanely attracted to a man she
cannot and should not want. If I'm going to maintain my self-
control, I need to establish boundaries with him. Now.

Supposedly, he's one of the few good men out there, so
what a bitch would I be to open up this can of worms? I don't
want to do harm, because I can't ever be the kind of woman a
man needs and wants for more than a night.

Me: No that's OK. Just leave it up front with
Jenny, I won't disrupt your day. You don't
need to keep trying to make up for this
morning. We're good.

It was a tad manipulative putting it back on him like that,
but if I achieve success, it was worth it. His reply is immediate.

Reed: I'll do no such thing. Please text me
when on your way. Dang, 4 months feels so
long away, I'm anxious to get this started!

Without permission, a stupid, goofy grin takes over my face. I should be digging in my heels right now. Instead, my fingers start punching a response, and my smile grows with every word.

> Me: It'll be here before we know it and we'll kick ass on this project. Women athletes will be lining up outside your office in no time. ;)

After pressing send, I reread my message and toss my phone on the bed. I roll out my neck and try to regroup. If I'm going to keep this professional, no more winky faces and no more flirting, or what could be perceived as flirting. Sure, I don't doubt women will bang down his doors to work with him after this. Between the many stories Jenny and Aubrey have shared about him, it appears he's a decent person. My own experience with him at dinner was pleasant, but I don't need to stroke his ego.

Get it together, Beverly.

> Reed: Did Nell steal your phone? I didn't picture you as the winking face kind of woman.

Perceptive man, isn't he? I was hoping that would've slipped by unnoticed or at the very least he wouldn't call me out on it. Of course, he's right, a smiley face, let alone a winking face in a text isn't me. I rub at my tense left shoulder, thankful I have an appointment this weekend with Holistic Sports & Injury Massage in Encinitas. My favorite massage therapist of all time owns it. I never would've survived my competitive years without her.

Me: Talk tomorrow. Goodnight, Reed.

I opt to ignore his comment. Good job, Beverly, way to not overthink it. I pat myself on my shoulder.

Reed: Looking forward to it, Beverly.

My breath catches in my throat. Before I turn out the lights, I quickly text Stan to make an appointment. He needs to help me make these feelings go away.

— 13 —

Gavin

After three disturbing and eerily similar nightmares, I rub the sleep out of my eyes and give up, climbing out of bed at 5 a.m. In each dream I was lost, but looking into Beverly's beautiful brown eyes. Her eyes appeared sad; tortured eyes filled with tears. When I reached out to her, she turned and walked away.

No matter how fast I ran, I couldn't catch up to her. Eventually, she disappeared from view altogether.

It's 6 a.m. I'm sitting outside in my favorite hammock chair, drinking coffee, and waiting for the sun to rise. As I ponder the agony of my dreams last night, an ominous feeling touches a fear deep inside me that says this was more a prediction of my future than some random dream. My grandma would have a field day with this one. She's an old spiritual kook who believes dreams have profound meanings that need to be evaluated.

Not even three cups of coffee can break the funk I'm in. Lately, it's becoming difficult to keep up with my ever-shifting moods. At this rate I fear my Y chromosome will be lost for good. My stomach churns, no doubt from the copious amount of caffeine and lack of food this morning.

After a large bowl of hot oatmeal and berries, I leisurely prepare for the day. Not keen on waiting in my office, obsessing over when Beverly will text me. I suspect I'll be doing a lot of waiting when it comes to this woman. As much as I hate waiting to ask her out on a date, I dread the thought that she could slip through my fingers before we get a chance to see if we could be something great together.

—

WAITING AT HOME isn't working for me. I head out, arriving at my office around 9 a.m. Two hours pass. After forcing myself to concentrate on emails, draft contracts and reaching out to new recruits, my time at my desk is productive. It hasn't stopped me from checking my cell phone every few minutes or from the anticipation of seeing her name across my phone.

Correspondence caught up and contracts approved and sent to my staff, my thoughts begin to wander. As I fantasize about Beverly's mouth, I recall the multiple cups of coffee I drank and the onion bagel I ate this morning when I got to the office. Time to brush my teeth.

Grateful for the personal bathroom attached to my office, I open a new toothbrush, squeeze some Spearmint toothpaste on top and brush vigorously. Even with this small distraction, my thoughts stay in Beverly Land, and I idly wonder how her lips would feel against mine.

Back at my desk I peer at my phone, and I discover a message from Beverly.

> Beverly: Be at your office in 45. Leave it with
> Jenny if you're busy.

She's still hinting for me to leave the contract up front, probably because she thinks the only reason I'm making time to see her is to atone for my sour mood of yesterday morning. If only she knew the truth. I want to see her again. It's that simple. And complicated. I smooth down my shirt and run my fingers through my overgrown, wavy hair, hoping to make a better impression than yesterday morning.

I wonder if this is a regular occurrence for her. Jenny said she always gets hit on. Do other men go out of their way to see her? Am I acting just like them? I can't focus on that. I'm making this complicated. It's simple. I like her. I want to get to know her, and I'm not going to deprive myself of that.

Me: Perfect. I'll be here.

I sit down at my desk. My palms sweat, while my stomach does back flips again.

Get a grip.

I dial Jenny's extension to give her the heads-up.

"Hi, Mr. Reed."

I nervously stand and do deep knee bends as I talk. "Hey, Jenny. Beverly Morgan will arrive in about forty-five minutes to finalize the contract terms. Please send her right in and hold all calls until she leaves."

"Really?" Jenny exclaims. "She's actually stopping by? I'm impressed."

Her praise gives me hope, and I sink back into my chair as a sense of calm washes over me.

"You didn't think I could get the contract?" I ask, fishing for more information. I need the boost of confidence.

"I didn't doubt you'd land the deal. You persuaded Miss

Morgan to meet over dinner last night *and* to come into the office today. She never hand signs contracts in person, so you must have made quite an impression on her."

Hope explodes in my chest. Is Jenny right? Is Beverly Morgan going out of her way to see me? Is she attracted to me? The uncertainty I feel is driving me nuts. It's impossible for me to figure out what she's feeling or thinking without knowing anything about her.

"Must have been your advice before dinner."

"Maybe. I'll send her in when she arrives, sir."

"Thank you."

I check my watch. Only ten minutes since I received her text message.

Feeling fidgety and pent-up, it's possible I'll develop an irreversible twitch waiting any longer in this room for Beverly to arrive. Maybe I should go for a walk and watch the downtown morning buzz to distract myself. I pause at my office door, Jenny knows my habits. When I'm nervous, I can't remain still. She will be suspicious if I leave before Beverly arrives. Damn it. I'm trapped.

I decide to call Trevor. I wonder if he's staying at the same hotel as Beverly. Maybe he's bumped into her and has some further intel. I dig my cell phone from my pocket. As Trevor's phone rings, I hear a knock on my door.

Assuming it's Jenny, I yell, "Come in."

Just as Trevor answers his phone, Beverly glides through my office door. Her long dark hair and white silk blouse cause my mouth to go dry. I hear Trevor say, "Gavin, are you there?" I hang up on him and turn off my phone.

"I got here a little faster than I anticipated. Am I interrupting?" she asks in a low voice, gesturing to the phone still gripped in my hand.

"No. No, not at all. Please come in." I walk toward her, eager to clasp her delicate hand in mine.

She looks striking with her glossy, chocolate hair tumbling nearly to her waist. Her petite frame is all legs, and she's dressed more relaxed today in jeans, but then there're the shoes. Black high heels. I'm a sucker for a woman in heels. With a colossal amount of effort, I force my eyes to stay focused on her face.

"Great to see you again. Would you like something to drink?" I give her a warm smile all while maintaining steady eye contact.

"Water is good. Thank you." A slow blush creeps up her face, but she doesn't back down from my stare. Her confidence is sexy.

"Of course. Please, have a seat at the conference table. I'll grab water and the paperwork."

When she turns to walk toward the table, I sneak a peek at her perfect backside. She should wear those pants and heels every day. Scratch that. She should only wear them around me. I don't want any other man enjoying that view. Reluctantly, I turn away to fetch the water and the final contract.

Once she takes a seat at the conference table, Beverly stares out the window, her brow furrowed. She's so lost in thought, she doesn't notice me setting the water down in front of her. I sink into the chair across from her and enjoy the opportunity to observe her. As much as I want to sit next to her, it would be torture to put her within reach and not touch her. She still hasn't noticed me. *What is she thinking?*

"Do you have any other questions about the contract for me?" I quietly ask a few minutes later.

She flinches. My voice seems to have ripped her from her thoughts. She flushes with embarrassment before she recovers and taps her fingers on the contract.

"No, it looks good. However, I do have a request."

I lean forward. "Anything." Little does she realize, she owns me right now.

"I want your team to book me a flight for five days in advance. I'll cover the cost of the room for those nights."

Her request piques my interest. "Sure thing. May I ask why?"

Uncertainty fills her eyes, and she chews on her bottom lip.

A major distraction for me. I take a steadying breath.

"My team doesn't know this, so I'd appreciate it staying between us." Pausing, she searches my face.

"Beverly, your secrets are safe with me," I assure her, because deep in my gut I am certain Beverly Morgan has too many secrets to count.

Another rule of mine is that any woman I date needs to be an open book. I saw what secrets did to my family. What the secrets did to my mom, day after day, as she hid Dad's unforgivable behavior. Oddly enough, Beverly makes me want to rip up my list of rules.

She squirms in her seat at my response. "It's not a big deal, but I like to arrive well before my team. It's an integral part of my process to inspect the areas where we'll work. If my assistant knew, she'd pester me to bring her and other employees along to assist."

I chuckle. "Did Jenny put you up to this?"

It's a solid joke around here, because I do the exact same thing before important projects. In my case, my staff knows about it and makes fun of me. They call me 'persnickety'— leave it to Jenny to draw a word like that off the top of her head. All because I prefer to choose each spot alone. My staff says it's so I don't have to hear other points of view. I wonder when

Jenny had time to concoct this with Beverly and how she got her to agree.

Beverly purses her lips, and that impeccably plucked eyebrow twitches just like yesterday morning, either confusion or irritation written all over her face. Even now, she's adorable, although I think I've said something wrong.

She folds her hands on the table. "I'm not kidding, Mr. Reed."

Crap. She's offended. She thinks I'm laughing at her. If what she says is true, we have more in common than I ever expected.

I clear my throat. "Forgive me. I thought Jenny told you to joke with me because she knows I always get to the location a few days early. I check out all the spots my team has booked, weed some out, then give final approval before anyone else arrives. Why don't you tell anyone?"

She stares at me. And for the first time since she stepped into my office today, her detached, imperturbable mask appears firmly in place. I had hoped not to see it again.

You can trust me.

Please don't hide from me.

Beverly tucks her hair behind her ears and, after an uncomfortable pause, she answers. "I've always just kept it to myself. I guess so no one can disturb me. I would appreciate it if you don't tell Jenny about this. She and Aubrey are friends, and Aubrey assumes I take a vacation before a project. She already hassles me enough about working too hard... sorry, I'm rambling."

Interesting that her employee gets on her case, too. After hearing more about Aubrey, I suspect they're also friends. Beverly sure does like mixing friends and business.

"Why do I get the feeling there's more to the story?" I'm not going to beat around the bush. It isn't in my nature, even though I've tried to make an exception for Beverly, but I guess twenty-seven hours is my limit. If I want her to get to know me, then I need to show her exactly who I am.

"Maybe you're looking for a juicer reason than the one I gave you." She grins at me, then turns her attention to the papers in front of her.

"Perhaps. But don't worry, my lips are sealed. I will personally book your flight. Also, I won't bother you before the campaign starts. Unless you're interested in seeing some of the locations with me?" I try to keep optimism out of my voice.

"Thanks." She picks an imaginary speck of lint from her shirt. "Sure, I wouldn't mind viewing some spots with you. Ya know, if it works out." She avoids eye contact, fidgeting with the stack of papers in front of her.

I was expecting a lame excuse on why she'd rather we check things out separately. Man, she's full of surprises. This will be perfect, I tell myself as I mentally start orchestrating a plan to schedule our flights for the same day. Five days. Just the two of us. No employees. No responsibilities.

I clasp my hands together, allowing my excitement to drive me. "I haven't eaten lunch yet, have you? Feel like joining me?"

My enthusiasm is getting the best of me, but I don't care. I want more time with her, because doubt keeps hammering at my confidence. What if she heads back home and someone catches her eye before I see her next? Where does she even live?

Those big beautiful brown eyes keep darting from my face to the door, and I see the struggle playing out in her head. At this moment, I feel sorry for her. She needs to weigh every move she makes in business. Every step could be construed as

leading someone on or crossing that invisible professional line. I don't envy women in the business world. I admire them, but envy them, I do not. I try to remain aloof and curb my eagerness while she considers my invitation, but inside my head, I'm screaming, "Yes! Yes! Yes!"

Please, say yes.

"I could eat." She offers a faint smile. "Do you have somewhere in mind?"

My mouth lifts into a huge grin. Beverly's smile grows bigger in response.

"There's a café on the first floor." I march over to my desk, yank open the top drawer, find their menu and hand it to Beverly.

"Are you okay with ordering food to eat here? I can have it delivered."

"Absolutely. It'll give your employees a lot less to gossip about."

I chuckle. "True point."

— 14 —

Gavin

Less than twenty minutes later, Jenny taps on my half-closed door and delivers our lunch. Never have I loved the convenience of a café in the building more than today.

Jenny places the bag of food on the conference table, then adjusts her black-rimmed glasses on her nose. "Is there anything else I can get for you before I leave for lunch, Mr. Reed?"

"No. Thank you, Jenny." She nods and quickly departs my office, glancing back at us a few times with a curious smile on her face. If I didn't know the quality of her character, I might be worried that she'd run off to gossip.

My stomach grumbles as the promising fragrance of a good meal reaches my nose. "I'm famished."

I unpack our lunch, placing Beverly's hummus and avocado wrap in front of her. I position my chicken salad sandwich across from where she sits, still giving her space and remaining professional.

I rip open my bag of chips and pop one into my mouth. I take a closer look at my sandwich, which without the onions still looks amazing.

Why can't I make a sandwich this good?

"Thanks for lunch," Beverly says before she sinks her straight, white teeth into her wrap, briefly closing her eyes and allowing a small sigh to escape her lips. Then, she adds, "You should've let me pay. After all, you are *my* client." She flashes me a pointed look.

When watching her eat last night, I noticed her appreciation for food. At this moment, I'm loving her sensuous enjoyment as she savors each bite.

"You're welcome. And I'm not your client. We're business partners, at least for this campaign." I'm uncertain if I'm trying to persuade her it's okay to be interested in me, or if I'm attempting to convince myself.

She sets aside her food and presses a napkin to her lips. "You can't keep being so kind to me." She shakes her head.

"Who says?"

"Me. I can't get used to this kind of treatment from 'business partners,'" she quips.

I struggle to swallow my food. "Are people that terrible to you?" I should've paused before responding, because I know my anger is written all over my face and evident in my voice.

She cocks her head to the side. She scans my face, examining me, looking for . . . what, I don't know. A heartbeat later, she apparently finds what she's searching for.

"It depends."

Typically, cryptic responses annoy me, but not with Beverly. I already know she needs to be cautious, drip feed information, and read people's reactions before oversharing. The thought that she's forced to function this way pisses me off yet again.

Warmth floods my body. I push up my sleeves. "On what?" I try my best to ignore the tension building in my neck and shoulders.

Beverly folds her hands in her lap. "What they know about me. Besides, this is a man's industry. Some of the men I work with are jerks with overblown egos. They seem to think any woman who steps into their office wants to sleep with them or needs to sleep with them to get to the top. Others are overly helpful and kind. A few treat me like a little girl because I'm young. Guess it just comes with the territory. But I'll tell you what, the thrill I get from the many CEOs who hate that I'm in demand helps make putting up with their garbage all worth it," she explains, shrugging her shoulders.

I throw down the chip I'm holding. "None of this should come with the territory, Beverly."

Her back straightens, and her eyes go wide.

"Those jerks need to get with the times. You're transforming the industry, and they're burning their bridges with you. I look forward to the day you can tell them all to go screw themselves."

Her nonchalant attitude only fuels me further. This is bullshit. I cringe, remembering how I checked her out yesterday, and even today I took the first opportunity I could to look at her backside.

Damn, I'm part of the problem.

She sighs, then folds up her food wrapper. "Well, that was delicious."

Smooth, Beverly, real smooth. I understand her cue and am about to change the subject when she grips the edge of the table and speaks again.

"Look, please put away your sword and shield. While I appreciate your outrage, I'm fully capable of taking care of myself. The best thing you can do to help me, and other women like me, is be the respectful man everyone raves about.

And if you see someone being mistreated, male or female, speak up for them."

Baffled that she considers me a good guy, I'm tempted to let her in on the truth, to confess my sins because the thoughts running through my head about her haven't all been honorable. Instead, I take the easy way out and change the subject.

"That I can do, but so you know, if ever needed, I'm prepared to pick up my sword again and fight for you." Not giving her a chance to respond, I continue, "Anyway, on to more pleasant subjects, tell me about yourself."

She leans back in her chair, crossing her arms over her body. "What do you want to know?"

"Anything . . . everything."

A sweet, soft laugh escapes her. "Come on, give me a starting point." She relaxes in her chair and runs her right hand through her silky hair.

I want to do that.

"Okay. Let's begin with the boring stuff to warm you up. Where do you live?"

She nods. "Portland, Oregon."

I hold up my hands. "Whoa, easy there, Miss Morgan, please don't overshare." Evidently, I'm feeling more comfortable, because my sarcastic self is making an appearance. "Do you like it there?"

Her lips curve into a toothy grin. "Love it. I love the trees, the river, great food, and, of course, the coffee." She sighs, and I wish I could see the images floating around in her head. "Do you like living here?" she asks.

"Honestly?" I rub the back of my neck.

"No. Please lie to me." She rolls her eyes, matching my sarcasm from a moment ago. Yes, she possibly breaks every rule in my

book, but her sass and pretty little face could persuade me to break all the rules.

"Just checking," I reply, raising my hands in surrender. "No, I don't like living here, at least, not as much as I feel I *should*."

She frowns. "I don't think you should feel anything. Why do you think that?"

Fidgeting with my cup, I break eye contact for a moment, considering how real I should be right now. "Guilt, I suppose, for not loving life here. My backyard is practically on the beach, and people perpetually say I'm blessed to live in amazing weather all year long, but truthfully, I miss the seasons. Everyone thinks I'm insane, but San Diego's never felt like home to me. Eventually, I'll move," I say, as if to justify staying. "I haven't been to Oregon yet, but I've heard amazing things. It's definitely on my bucket list." I sip my iced tea.

"Why do you stay?" Beverly challenges, not accepting the weak answer I provide.

"I ask myself that very question, and often. I guess it's because I haven't found my true home. Not yet, anyway. I want to feel like, *ahh*, this is where I belong. Where I'm supposed to live and grow roots. I need to feel it in my bones, and I think I'll know when I find it, but for now, I wait." I shrug, because really I don't know if that's why I stay or if it's an excuse.

She studies me for a long moment. "I'm beginning to understand why Jenny is always raving about you."

My heart drums deep in my chest at the look on Beverly's face. And the news that Jenny's talked about me with her spreads warmth throughout my body. Hopefully only good things. Jenny's been around for a long time, and she's seen me at my best and my worst.

The small, shy smile on Beverly's face and her use of the word "raves" tells me Jenny spoke highly of me.

I shift in my chair, trying to maintain eye contact while containing my excitement. "She's one loyal employee. How well do you and Jenny know each other, anyway?" She never mentioned Beverly or Aubrey to me before yesterday. Then again, she's overall a private person. Still, I want to get to the bottom of this. How could I have been so clueless about Beverly, and about Jenny's relationship with Beverly?

"Not well. Aubrey's worked with me since I started the company, but before that we were friends. She was actually my first friend in Portland. She's been pestering me to work with your company. Aubrey's said more than once that, if we could impress your company, we'd be unstoppable. Although, I also imagine she and Jenny chatter about how male CEO's treat me and both thought working with you would be a nice change of pace from what I'm used to. My friends take things very personally where I'm concerned."

Pausing for a moment, she inhales deeply. "As for yesterday morning, you should know Jenny forewarned me you were out of sorts."

I chuckle with relief. "So, were you messing with me when you wouldn't sit down or barely answered my questions?"

Smoothing her silky hair behind her ear, she flashes a playful smile. "A little. My night was rough, and I was irritated you were late."

God, she's beautiful. "Did you enjoy teasing me?" My eyes slide down to her soft lips.

"Undecided." She bites her lower lip.

I force myself to breathe slowly. How am I going to navigate through a business relationship with this woman when I already

want more? Even though it goes against every fiber in my body, I can't tell her I'm interested in her. That would make me like every other man she's ever worked with. If I can buy us some time to become better acquainted, eventually I'll take a chance. Sharing my feelings is who I am. I don't allow good things to slip through my fingers.

For the time being, I will manage to be happy with any extra time we can share. "What do you do in your free time?"

Beverly grins like she can read my mind. I suspect she knows I want to ask more, need more details, and that I'm trying to figure out how I can prove I'm not like everyone else.

"I love hiking and reading. I often just wander the city, finding new places I didn't know existed or checking out stores I've passed thirty times but never explored. Oh, and there's an amazing farmers market I go to on Sunday when I'm home. If you're ever in Portland, give me a call and I will be your personal tour guide."

I blink in surprise. Did I hear her correctly? Did Beverly Morgan just offer to see me outside of business?

"I plan on holding you to that offer."

Glancing out of my office window at the beautiful sunny day and feeling exhilarated by her offer, I ask before thinking, "What are your plans for the rest of the day?"

Beverly massages the back of her neck. "I'm hoping to fit in a workout and enjoy this beautiful weather. Why?"

Yes! The stars have aligned, and my life is back on track. I ask my next question. "What would you say if I invited you to join me on a hike?"

Shifting in her seat to look outside, she murmurs, "Maybe."

"Really?" Screw hiding my excitement anymore. For starters, I suck at it, plus it's damn exhausting.

She smiles at me. "A hike sounds fun. But I need to go back to the hotel and change. Where should I meet you?"

Oh, no, you don't. You're not going back to your hotel alone to then cancel on me. I wouldn't put the slip past Beverly. From what I've observed so far, she is a detached, strong, yet introverted woman.

"How about we just finish up here, then swing by your hotel to grab your clothes and drop off your car. We can get ready at my house. That way, I can change clothes, too."

Beverly straightens her back. I know she won't agree to my proposal.

"How about I drive to my hotel, change, then we can meet wherever you want to hike?"

"Deal," I say quickly. No way do I want to scare her off. I throw our mess from lunch back into the bag and toss it in the trash.

Beverly stands and smooths her shirt. "Well, I'm going to get a head start. Just text me where I should meet you."

— 15 —

Beverly

"*Great,*" I mutter under my breath. I bend down to pick up my car key, which I dropped because my hands won't stop shaking.

What are you doing? an angry voice shouts inside my head.

I climb into my tiny, uncomfortable rental car and throw my purse and papers into the backseat. Thankfully, I don't have to actually drive back up to Carlsbad. I planned to work out today, so I brought workout gear, plus an extra outfit in my trunk. My whole always-be-prepared routine never fails me.

"Where's my phone?"

I roll my eyes. "Why am I talking to myself?"

I reach back and snatch my purse, dig around, and latch onto my phone. Quickly, I dial Nell's number.

"Hey, Boo," she answers on the first ring.

"Hey, are you home?"

"What's wrong?"

Her concerned voice forces me to calm myself. I draw in a deep breath. "I'm fine, Nell. I just want to know if you're home. I'm downtown at Reed's office."

She blows out a loud exhale. "*Oh.* No, I'm out shopping. You can come meet me if you want?" she invites.

"I'm actually going to go on a hike, but I need a place to change and kill some time. Is it okay if I go to your place?"

"A hike sounds nice..." She leaves a pregnant pause, fishing for an invitation.

"You want to come with us?" I grin and cross my fingers like I did when I was five years old and would ask my mom if Nell could come over to play. This is perfect, I can still hike with Gavin, but with Nell's prying eyes constantly observing, I'll stay on my best behavior and keep myself from leading Gavin on to something that will never happen.

"*Us?*" she asks.

Crap. I chew on the inside of my cheek, "Yes. Mr. Reed invited me."

Nell doesn't say a peep. I check my phone to make sure I didn't drop the call.

Absolute silence. I picture Nell at Fashion Valley Mall, stopping dead in her tracks and dropping her bags.

I pinch the bridge of my nose. "Nell?"

"You're serious?" she demands.

"Don't make a big deal out of this."

I jerk the phone away from my ear as Nell unleashes, "OH MY GOSH!"

"Sis, I can't crash your first date in years! Go to my condo, you know the front door code, get fresh, then go enjoy yourself! OH MY GOSH!" she shouts again. "And you better call me later and tell me everything!"

"It's not a date," I say through clenched teeth. "Come with us?"

"Have fun, Bev. Talk later." Nell hangs up before I have a chance to say anything else.

On the drive to Nell's condo, I try to devise a plan. Usually, I'm a skillful avoider capable of dodging all sorts of obstacles. What the hell was I thinking? Agreeing to go on a freaking hike with a CEO who is hiring me for the biggest project of my career, the same CEO I want to strip naked and take advantage of?

Think, Beverly, think.

My brain rebels. I picture us alone, my hands running through his unruly hair, and his sexy lips fused to mine, his strong hands gripping my hips, pinning me to him . . .

I bang my hands on the steering wheel, baffled by my own thoughts.

Even if I did initiate a hookup, which could put our collaboration at risk, Jenny insists Reed's on the hunt to find a woman he can share his life with, and he doesn't do one-nighters.

Put this man out of your head and get your act together, Beverly.

—

I WALK INTO NELL'S pristine condo, and flop down on her comfy cream couch. I'm desperate to get my mind off of Reed and back into reality. My reality. I call Aubrey.

"Hey, how are you holding up?" she says when she answers her phone.

"Umm, that's my line." I feel confused and rub my right temple. "How's your dad doing?"

"He's feeling a little better, and he's looking forward to your visit. So really, though, how are you? Jenny told me our new business partner was sort of a mess yesterday morning. Then last night your brother texted me to tell me your dad bailed on you. Again."

I sit up, put my phone on speaker and place it on the table in front of me. Covering my face with my hands, I say, "The meeting was fine. Whatever you heard was probably an exaggeration. It started a little rocky, but he recovered. As for my brother, tell him Dad didn't bail on me, he needed to work on a case. When is he going to stop reporting everything to you? I'm *his* older sister. Shouldn't I be worrying about him?"

"Your brother loves you, so cut him some slack. And he has a point. This is like the third time in a row your dad's had to work when you're in town. Couldn't he have cancelled this one time?"

I yank at my hair. Why would my dad postpone his search for a missing girl? What would make me more important than that? A young teenager is missing, her parents weighed down with grief and the unknown. I'm a grown-ass woman, for goodness sake. I'm grateful my dad puts his work first at this stage in his life, and I'm proud of his devotion. His dedication saves other families from shattering like ours did.

Of course, I don't say any of this out loud.

"Aubrey, I called to check on you. Also, I wanted to let you know that I signed the final contract today. We fly to Hawaii in early January."

"Damn, that's faster than I thought. Jenny told me it would be in late February. Why the rush?"

— 16 —

Gavin

As I tug on my T-shirt, a text alert sounds on my phone.

> Beverly: Where should I meet you?

I run my hand through my hair a few times before deciding on the best way I can ask her to meet at my house. Even though Del Mar doesn't feel like home to me, my house is still killer. If nothing else, we can admire the view of the ocean together.

My time is limited with Beverly, and I'm prepared to pull out every trick I have available. Not to mention, it'll be way easier if we drive together in my car.

> Me: I'll send you my address. We're going to Torrey Pines, but the parking can be a nightmare, I have a parking pass. Let me know when I can expect you, and you can hop in my car.

I'm worried she won't believe my story, even though it's the

truth. If she isn't familiar with this area, she'll assume I'm trying to manipulate her.

I pull on shorts, socks, grab a sweatshirt from my closet, brush my teeth, and hear nothing. No response from Beverly. I snag my foam roller out of my closet and get down on the floor in an attempt to work out the nervous tension building in my neck and shoulders.

My phone pings, and my upper back cracks when I spring off of the floor and foam roller like a rabbit. *Ah, shit.* I reach back with my left hand to try to massage the area as I grab the phone from my bed.

Beverly: OK. Send address.

Like I promised, I'm waiting outside when Beverly pulls up. She climbs out of a black hatchback Audi A4 and smiles when she sees me waiting by my truck. I love her smile.

We drive along the coast in comfortable silence. I notice she grips the door handle as she peers out the passenger window at the Pacific Ocean. The waves are on fire this time of year, the water brimming with surfers catching perfect tubes. Would Beverly surf with me?

I interrupt the quiet, "Torrey Pines State Park's just up ahead. It's one of my favorite hiking spots in So Cal. The trails get kind of overrun on the weekends, but it's pretty mellow this time of year. I'm excited to show you, it might not be as great as the trails you've got back home, but the view of the coastline is stunning."

"Do you come here often?"

I pull into the parking lot, and she releases her grip on the door handle. *Is she nervous?* I wonder.

"I try, but I travel a lot for business," I answer as we climb out of my truck.

We tackle the steep road that leads to the trailhead located at the top of the cliffs. I notice, being side by side, just how small she is. With the ocean roaring behind us, I steal glances at her as often as I can. Beverly ignores me, maintaining total composure.

How old is she?

Out here in the sunshine, in her yoga pants and loose-fitting pink tank-top, her hair piled high in a messy bun, she looks way younger than I thought and more carefree.

The road narrows ahead. A group of guys descend the hill we're climbing. Like dominos collapsing, each set of eyes fall on Beverly and their energy shifts. Some of them stand a little taller, puffing up their muscles the best they can, just hoping her eyes will land on them. My eyes remain locked on these dudes who haven't noticed me yet. I pull back to allow Beverly to walk ahead, and only once the group has passed us, do I start to relax again.

Then, I take a quick peek at Beverly from behind. Man those tight, hug-every-curve yoga pants are pure torture. Half of me wishes I hadn't looked, the other half is dying for another glimpse.

We reach the top of the hill and take a narrow sandy path edged in wildflowers, heading to one of the many lookout points. She exclaims in delight when we come to a stop at the edge of the cliff. On the horizon, she spots a pod of dolphins leaping in the ocean. My eyes should be on the water, taking in the graceful dolphins and the breathtaking scenery. Instead, my gaze is locked on Beverly's smile. In this precise moment, I recognize exactly how screwed I am.

In her delight, she grips my forearm. A hot, spine-tingling, current of desire surges up and down my back.

"This is amazing! Thank you for bringing me up here." Her wide smile encompasses her beautiful eyes. Between her genuine happiness, and her hand against my skin, it's impossible to slow the rapid beating of my heart.

She looks down at her hand, and abruptly removes it, giving me a sideways glance. "You okay?"

My mouth goes dry. Before I attempt to speak, I pull two waters out of my backpack. I hand one to Beverly and guzzle the other. Her penetrating eyes never leave my face, and I don't want her to stop looking at me. I want her to see the raw emotion I'm feeling right now, the part of myself I've never shown anyone. But mostly, I want to keep our connection.

I toss my water bottle into my bag and tug on her hand. "Come on, we aren't done yet." The level of pleasure that swells in me when I hear her suck in a deep breath as I clasp her hand is beyond description.

After nearly an hour of trekking through a couple of the trails and stopping to take in the views, we descend the path that leads to the beach. The salted air and sweeping views are invigorating. During our time together, my body's become keenly attuned with hers, as if I can sense each path and direction Beverly is going to walk before she does.

Keeping up with her is no easy feat. She's speeding through, making this relatively easy hike hard work, and her endurance is remarkable. I wonder if she is or was an athlete of some sort, but I haven't been able to catch my breath enough to ask her.

I'm soaked in sweat, and Beverly's skin glistens with a fine sheen. Her mouth is slightly open as she pulls in oxygen. The fire in my lungs has simmered to a low flame. As soon as we hit the sand, a new wave of energy floods me. Squatting down, I

start taking off my shoes and socks. Beverly glances down at me in question.

"Are you up for my favorite part? The water cools off this time of year, but I love . . . " Before I can finish my sentence, she is kicking off her shoes. Realizing her intent, I pop to my feet and shout, "Race you!" I start to run before she gets her last sock off.

Thinking I am in the lead, I turn around, grinning. She's right there, speeding by me, reaching the water in seconds.

Whoa, easy there, Speedy Gonzalez.

I slowly jog my way out to her. When I reach her, she's laughing and kicking up water along the shoreline. Her hair has come undone and loose waves frame her beautiful face. A warm feeling that eases the cold bite of the ocean takes root and expands in my chest.

Our time together outside has unleashed the fun side of her. That business mask she wears must've been left in my office. Without it, I am treated to a glimpse of a relaxed Beverly. No stuffy business clothes confining her, and the high, seemingly impenetrable walls surrounding her lowered at least a few feet. Her eyes sparkle as whatever fears or memories usually restrain her slip somewhere into the depths of her mind.

The tide comes a little higher and she plants her hands on my forearm as she tries to jump out of the way of a wave hitting her calves. To avoid her pants getting soaked, we slowly make our way back to shore where we left our shoes.

"You're quick on your feet. Did you play sports growing up?" I feel her energy shift before I see it. She freezes, her shoulders tense, and she gnaws on her bottom lip.

I watch her, watch all of the joy drain out of her. My heart hurts for her. *What did I say?*

She stares up at me with wide eyes. She searches my face, the same way she did at the restaurant last night. Feeling uneasy and confused by her reaction, I say nothing but maintain eye contact.

"Yes, sports were a big part of my life," she states in a flat tone reminiscent of her business voice.

"Guess they still are, right? I mean, isn't part of your message to encourage people to be active in life?"

"Yeah, but it's different now. It's not a part of me like it once was," she counters, sounding miles away as she stares out at the ocean. So many questions stir inside my head, but a more prominent part of me wants to change the subject. I want the happy Beverly back.

"Are you ready to head back, Roadrunner?" I grin, pleased with my nickname for her.

Beverly gasps and claps a hand over her mouth.

I place my hand on her upper back, eager to understand what's happening. "Are you okay?" God, you'd think I told her I kick puppies.

Beverly swallows, twists her hair together and pulls it over her right shoulder, then nods and plasters on the fakest smile I've seen since my mom tried to pretend to like my first girlfriend.

"Just cold," she mutters, and wraps her arms around her chest as we stand in the damp sand. I offer her my sweaty T-shirt.

She shakes her head to decline, and I don't blame her.

It's glaringly obvious I've said something that's causing her turmoil. At this point, her reactions are becoming a little ridiculous, and it's time to call her out on it. I've treaded cautiously, mostly because we got off on the wrong foot, and I'm into her, but it's time for me to do me.

"Beverly, you're as white as a Beluga Whale, and it's not just that you're cold. Please tell me what I said wrong."

She clamps her lips together to suppress a giggle. Again, I have no clue what I said, but her expression is funny, and I can't help but chuckle. Although, somewhere in the back of my head, I'm concerned I've picked another crazy chick.

"What's so funny?"

"Beluga Whale?" She arches an eyebrow and digs her feet into the sand as the tide comes up. "Seriously? Isn't it white as a ghost?"

"No," I scoff. "That's a stupid saying. Ghosts are see-through or invisible. Beluga Whales are actually white, and that's how you looked a minute ago."

"Fair enough," she concedes with a soft smile.

"Beverly, what's wrong?"

She looks serious at the tone of my voice.

"I'm sorry." She kicks at the sand, tugging her hair back into a messy bun. "It's just, a long time ago someone used to call me Roadrunner. It took me back a bit, that's all." She avoids my eyes and smooths down her T-shirt.

The tortured look on her face lets me know she's telling the truth, but I sense she's leaving out a huge chunk of the story. My money's on an ex-boyfriend. Does she still have feelings for him? That would explain the extreme reaction. At the thought of competition from another man, my gut plummets into a dark, uncharted pit in my body.

— 17 —

Gavin

We're almost back to my house. I dislike that our time together will soon end. As I pull into my driveway, I avoid the far left side where the garage windows are still boarded up from Peyton's break in. Beverly shifts her body toward me and tilts her head in that unnerving investigator way she does. She folds her hands in her lap and prepares herself to speak.

"So, did you research me after last night?"

I shake my head in response.

Her shoulders sag, and she exhales. "And Jenny still hasn't told you anything about me?"

What is she so afraid of me learning? Her past means nothing to me. It's not my job to judge her. Unfortunately, many people feel entitled to make judgments. In a cut-throat industry like ours, some will exploit the faults and mistakes of others to their benefit, then twist their unethical behavior back onto you in an attempt to cause you to believe you're to blame.

"Honestly? Jenny asked me if I wanted information on you before our dinner meeting yesterday."

Clearly startled, she waits for me to continue.

"But I told her no. Normally, that's a routine part of her job. But, for a reason I can't explain, it felt wrong, and I wanted to get to know you organically. That's part of the reason I've been eager to spend time with you. Although Jenny did make it clear I shouldn't hit on you." I grin. "I think I might've failed with that. And, if I'm being honest, after dinner I was itching to Google you."

"Why didn't you?" She fidgets with her hair.

"My gut was telling me not to. After you texted me last night, I knew I did the right thing. Although, now you've definitely piqued my curiosity again. What are you hiding?"

Pressing her hands together, she tangles her fingers together and stares at them. Her insecure look isn't an expression I've seen before from her, and it makes me realize that, even though she's tenacious and confident, she is also vulnerable.

Beverly draws in a deep breath and meets my gaze. She doesn't break eye contact. If anything, she is reaching inside of me—deep inside. "Look . . . Reed . . . it's just refreshing to meet someone in our industry, hell, in life, who doesn't know every detail of my life. Most people jump to conclusions without knowing me or even trying to know me. It's rewarding to land a contract based upon my own credibility. I assumed you wanted to hire my company, in part, because of my past. It could cause some media attention." She shrugs.

Before I can respond, she adds, "Also, I didn't know you were hitting on me. I thought you were being kind." She bites her bottom lip, attempting to hide her burgeoning smile.

"Come on, I'm pretty sure you can tell I like you. I wasn't going to say anything, because I don't want you to feel uncomfortable. I won't make a move on you or anything. At least, not until you make it crystal clear you're interested in me, too."

She arches one delicate brow. "You say that like it's a foregone conclusion."

"Because it is. Someday, it might not be today, or a week from now, or even a month from now, but someday, you will fall for me."

Her eyes widen, and her jaw sags briefly in surprise.

"Let's make a deal. I won't dig for any information about you, and you'll join me for dinner tonight." My heart quickens. With enormous effort, I force my breathing to remain steady. Feeling so nervous is equal parts thrilling and irritating.

"If I say no, will you look me up? Because isn't that blackmail?" She crosses her arms and waits for my reply.

I pretend to ponder her question, silence settling around us, even though I know I won't. She's probably made choices she isn't proud of, and I'm sure some sleazy journalist exploited her mistakes. Sadly, I see it all too often with the athletes I manage.

Whatever she's hiding, it doesn't matter to me. We all have pasts. I'm not pleased with all of my choices, but I know they don't define me. I've learned to forgive myself. Now I pride myself on knowing how to live in the moment. I won't end up like my grandfather, who lived each day on autopilot. Until his cancer diagnosis woke him up and motivated him to rebuild that car with me.

"No. I wouldn't," I assure her.

"Okay, you have a deal." She smiles shyly.

I have to look away to stop myself from kissing her. "Great!" I glance at my phone. "It's almost 4:30 p.m. Shall I pick you up at your hotel, and we can find something to eat up there?"

Beverly hesitates briefly. "Actually . . . I'd rather just stay around here. I'm hungry, and I brought a change of clothes."

She tugs at the ends of her hair. "My hair's a disaster, so why don't we go someplace casual?"

I can't contain my wide grin. Hope prompts me to think she brought a change of clothes, because she wants us to spend more time together.

I guide Beverly into my home and upstairs to one of the guest bedrooms, which has its own private bathroom. "You're more than welcome to shower if you'd like. Here's a stack of towels. Under the sink, you'll find shampoo, conditioner, and soap."

Beverly settles her tote bag on the floor. "Thanks."

My cheeks ache from the smile plastered on my face. "I'm going to grab a shower in my bedroom to get the saltwater and sand off me. Meet you downstairs when you're done." I click the door shut behind me. Then I hear the guest room door lock. I head down the hallway to my bedroom.

Once inside my room, I lean back against the closed door, exhale and try to curb my enthusiasm. As I think about the range of emotions I've experienced today, exhaustion cuts right through me.

These past two days—a bona fide roller coaster ride—have drained me, while Beverly continues to intrigue me. Juggling Peyton's psychotic inclinations and dealing with the bewitching Beverly Morgan translated into zero sleep during the past fifty-five hours. But hey, who's counting?

I'm afraid the more time I spend with Beverly, the sooner I'll reach my boiling point, and my feelings for her will burst out of me. Which could be destructive to any chance I have with her. I suspect the walls she's built around herself need to be taken down with care, brick by brick.

Straightening, I make my way into the shower. My mind

never strays from Beverly, replaying our first meeting, then dinner, the nerves I felt when she texted me last night and the fact that she's just down the hall from me here in my home.

Maybe there are nude photos of her online. That could explain why men in the industry brazenly hit on her, why she doesn't want me to research her, and why she's so careful about everything she does and says.

Trevor would've mentioned dirt like that to me. He's into gossip, and he's definitely into hot-looking, naked women. I remember his behavior the first time he met Jenny at my office.

How long have I been in here?

— 18 —

Beverly

You've got this.
You made the right decision.
You're just getting to know who you're working with.
This is the pathetic pep talk I give myself while looking into the enormous, distressed-wood-framed mirror of Reed's guest bathroom. I can't believe I'm here, in his house, and that I took a shower in his spare bedroom.

When he mentioned having dinner in Carlsbad, panic took over. The last thing I want is to increase the chances of running into an old friend or my brother. He would blab immediately to Aubrey. I get that the poor guy is in love with her, and he can't stop himself from using me as an excuse to reach out to her, but Aubrey is engaged to another man.

I fix my wet hair into a side braid, put on a quick layer of mascara, and one coat of lip-gloss.

This will do.

In the hallway, I hear water running. Following the sound, I walk down the smooth hardwood floors to the bedroom at the end of the hall where the shower is definitely on. Either he's taking

one long ass shower, or he had other things to do before getting ready. I make my way downstairs.

To the left of his gorgeous kitchen, complete with white quartz countertops, a massive island, and sleek black modern farmhouse cabinetry, I spot beautiful French doors that lead to his backyard.

I step out into the cool San Diego fall air, and I feel a sense of longing for an area I left so many years ago. Today during our hike, I didn't tell Gavin that I used to go to Torrey Pines as a teenager. Mostly with Nell and my mom. It was one of our favorite spots. We'd spend the day exploring each of the looping trails near the cliffs, search for dolphins along the coastline, and then finish up with a picnic on the beach.

Today, when the huge pod of dolphins suddenly appeared, it took me back to a time in my life when I was unbroken. I could hear Mom's laughter in my ears and, for a split second, I forgot who I am now and what kind of times I allow myself these days. It wasn't until we made our way down to the beach that I felt reality, ugly bitch that she is, slap me across the face again.

Gavin's questions about sports churned up anxiety, but when he called me Roadrunner, I nearly fainted. Was the universe playing a sick joke on me? More likely, it was reminding me of my current place in this world. Patrick adopted that nickname for me when we were nine, and no one has used the moniker for me since before my race on *that* day.

Casting my gaze out over the ocean, I momentarily allow my mind to wander, and I wish things were different. Gavin Reed makes me long to be a different Beverly. Not the Beverly I once was, and not the heartless Beverly I am now, but a stronger, happier, healthier Beverly.

Still, I am positive if I let go, if I move on, then I'll be letting go of the people I loved most. Letting go of the happiest years of my life. It would be me saying my happiness is more important than treasuring their memories. Being honest with myself, if I move forward, grow, and change, I'm afraid I'll no longer want to fulfill Mom's dreams. I might be selfish enough to resume the pursuit of my own dreams, especially the dream which ultimately caused her to lose her life.

My phone rings, making me jump in the comfortable lounge chair I'm sitting in that overlooks Reed's pool and the ocean.

Ugh. My brother, Ian.

"Hey."

"Bev, where are you? Aren't we going to get together while you're in town?"

"Yeah, sorry. Work's kept me busy with Aubrey leaving early and all." At least part of that's true. "Tomorrow morning I have a commercial shoot near you, let's do lunch."

"You're not gonna flake?"

"No, Ian," I huff, and roll my eyes. "Name the place."

Noticing movement near the door, I glance over and see Reed, standing there in jeans and a black T-shirt that shows off his sexy biceps and forearms. My mouth waters, and I allow my eyes to slowly skim the length of his body.

How long has he been there?

Still, with my phone pressed to my ear, Ian's voice sounds far-off. "Just text me where. I've got to go."

I hang up on my brother, my eyes fixed on Reed.

He pulls a chair over to sit by me, and I can feel that he wants to know what guy I was talking to, but I skip informing him that Ian is my brother. Maybe if he believes I'm involved, that will dampen his attraction to me.

Gavin leans in toward me. "Everything okay?"

"Yes. What about you?"

"What about me?"

"I was worried you passed out or something. It took you so long to get ready, I almost sent in search and rescue," I quip.

Gavin chuckles.

I love the small crinkles that form around his eyes when he laughs.

"Sorry about that." He doesn't provide an explanation on why it took him so long. And I like that.

I rub my stomach. "So where are we going for dinner?"

A slow smile animates his face. "Let's go, and I'll show you."

I decide that his low husky voice probably makes most women swoon, and it would probably make me swoon if I were capable of that kind of emotion.

— 19 —

Gavin

We eat dinner at Cardiff Tacos, a little hole-in-the-wall, actually more like a hut on the beach. Beverly's sipping another Arnold Palmer. Just as I did last night, I follow her lead and cradle a glass of lemonade. The condensation coats my palms, leaving my hands damp.

Does she not drink alcohol? Or is she still sending me a clear message that our relationship is strictly professional?

"I really like this place," Beverly says after she polishes off her last taco.

"It's one of my favorite local spots," I reply.

"This is more my kind of place than where we ate last night."

Hallelujah! Even with her reserved personality, I didn't pin her for being pretentious. However, I hesitated to bring her here, on what I consider the continuation of our first date.

"Don't look so surprised," she swats my arm. "This is the kind of place my dad would always bring me to and the exact type place I search for all over in Portland."

Would take her? This is the first time Beverly's mentioned her dad or anyone in her family.

Before I get the chance to ask her more, our conversation is interrupted when I hear my name shouted from across the tiny restaurant. I look over to the front door, maybe twenty feet away, and spot Jeremy, my least favorite colleague in the sports industry. He's standing there with a proud grin as he waves at me.

"*Ugh,*" I grumble under my breath. This can't be real. Jeremy's the last human I want to deal with right now. After correlating his past comments to Beverly, I want to throat-punch the guy.

Beverly's back is to Jeremy. I nod once in his direction with a tight, forced smile. I pray Jeremy doesn't approach our table. Before I can tell Beverly who it is and not to turn around, she glances over her shoulder.

Jeremy looks stunned, his mouth drops open, then his facial expression darkens. Beverly turns back to me, her disgust apparent. *Trust me, the feeling's mutual.*

Jeremy stalks toward us, his long legs carrying him quickly. I can see his desire for a fight written all over his narcissistic face. Bad decision. Hopefully, he's at least smart enough to pick it with me and not Beverly.

The insolence of this clown, believing he is good enough to even share the same air as Beverly, infuses me with rage.

Jeremy stands before our table, hands on his hips. "Well, well, well, it's nice to see someone's finally caught this little thing's attention, Gavin. I hoped it would be me." His predatory gaze shifts to Beverly. "No worries, sweetie, and no hard feelings."

His chauvinistic attitude brings me back to when I was a boy and Father would belittle Mom. The only difference now, I'm old enough to put a stop to it. Before Beverly can speak, I jump up from my chair and tower inches above Jeremy's smug

face. With my six-foot, three-inch frame looming over him, he's finally smart enough to put his hands up in surrender.

"Apologize to her now. Miss Morgan and I are in a business dinner meeting and discussing a future project," I add the last part for Beverly's sake. I couldn't care less if this idiot thinks we're together, but I don't want her reputation tarnished.

"Whoa." Jeremy takes a step backward. "Hey, Gavin . . . I-I, I'm sorry, I-I . . ."

"Wrong person!" I shout as our startled fellow diners turn toward us. I clench my hands into fists at my side, trying to control my fury. "I don't need the apology, you idiot! She's the one you insulted."

Composing himself enough to speak to Beverly, he says, "Right—Beverly, uh-umm, Miss Morgan, I'm—"

She cuts him off. "Just walk away, Jeremy. Once the last set of the *Prove Them Wrong* commercials are wrapped, we're done. I won't work with you again." Her voice is calm, yet firm. She remains unruffled, staring him down with confidence and poise.

I'm shocked when Jeremy turns around to leave. His cute date, whom I hadn't noticed hovering behind him, slaps him across the face.

"You're a pig," she seethes and stomps her way to the exit.

"Beth . . . Beth, wait," he says as he chases after her.

Easing back down into my neon green plastic chair, I blow out a frustrated gust of air and close my shaking hands into fists as adrenaline pulses through me. *I should've kicked his ass.*

Beverly stares out at the ocean, appearing calm. I expect her to be as enraged as I feel. Although, now that I think about it, yesterday morning in my office she responded to my behavior with similar detachment. She's clearly well practiced at being treated like crap in this industry.

To think I could've been different, I could've stood out. Instead, I was a jerk. Like everyone else. I pinch the bridge of my nose, wishing for something stronger than damn lemonade.

Beverly's gentle hand settles on my forearm. "Don't," she whispers.

Confused, I study her face, searching for answers.

"Don't let him ruin your night. Come on, let's get out of here. Feel like a walk on the beach?"

"Sure," I reply, still trying to shake off the impact of the rage roaring through me.

When I don't move, she stands up and tugs on my hand. Her touch is all it takes to suppress my fury—at least, temporarily.

— 20 —

Gavin

In unison, we kick off our shoes right when we hit the sand. We stroll to the hard-packed, wet sand at the edge of the Pacific. I notice, yet again, Beverly's height. I must be at least a foot taller. Generally, I'm drawn to tall women, who don't make me feel like a giant, but Beverly carries herself in a way that I sometimes forget about her height.

We cruise along the water's edge in silence, the moon resting high in the darkening sky, bright and almost full. Then I stop and turn to her. I can't hold back my questions any longer.

"How are you not pissed? Why didn't you let him apologize? You deserved an apology," I insist.

Her facial expression remains serene. "Of course, I'm upset, but I refuse to give him the satisfaction of knowing that. Besides, you didn't give me much of a chance to react." She crosses her arms, but her eyes remain soft.

"He's a misogynistic pig, and I don't care one bit about his opinion of me. And why should I let him apologize? *Screw that!* No way will I give him a chance to redeem himself," she says, surprising me with the fire I hear in her voice.

"Is this how they all treat you?" I stuff my hands in my pockets, scared of her answer.

What will I do if she says yes? I can't stop working with everyone in the industry. My business would collapse. I can't protect her from everyone, either. Not that she would even accept my protection. The thought of another woman I care about being hurt isn't something I'm willing to ignore.

Beverly lets out a frustrated sigh, aiming a hard kick at the sand between us. "No. Jeremy is one of the worst. I knew, getting into a male-dominated field, there would be some pricks out there. I can handle myself."

I rest my hand on her shoulder. "I know you can, but you shouldn't have to. Even I could've treated you better yesterday morning."

"Just stop." She shrugs my hand off of her shoulder. "I already told you, you weren't even rude. Never did you say a degrading word to me. So, please stop. I don't want you to view me as some little girl who needs rescuing. I don't want or need sympathy from you or anyone else."

"Sympathy? You think this is sympathy? No, Beverly. This is rage. Rage toward Jeremy and every other pathetic man like him. Rage that you have to go through this shit. Rage that you even have to utter the sentence 'I can take care of myself.'"

Her face softens. She reaches up and presses her palm against the side of my face, gently stroking my stubbled cheek. My stomach muscles tighten and my heart rate accelerates.

"Thank you, Gavin. I'm used to handling these things myself, and I didn't thank you for having my back." Her gaze slides from my eyes to my lips, and her hand slowly slides from my check down to my chest.

Kiss me, kiss me, kiss me!

She looks away and shakes her head.

I'm a fool; I should've kissed her. No, she needs to make the first move. I did the right thing. She's in control here. She's driving me crazy, but I think she needs to be in control.

"Do you want to sit down for a bit?" she asks.

"Okay." Still in a daze from her hand on my chest and the look in her eyes, I plop down on the cool sand next to her. We stare out at the dark ocean, and my hand grazes her jean-covered thigh.

"Sorry." I shift sideways to give her more room.

"Gavin, you don't need to make such an effort not to touch me. I'm comfortable with you, and I trust you're not going to pounce on me."

"It isn't only for you, Beverly." I lean back on my hands with my legs stretched out long.

I can't bear touching her without knowing I don't have to stop.

"What do you mean?"

Feeling her gaze on me, I turn my eyes to meet hers. "I think it's pretty obvious, I'm attracted to you. I really like you."

She bites her full bottom lip, and she remains quiet. I know she's into me, too. I hate waiting, but I won't rush her. As much as I feel her attraction to me, I also feel her resistance.

Not able to handle her big brown eyes staring at me with longing for another second, I ease back onto the sand and stare up at the night sky.

"Tired?" Beverly pokes my side.

"Yeah, I went on a grueling hike today with this fierce, tiny, inexhaustible, beautiful woman," I tease. Yes, I plan to take it slow, but playing by her rules is exhausting.

"Hey! I'm not *that* little. You're just abnormally large." She pokes me in the ribs again.

I grab her hand, pulling her atop me. She smells like sweet wildflowers and vanilla. Possessed by the alluring Beverly, I tickle her and am rewarded with the biggest howl of laughter and one very wiggly Beverly.

Like a masterful escape artist, she manages to break free of my hold. My hand shoots out, but I miss her. Now, she's on her feet, daring me to try and catch her. But that's a dare I don't take, because that girl can pump those legs like nothing I've ever seen.

—

HUNDREDS OF THOUGHTS invade my brain on our drive back to my house.

I don't want tonight to end.
Should I have kissed her?
I want to kick Jeremy's ass.
I wish she had kissed me.

Her voice pulls me from my thoughts. "Are you okay?" she asks with concern.

"Why do you ask?" My gut feels like I consumed a dish of anxiety with a dash of acid.

"Well, for starters you're gripping the steering wheel as if it were Jeremy's neck. Then, there's the fact that you haven't said a word since we got in the car."

I chuckle and loosen my grip on the steering wheel. "I wouldn't mind strangling that guy. Sorry, it's been a long couple of days, yet I don't want tonight to end."

As I pull into my driveway, she unbuckles her seatbelt and shifts to face me.

"I had a great time, but I think we both need to get some sleep. I have an early obligation in the morning. I'll have some pissed off people if I come in looking haggard."

"I don't think that's possible. But don't worry, I have an early morning, too."

I decide not to tell her we have the same destination tomorrow morning. I don't want to add any stress to her day, or make her feel obligated to go out of her way to chat with me. I wonder what she's doing there. I'm going to make sure Trevor doesn't harass Beverly. At least, that's what I've told myself.

"Then it's settled." She pats her knee, and I think it's to convince herself to call it a night. "I just need to grab my bag. I left it inside your front door."

We climb out of my truck and slowly walk up the paver path that leads to my solid oak front doors.

"Are you sure you don't want to come in?" I ask as we reach the front.

She shifts from foot to foot. "I really should be going."

I nod, step inside to grab her bag, and then walk her to her car. Once her bag is secured in the backseat, we pause and look at each other.

Then, with an awkward handshake, I try to say goodnight, but she draws herself closer, raises up on her tiptoes, and gently kisses my cheek.

"Thanks for a great time today. I'll see you in January."

Stunned, I let her turn away without another word.

As I watch her drive away, my phone rings. It's a number I don't recognize.

"Reed," I say into the phone.

"Why are you ignoring me?" Peyton whines into the phone.

Good God!

"Peyton, stop contacting me!" I hang up before she can respond.

Nothing like an ice-cold bucket of crazy dumped on my euphoric day.

Even after Peyton's disruptive call, once inside my home I feel the happiness of the day wash over me again. Tonight, the first night in months, I skip my nightly swim. Opting to sip on a glass of Cabernet Sauvignon, instead, and relive the feel of Beverly's hand on my chest, her face inches from mine, her eyes scanning my lips as she waits for me to make a move.

I'm startled from my vivid memories by my phone buzzing on the wooden patio table next to me. Checking the screen, I am shocked when I see Beverly's name across the screen.

Beverly: Thanks again for today. I had fun.

She might not want to admit it, but she likes me.

Me: Me too. Goodnight, Beverly.

— 21 —

Beverly

A strange blaring noise jolts me awake. I almost tumble out of bed and onto the floor of my fancy-schmancy hotel room.

What the . . . ?

Is that my alarm?

I can't remember the last time I slept more than a four-hour stretch, let alone straight through the night. Thank God I'm a punctual freak, and I never forget to set my alarm. Without it this morning, I might've slept my way right through the commercial. I need to be there in less than two hours.

I call room service and order more food than a person my size should be capable of eating. Eggs, hash browns, sourdough toast with extra butter, a full order of fruit, a glass of water and, of course, coffee. Always coffee.

Rested and stuffed, I take the hottest, most cleansing shower of my life. My mind's clear of my obsession, and I'm thankful for the start of a new day, free of the tempting Mr. Reed.

I apply a fresh and simple makeup look, although I'm sure the producers will have the makeup artists attack my face. After drying and curling my hair in large loose curls, I unzip the bag

containing my wardrobe for the commercial that *Stand Up,* the nonprofit organization, delivered to my hotel last night.

Their stylist, whom I've never met, did an astounding job choosing an outfit that suits me but is also appropriate for a Domestic Violence Ad. I slip into the beautiful deep eggplant purple sheath dress, topping it off with a tailored black blazer. Then, I'm out the door.

Shay, the owner of *Stand Up*, approached me last year about working with her organization. She did her research, learning about my involvement in the domestic violence community and the donations I've made to *Walk for Enough,* a small high school walk here in Southern California where all proceeds go to victims of domestic violence.

What she doesn't know—no one knows—is why I'm involved in this community. Some people make assumptions about me, figuring I'm a survivor. Not true.

This is another goal Mom wasn't able to fulfill, another secret of hers I found on her computer. Learning about Mom's childhood and her goal to help others after she died were agonizing reminders of a beautiful life ended too soon.

"I hope this is what you had in mind about helping victims, Mom," I say aloud. The pain of her death rips through me again.

—

ARRIVING THIRTY MINUTES early, I head into the massive commercial building space we'll use for shooting. Following the signs leading me to the room I need to be in, I almost crash into someone walking through one of the doors.

"Whoa, sorry," a familiar voice acknowledges. "Hey, Beverly!" Trevor, Gavin Reed's cousin. Crap, I didn't realize we'd be here at the same time today.

"Hi, Trevor, how you doing?" I ask, following his lead when he hugs me. A friendly guy, he's also one of the nice ones. Maybe it's because he's dating Jenny, Mr. Reed's assistant, or perhaps I'm not his type. Either way, he's never hit on me.

"I'm good. Are you ready for today?" he asks with an odd warning look on his face.

He steps to my side, and my heart plummets. Standing behind him is the delicious Gavin Reed, his eyes darting back and forth between Trevor and me. He looks tense.

I now understand what Trevor was trying to tell me. *Don't mention Jenny.* I remember that Gavin doesn't know about their relationship. He forbade it years ago. As for Gavin, he remains tense after observing my friendly greeting with Trevor.

Oh, boy.

"Mr. Reed," I acknowledge. He flinches at my formal greeting, but I ignore his reaction. I know anything that happens here today will get back to Jenny, which will also reach Aubrey. I quickly realize our lives are all tangled together.

Does this mean something? I wonder.

Gavin doesn't follow my lead today. "Hi, Beverly." He leans in to hug me.

God, he smells delicious, like the woods, jasmine, and cinnamon blended into a tempting concoction. Like a saving grace sent from the heavens, my phone rings. I excuse myself.

"Hey," I say to my brother.

"We still good for lunch today?" he asks.

I'm in hearing distance of Gavin and Trevor, so I keep my response vague. "Yeah, I'll text you when I'm done here."

"Okay, is one still a good time?" Ian asks.

"Yes."

My brother thinks nothing of my short responses, because

that's my usual style—direct with no extra fluff on the phone.

"See you soon, sis."

"Okay, bye." I end the call.

Turning back to Gavin and Trevor, I notice Trevor slip back into the next room, leaving me alone with Gavin in this tight, airless waiting area.

"It's good to see you again today." He places a gentle hand on my shoulder.

My breath hitches as a hot current of electricity seems to flow between us. "Yeah, what are the odds? Are you in the commercial, too?" I ask.

"No. I'm supporting Trevor. He does these types of things for me, so the least I can do is be here."

What does he mean?

"You don't like being on camera?" I ask, trying to determine his meaning.

"Not my favorite thing, but that's not what I meant. My mother and I are survivors of domestic violence. Trevor donates his time every year on our behalf."

Oh. Umm ... words, where are you? Please enter my brain again, and please be appropriate and not the cold words of a detached woman with a dead heart.

I twist my hands together. "I'm sorry. It's nice of him to recognize the struggle you went through."

Good job, Beverly! Congrats on being human!

"Yeah, he's a good guy," Gavin replies, scrutinizing me.

I know what he's doing. He's searching for any hint that I might be into his cousin. While Trevor is handsome, kind, and a successful baseball player, there's only one man that's ever tempted me to disregard my commitment to solitude, and he's standing right in front of me.

Lies! The dead-hearted witch who runs the show screams in my head. Something about this man makes my split personalities emerge more frequently. Frankly, after only a few days, I'm exhausted by the bickering. I can't wait to escape back home to Portland. The fresh air, trees, and rain will cleanse me of all this Gavin Reed nonsense.

I shift under Reed's intense blue eyes as he searches my face. "Well, I should get in there," I announce, feeling reluctant to walk away from him.

"Oh . . . yeah . . . right . . ." he mutters in a very un-Reed-like manner. He takes my hand, stopping me from walking past him. "Want to grab some lunch after we're done here?"

I glance down at his strong, yet gentle hand, holding mine. I'm terrified that, if I leave with him, I'll destroy this sweet man. Never have I been more grateful for my little brother.

"I'm sorry, I already have plans."

For a split second he lets his disappointment show, but like the persistent man he is, he asks about my dinner plans. I freeze. He knows he's got me, and he pounces.

"It'll be casual. Just as friends," he says, then adds, "You're probably leaving town soon. It's good to get to know your co-workers."

He almost has me, but looking into his beautiful eyes, the desire not to hurt him trumps my desire to have my way with him. "I'm sorry, I have an early flight in the morning, and after lunch, I need to meet a prospective client."

Thankfully, all of this is true. I have lunch plans with Ian, and earlier this morning I texted Blaire, a gorgeous model I've been dying to persuade to sign with me for months now.

She's constantly telling me she wants to be "fabulously famous"—her words not mine—and she doesn't know if my

company can get her there. She doesn't yet believe that my vision will become what I know it will. If she agrees to meet with me today, I plan on giving it to her straight. I'm not in the habit of begging anyone to join us, but her voluptuous curves attached to such a stunning all-American face tugs on something deep in my gut.

Plus, I'd hate to see another beautiful, healthy woman fall into the hands of a traditional agency, which will make her drop fifteen pounds minimum because some tool tells her that's what beauty looks like, and what sells.

"Excuse me, Miss Morgan?" a timid sounding young woman says.

Both Reed and I jump.

I clear my throat and croak, "Yes."

"I'm sorry to interrupt. We're going to be ready for you soon, and I'm supposed to bring you to the makeup artist," the lanky brunette carrying a clipboard, pencil tucked in her ruffled hair, and wearing large clear-rimmed glasses explains.

"Okay. Thank you. I'll be there in a moment." I nod at her. She ducks out of the room, and again I'm alone with the unfairly gorgeous Gavin Reed.

"Well, good luck today. And Beverly?" He pauses, his eyes roaming over my face.

I manage to force out a breathless, "Yes?"

"You're beautiful." And with that, he opens the door for me to enter the set of the commercial.

— 22 —

Gavin

Unable to keep my eyes off Beverly, I watch as she gives the camera a moving statement about domestic violence and its long-lasting effects on victims. With so much emotion couched in her words, I wonder if she's suffered through something in her home.

Could that be why she doesn't speak about her family?

During a part of the commercial, Beverly and Trevor speak together. In between takes, I study their interaction. Trevor speaks in low, hushed tones so no one can overhear. Beverly seems comfortable with him, like she's been around him many times. If that's the case, it would mean my cousin, the closest person to me in my life, lied to me. He told me he met her once in Jeremy's office.

The only reassurance I get from the doubts swarming in my head is the many glances Beverly sends my way. I see no interest on her part in Trevor. Her body doesn't angle toward his, she doesn't flirtatiously touch her hair, the way she did with me last night.

After only a few retakes, the commercial wraps, and Trevor strolls over to me. "So, what did you think?"

My eyes remain anchored on Beverly as she speaks to Shay. She removes her blazer, revealing the tight dress below that hugs her every curve.

"It was great," I mumble to Trevor. "I'm happy I came."

"Yeah, I bet you are." He nudges me hard with his elbow to get my attention. Shifting toward him and away from Beverly takes all of my strength. When Trevor gives me a knowing look, I realize I should tell him about my feelings for Beverly.

"Let me say goodbye, then we'll go out to lunch and catch up," I say.

"I'll wait downstairs for you," he responds. Then he shouts across the room, "Bye, Beverly! Shay, always a pleasure." And with a cocky grin, he's out the door.

There's no way I'll leave without saying goodbye to Beverly. It's possible I won't see her again until January, and a lot can happen in four months.

I don't need to wait long for her to finish her conversation with Shay. When they're done, it's Shay who comes over to me, not Beverly. The flirtatious Shay holds nothing back.

"Gavin, I'm so happy you came," she exclaims while caressing my forearm.

"Me, too," I respond, looking over at Beverly.

When our eyes connect, she offers me an encouraging smile. She can't possibly think I'm into Shay. Not after the day we spent together yesterday.

Well, you didn't kiss her when she was practically in your arms begging you to.

"Excuse me." I leave a startled Shay in my wake.

Crossing the room in a few long strides, I place a gentle hand on the middle of Beverly's back. She freezes. "You were great," I tell her.

Turning to face me, her warm honey eyes sparkle for a moment, but her features quickly shift into a detached, distant gaze.

"Thanks," she says. "Well, the last few days have been nice. If you have any questions from now until January, you know my number."

That's it, she's saying goodbye. I feel her pushing me away—she's lacing up her running shoes and sprinting away from the chemistry we have. Well, I've got bad news, baby, I might not be as quick as you, but I've got endurance, and I'll go the distance. "I'm sure I'll reach out to you a lot from now until then. Details need to be finalized, plus we're friends now, right?"

A faint smile softens her face. "Friends."

Without hesitation, I lean in to give her a friendly hug. One that others wouldn't think twice about.

"Talk soon, Beverly," I whisper. "Oh, and don't forget, if I'm ever in Portland you promised to be my tour guide."

"Yes, I did." She chuckles. "Bye, Reed."

I'm not sure why sometimes she calls me by my last name, but I dig it. Little does the beautiful Miss Morgan know, I have a meeting in Seattle in a few weeks. It's time for me to extend the trip and take a few personal days in Portland.

With one more glance, I stride out of the building with a new objective that will secure me more time with Beverly.

—

THE SUN HITS ME WITH an unusual intensity for late September, even by Southern California standards. Walking over to my truck, it takes me a moment to spot Trevor. He's on his phone, tucked under the shade of a large oak tree near the street. He

sees me, turns away and quickly ends his call. Then jogs over to me.

"Who was that?" I ask when he reaches me.

"Just some chick who's got it bad for me." He pats my back.

We stare at each other for a long moment. He knows that I know he's lying, but instead of getting into it in the parking lot of an office building, I bite my tongue. We'll talk about it at lunch.

We climb into my truck, and immediately Trevor inserts his iPhone into my dock on the dash and plugs in. I'm backed into a parking space, facing the entrance of the building. As I start my Tacoma, the doors swing open in front of us. A very differently dressed Beverly Morgan emerges.

Her tight and tiny jean shorts show off her amazing, no incredible—no, there are no words to describe what her legs are. They are everything and have shot up the list to my all-time favorite legs. The thin, loose mustard-yellow tank top flatters her olive skin tone, and her hair is in a high ponytail swaying with every step.

Who are you going to see dressed like that?

Trevor whacks me on my shoulder. "Man, you got it bad." My pain in the ass cousin is cracking up. "I knew you had a thing for her the moment I saw you two together."

His laughter is quickly cut short when his phone rings with a ringer I've never heard before. My eyes move toward the sound. Trevor jumps and reaches out to grab his cell, but it's too late. I saw it. A picture of a familiar, cute girl blowing a kiss, with an unfamiliar title lit up on the screen, 'My Love.'

My jaw goes slack in disbelief. I rub my eyes with the back of my hands and turn to my cousin, who's staring down at the phone he's cradling in his hands.

"Why is Jenny calling you? And how do you have that picture of her?"

— 23 —

Beverly

Day five back at home, the fresh and cleansing Oregon air is supplying my brain with the appropriate amount of oxygen and freeing it from foolish desires. Without hearing a word from Reed or his team, I'm grateful to slip back into my relentless hustle.

For a moment there, I went soft, but that isn't something I'll allow to happen again. After all, I have a reputation to uphold. Often I'm called a bitch or uptight, but the truth is I'm operating my business just like any male CEO. Yet, because I'm a woman, I'm categorized and receive incessant pushback from men with oversized egos.

The fight has been challenging, but now I officially know I've made it in this industry. My email and phone are under assault by the biggest jackass in the industry, Jeremy, pleading and groveling for my forgiveness and continued partnership. Some might say it's vile or even unladylike for me to revel in his pathetic emails, or the pitiful fear evident in his voicemails. Too bad for Jeremy I don't value those opinions.

I've had to suffer through offensive comments, detestable

looks and actions from this man. I've protected and defended my models from his sexual harassment and now, finally, I can kick his revolting butt to the curb. I've printed out his emails and saved his voicemails to my computer to use as a pick-me-up the next time I encounter another predator like Jeremy.

My office line rings, and I admit it's a little sadistic that I hope it's Jeremy again.

"This is Beverly," I say much too cheerfully into the phone.

"Miss Morgan, there's a Peyton Hollis on the line, insisting she speak to you." Andrew, my temporary fill-in, says.

"Andrew, I don't know Peyton Hollis. Take a detailed message, including her contact information, and if I feel she warrants a callback, I'll contact her."

"I'm sorry, but I've already done that. She's the one who called while you were in San Diego," he stammers. "She's the actress who wants to get her feet wet in modeling. I sent you her file, as you requested."

I completely forgot about her. "Right. I need you to buy me time. Tell her I'm unavailable right now, but I will be in contact soon."

"Okay. Will do, thank you."

———

THREE PROSPEROUS MEETINGS later, and two new major deals signed, my body feels lighter, and I'm gliding around the office feeling intoxicated. Before heading out for a relaxing routine-filled weekend, including my favorite Italian dinner, chocolates at Sal's and an early morning hike with Aubrey, I check out Andrew's notes on the woman, Peyton, who called earlier.

Turns out she really is a successful TV actress, who's interested in branching out to modeling. Andrew also forwarded me

an email that she sent after their conversation today. It includes photos of herself and the many reasons why she wants to work with my company.

Checking the time, it's already 7:30 p.m. on a Friday, so I make a note on my calendar to contact Peyton Hollis on Monday morning, then happily depart my office.

The drive to my favorite restaurant, which is actually over in Vancouver, Washington, is a typical Friday night ride, filled with gangster rap and hammering rain. Sitting at my usual table, my meal is delivered to me without the need to order, and a comforting sense of normalcy is fully restored.

After the delicious Caprese salad, I dig into my creamy, Penne alla Vodka pasta, sopping up the excess sauce with crusty bread and savoring every bite.

I sip Pinot Noir from the Willamette Valley, waiting for my dessert to arrive. My cell phone chimes. I dig it out of the studded-leather Kate Spade purse Nell bought for me last year.

Seeing Gavin's name across the screen, I choke on my wine. I blot my chin with the napkin and try my best to rationalize my overreaction to a text message.

You just don't like things you're not prepared for. I tell myself. *You're tired.*

Recognizing the ludicrous nature of my behavior, I skate a finger across my phone and open the text.

> Reed: Hi Beverly, just a heads up the new wardrobes for the tennis players have shipped to your office. I'll forward you the tracking number.

See, you idiot. All that worry over nothing. Although, I

know what I'm actually terrified of—what if Gavin Reed takes me up on my stupid tour guide offer?

— 24 —

Gavin

This is it. This is the week I hope to see Beverly again. I have a meeting in Seattle on Thursday morning with Robertson's, a men's underwear line. My goal is to land a deal for one of my most profitable athletes, and then to shift my attention to someone who matters much more to me.

From Seattle, it's only about a three-hour drive to Portland and, therefore, to Beverly. Since I haven't been able to get her off my mind since she left San Diego, I think it's time to take her up on her offer of a free guided tour. From the time she left San Diego fifteen days ago, we've talked mainly about work. I hope my showing up in Portland won't seem weird to her.

I shoot her a text, so I don't put her on the spot too much.

> Me: I'll be in your area Thursday. Will you be around?

I blow out a long breath and set down my phone, trying to focus on work. It's Monday and the middle of the day, so she

might be busy. I can't waste another workday fantasizing about long dark hair and eyes the color of honey.

I start going through my never-ending emails. First, an email from the assistant at Noel's Media, requesting a phone conference with Noel. After replying with the times and days I'm available, I check my phone to make sure it's not set on silent.

Probably in a meeting. Keep working.

Seventeen emails, six phone calls, two bathroom breaks, three more cups of coffee, one water, and a meatball sub later, my phone chimes with a text message. Just like every other time I hear that specific alert I had set up for her, my heart rate accelerates and my palms sweat.

> Beverly: Is it regarding work? I'm free after 3 p.m.

I didn't expect her question. I should've. Do I make up something about work or . . . be honest, Gavin. I'm looking for a free and hot tour guide to show me around.

Maybe not that honest.

> Me: After 3 p.m. is perfect. No, not work-related. I'll be in town and want to take you up on your offer. I promise to pay my volunteer tour guide with dinner.

> Beverly: How long will you be in town?

> Me: Until Sunday night.

Damn! Not enjoying this texting routine. Her Miss Aloof act isn't a good sign. Perhaps she's no longer attracted to me. What if she's met someone else?

Even if she has, it won't deter my feelings for her. Bottom line: my heart is a lost cause when it comes to Beverly Morgan. My mother told me someday it would happen, and when it did, I would immediately know and nothing would dull my emotions. She was right. Then again, she usually is.

> Beverly: Cool. Bring your hiking boots, and we'll go to my favorite spot.

Whew! My insecurities were getting the best of me. I mean, come on, she's an insanely successful CEO, who doesn't waste her time writing elaborate texts. She's efficient and direct.

Now, this weekend will be the ultimate test. If my feelings for her remain the same or grow, I'm going to let her know before I leave. I refuse to continue to live like this. I will lay it out for her, and the ball will be in her court. She'll need to make a decision.

She's all I think about, all I dream about. I'm losing my mind over her. I want to be with her. I don't want her to meet someone else before she understands how much I care for her, and that I'm not some jerk looking for a hookup. I want a real relationship with her, something authentic and meaningful.

> Me: Can't wait. Talk soon.

The rest of Monday and Tuesday move in slow motion. My mind repeatedly wanders to Beverly and Portland, making con-

centrating on anything impossible. It can't be healthy to think about someone this much.

I even change my flight from Wednesday to the red-eye on Tuesday night. Now, I'm sitting in my hotel room at Alexis in Seattle, just as on edge here as I was in San Diego. I need to get out of this room, but it's almost midnight. Worse, I have nowhere to go.

Instead, I order room service, clam chowder soup and a bottle of wine, hoping it'll make me sleepy. After eating and pouring a second glass of wine, I run a hot bath. Trevor would have a good laugh at this. I can hear him now, with his jock mentality. *Only you can get away with the girly shit you do and still have women all over you.* He's told me this since we were kids.

He justifies it as my mom raising me alone, and I let him believe whatever makes him feel comfortable. Truth is, some men are just idiots who should learn from women about some of the simple pleasures in life. I feel bad for anyone who thinks something as relaxing as a soak in a hot tub is for one gender and not the other.

—

FIVE HOURS. THAT'S ALL the sleep I manage. I'm up before the sun. With my meeting not until tomorrow morning, I regret my decision to arrive in Seattle a day early. I can't stay in this room. I guzzle a bottle of water, throw on a pair of jeans, comfortable shoes and grab a warm jacket with a hood, because it's Seattle. Although it's not raining, I know it will.

I'm on the street and trekking in the direction of Pike Place Market. I'm likely to find a café or bakery opening fairly soon. The cold, crisp air soothes my anticipation about seeing

Beverly tomorrow. It helps to ground me in the present.

I like it here. The vibe, the air, and the people—they all make me feel comfortable. The inner stillness filling my body is the most peaceful I've felt since Beverly walked into my office.

Settling into a café that sells only crumpets, I order a coffee, and an egg, cheese, and tomato crumpet. Unsure what to expect from the spongy cake, I'm grateful the coffee is rich and available in unlimited refills.

My first thought when my breakfast is delivered: I'll need two more to fill me up. Any reservations I had disappear when I bite into the delicious creation in front me. I spend the next hour in the café, sipping hot coffee and devouring another egg, cheese, and tomato crumpet, plus a sweet honey one.

I feel at ease with everything in my life, fully present in the here and now. I feel as though I'm returning to the sane and healthy man I was before a taciturn, brown-eyed girl stormed into my world.

For the rest of the day, I explore Pike Place Market. I examine every table at three separate farmer's markets, eating the best fresh raspberries ever. I browse an array of art galleries, then peruse several chocolate shops and book stores.

I'm blown away by the beauty and diversity of the area. The friendliness of Seattle separates it from any other city on earth. I've heard dozens of times that the rain and gloom of Seattle can be depressing. I've had the opposite experience. I'm falling in love with the Pacific Northwest.

— 25 —

Gavin

As soon as I wrap up my business meeting, I make a beeline for my rental car. Portland is about a three-hour drive. I plan to make it there in one shot. I ate a bagel and fruit in the meeting, knowing I won't want to pull over before I reach Portland.

Beautiful green scenery surrounds me throughout my drive south as James Bay floats through my rental car's speakers. I approach Portland, immediately hypnotized by the bridges that flow into the city. The euphoria I felt in Seattle intensifies into an unfamiliar feeling in my gut I can't immediately identify. The giant ball of nerves torturing me in San Diego vanishes.

The unique buildings, the Willamette and Columbia rivers, evergreens everywhere, and beautiful mountain backdrop render an undeniable beauty. I'm already falling in love with this city.

Pulling up to the RiverPlace Hotel, where the mesmerizing Willamette River flows, I know I've picked the right hotel. It's located just outside of downtown, yet still within walking distance of the lively urban buzz. I take a moment outside, inhaling the pristine air and watching cyclist and runners cruise by on the paved path in the waterfront park adjacent to the hotel.

After I check in and find my room, I text Beverly.

> Me: In Portland. At the RiverPlace. Want me to
> pick you up or meet you?

The room is homey, yet spacious, with a thoughtful, elegant feel that would appeal to both high-end and laid-back folks. I approach the large bay of windows near the balcony, peer out from my room, and take in the stunning view of the river, which showcases one of Portland's bridges.

The longer I stare, the more intense that warm feeling in my gut becomes. Before I can dig in and reflect on what it means, my phone vibrates. Eager to see Beverly, I grab it.

It's her.

> Beverly: Ahh, my favorite hotel. You're full of
> surprises. I'll pick you up at 3:15. We'll go
> around town a bit, then dinner.

Happy, I fist pump the air for choosing her favorite hotel. Through my elation, I do wonder why it surprises her that I'm staying here?

I glance at my watch—only forty-five minutes before she arrives. Since I'd like to woo this woman, it's best I start off the night smelling fresh.

I take a quick shower, then throw on jeans, a thermal, my Timberland boots, and my sweatshirt. I head down to the lobby and walk outside, drawing in a deep, cleansing breath of Portland's crisp, fresh air. Since there isn't much parking around the hotel, I wait out front for Beverly.

At precisely 3:15 p.m., a white Jeep Wrangler Unlimited

pulls up in front of the hotel. The passenger window rolls down, and I do a double take when Beverly leans over.

"Well, are you going to get in?"

I didn't see that one coming. I pictured her driving an Audi or Mercedes. A pleasant discovery. I climb into the passenger seat, close the door and turn to her. "Looks like you're full of surprises, too."

She gives me a genuine smile. "Oh, yeah? How so?"

"Didn't picture you in a Jeep," I answer.

"Well, I pictured you staying at someplace in the heart of downtown like The Nines. Maybe we have more in common than we thought."

The Nines? I'm guessing a hotel. I make a mental note to look it up online later tonight.

"I'll make you a deal. Let's stop the prejudgment and just get to know each other. I promise, I'm an okay guy."

"No wonder you're a sports agent. You sure do love to make deals." She grins at me. "All right." She nods her agreement.

Beverly bustles us through downtown Portland, clearly on a mission as she searches for an open parking space. I like that she's driving. Allows me time to admire her city. Although I'm spending most of my time admiring Beverly's beauty, instead of the main attraction.

I rub my hands together. "So, where're you taking me?"

"Sal's Chocolates. Normally, I would take you somewhere more fun, but it's Thursday," she says, as if that explains everything.

"Is Thursday chocolate day?"

She peeks over at me. "Either Thursdays or Fridays. Sometimes both. We're here." She smiles as she hops out of the Jeep.

I get my first good look at her since she picked me up. She's

wearing tight ripped jeans, dark gray combat boots, and an olive-green sweater that shows a hint of cleavage.

She's not like any woman I've ever been with. I love her original and ever-changing outfits. She dresses like a sophisticate for work, and now she looks edgy and hot, all while maintaining that no-nonsense attitude I dig. This woman is going to keep me on my toes and continue to make me work for her.

I hold open the door for her as we enter the chocolate specialty store, and it provides me with the ideal opportunity to admire her. An older man, maybe in his sixties, comes out from the counter and engulfs Beverly in a hug. He has a thick Italian accent. "Ah, my Gemma is here! Come, come, and let me get your usual ready. You're early, no?" He examines his watch.

"Grazie, Sal. My friend will also pick a few things." Beverly turns and gestures to me.

Sal peers from behind Beverly, slapping a hand to his cheek when he spots me. I step forward to greet him. He grabs hold of my hand, vigorously shaking it.

"Il Fidanzato? Il Fidanzato?" He dramatically throws his arms up in the air, then brings them down and together in front of his chest. "Oh, Gemma, you've met someone. Dolly will be very pleased. I should call her on the phone right away!" He reaches into his apron pocket and pulls out his cell phone.

Beverly waves her hands, mortified and desperately trying to interrupt him. "No. No."

Sal ignores her and turns his attention to me, pointing at me with his phone still in his hand. "You take good care of this beauty. She is special . . ."

Beverly finally insists, "Sal, we're friends. Amici." She laughs nervously and tucks her hair behind her ear.

Sal shoves his phone back in his apron pocket, and brings both hands in front of his stomach, pinching his fingers together, pointing them upwards, and bounces them around in front of his body. "You fool! *Amici.*" He practically spits the word out like he just tasted sour milk. "Don't wait too long. Women like her are rare."

Smiling at the animated man in front of me, I tell him, "You're a wise man, sir. But this Gemma requires patience."

Beverly blushes a deep red when I call her Gemma. I know only a little Italian from my maternal grandfather, but he loved the word gemma, meaning gem. He called my grandmother "Gemma" every day.

Sal, on the other hand, can't contain his excitement at my confession. He grins. With one hand he pinches his index finger and thumb together, then swipes it through the air. "Ahh, sì, sì!"

I wonder if they're related, they seem so close. For the first time since our first meeting, Beverly looks anxious and unsure of herself. Her gaze darts from me to Sal, then to the window showcasing the chocolates.

Sal finally takes pity on her. Shaking his head, he settles a gentle hand on her shoulder. "Okay, Gemma, what does your friend want?"

After picking out our chocolates, we say a long and drawn out goodbye, and finally head out the door. As we walk to her car, she slaps my arm. "Don't encourage Sal. He's been trying to find me a man since he discovered I'm single! He's even brought his sons and nephews to the shop in an attempt to hook me up."

So, Sal isn't family. I grip the bag holding our chocolates a little tighter. Sounds like I have competition.

Beverly laughs. The urge to kiss her is driving me crazy, but I remind myself she needs to make the first move.

"How does he know you're single?"

"Sal and his wife Dolly know a lot about me. They've been a part of my life for a long time now. I love them dearly, but they're obsessed with trying to find a boyfriend for me. Italians are big on romance, and I'm certain their final goal is to find me a husband. It's as if I'm incomplete in their eyes until I'm married." She chuckles and then climbs into her Jeep.

This is the first we've talked about relationships, and I grab hold of the conversation. "When was the last time you had a boyfriend?"

Her smile vanishes and her lips settle into a tight line. I regret asking the question. She shuts her eyes. I can feel sadness filling the car, but as quickly as it came, it changes again. She shakes her head and slips on her impassive mask. The mask that reminds me of the first day I met her.

She leans forward and looks out of her driver-side mirror. As she pulls away from the curb, she provides a vague answer. "It's been years." She's trying for nonchalance, and I might've bought it if her face hadn't just crumbled two seconds earlier.

Given her reaction, I probably should change the subject and not pry, but so many questions swarm in my head.

How does a gorgeous, successful woman not have a man in her life, and apparently hasn't had one in years?

As the city buildings float by the windows, my curiosity wins. "Didn't end well, huh?" I make an assumption, hoping that if I'm wrong, she'll correct me, and if I'm right, she'll confirm. I keep a watchful eye on her, trying to catch any emotions flashing across her face.

But she's prepared this time, and her mask stays in place.

"You could say that," is all she says.

"You must date a lot, at least."

"No, not really. How about you? You have a girlfriend?"

"What? No, I don't have a girlfriend. I wouldn't be here in Portland spending time with you if I had a girlfriend." I sound more offended than I am. I know she's trying to get off the topic of her and men.

"I just assumed. You're a good looking, successful guy, and in your late twenties now. Don't you want to find the right girl and settle down? Or . . ." She playfully taps her index finger on her chin. "Do you want to be a confirmed bachelor or something?"

I shake my head. "Definitely not. I guess I just want to take my time. The way I figure, it's a lot like finding the place I want to live. She should feel like home, and be so right I'll feel the rightness of her deep in my bones."

Too much emotion? Maybe. At least I left out the part that the Pacific Northwest feels like home. That would really frighten her, even make her think I'm stalking her.

She grips the steering wheel, checking every mirror before responding. "You're very forthcoming."

I wonder what she's thinking and feeling, but she's giving nothing away. "I haven't always been like this. But I learned I only get burned if I'm not truthful about who I am and what I want." My mother spent tons of hard-earned money on counseling for me to break out of the shell my father crammed me into.

She nods. "I respect that. I used to be more open." She frowns then changes the subject. "I'm happy you let me know you were going to be in town."

"You don't look very happy," I nudge her arm with my elbow.

Her full lips curve up in a smile. "It isn't something I'm used to." She doesn't offer anything more, and I don't push for more. I suspect she's trying to process her own words and feelings.

I have a sinking feeling something excruciating happened to her, and she's shut herself off from the world. Maybe, if I'm lucky, I can convince her to let me in.

I gaze out the window at the river flowing below us as we cross over the Portland-Vancouver bridge. "I'm glad to be here, too," I tell her. "I enjoy spending time with you. Which, I guess is a good thing since, in about three months, we'll be stuck with each other for three whole weeks."

I fake a shudder, and she giggles.

"Where to now, tour guide? And when do I get to try this chocolate?"

"We're going to my favorite Italian restaurant. It's in Vancouver, so don't tell anyone in Portland. Many Portlanders think there's no need to cross over to Washington. Unfortunately, I learned that the hard way." She laughs, glancing over at me. "Oh, and I always wait until after dinner to eat my chocolate, but you're free to have yours now if you want."

"I'll wait for you."

I'll wait forever for you, I realize.

— 26 —

Gavin

We pull up to a small curbside Italian café bathed in twinkling white lights. A white banner hangs in front. *La Bottega.* As soon as we walk through the bright red double doors, a tall woman with fair skin engulfs Beverly in a tight hug.

"Beverly! It's so good to see you!" The woman doesn't give Beverly a chance to respond before she's speaking again. "Your table's open. Go ahead and sit down, and I'll bring out your usual."

"Emilia, this is Gavin," she says, drawing me to her side. "He'll be dining with me tonight, so I think we'll both take a look at the menu."

Emilia's mouth drops open. She freezes, her shock apparent. Then she recovers, turns to me, and pulls me into a friendly hug.

"You're the first date she's ever brought here." She shoots daggers at Beverly. "In fact, I think you're the first person she's ever brought here. You must be very special," Emilia declares loudly enough for other diners in this small café to turn their heads.

And for the second time tonight, Beverly's face reddens

with embarrassment. "This is his first time to Portland, and I'm showing him all my favorite spots in the area," she explains.

"Trust me, you won't find Italian food like this anywhere in Portland." The woman smiles at me and hands me a menu.

We sit down along the window in this tiny hole-in-the-wall restaurant, which feels more like a home. So far, everyone I've met has been kind and cheerful. Causing that warm euphoric feeling in my stomach to grow stronger and stronger.

Beverly must be a creature of habit and go to the same places often. Either that, or she's great at making friends. But it's sad knowing she's never brought anyone with her. I wonder why.

"What do you recommend?"

"Everything's amazing. Usually, I get the Penne alla Vodka. It's creamy, delicious, and addictive."

"Excellent. I'll have that."

She grins. "You won't be disappointed."

I love that she doesn't doubt I'll be happy with what she suggests. Women I've dated in the past pressure me to study the menu, or ask me fifteen questions before suggesting something they worry I might not like. Beverly's confidence in her choices is a serious turn-on.

I set aside my menu. "How about you order everything for us. Whatever you normally would select."

She rewards me with that gorgeous smile of hers. "Okay," she says, smoothing her hair behind her ear.

She ends up ordering the Cheese Plate, Fig Salads, two plates of Penne and, for dessert, two coffees and a Ginger Crème Brûlée to share.

It's refreshing to watch her eat, especially when not a bit goes to waste. Beverly must enjoy a fast metabolism. I don't

know where she fits all this food. She savors even the extra sauce from the pasta by soaking it up on her bread. We've been here for two hours, yet it feels like twenty minutes. Spending time with her is easy and natural. It's as if we've always known each other.

"I still want to try those chocolates," I say.

"Oh, we will. I didn't forget about them."

Beverly drives us back to the hotel. Figuring our night is over, I'm surprised when she starts looking for a parking spot. We get lucky. She slips the Jeep into a space about a block away from the hotel.

"The hotel has an adorable courtyard. You can see the river, and it's the perfect place to enjoy our chocolates," Beverly says as she turns off the engine. My heart leaps with anticipation of spending more time with her.

Before I have a chance to respond, she's already out of the car, taking charge of our plans. It's a breath of fresh air to be with a woman who doesn't require reassurance.

Leading me through the lobby's double doors, past the fireplace and front desk, and right to the elevator, Beverly presses the button for level two. When the doors slide open, we walk down a narrow hallway and straight out through a side door, which opens to a deserted patio with a couple of wicker couches set out for guests. I guess she wasn't kidding about this being her favorite hotel. She really knows her way around.

We settle onto an outdoor sofa. Beverly reaches into the bag which contains our chocolates. First, she withdraws my box and hands it to me, then she pulls out hers and places it on her lap. Opening her box, she holds it out before me. "Try one."

I lick my lips, choose a piece, and pop the small milk chocolate nugget in my mouth. It melts on my tongue, and I hum my

appreciation. "Amazing," I say, ripping open my box.

Her face lights up. She bumps her shoulder against mine. "I know! I feel robbed I wasn't able to enjoy them my whole life."

"The injustice," I tease.

She giggles at the seriousness of my tone.

After she's satisfied I'm enjoying my chocolate, she places a piece in her mouth. Once her mouth closes on that piece of chocolate, her eyes shut. Hums of appreciation radiate from her throat, and she savors every last bit of it.

Damn. Talk about sexy to watch. I hope she eats another. Everything this woman does turns me on. All I want is more.

A crisp breeze blows strands of her hair across her face. Without thinking, I sweep a wayward lock away so I can see her again. At my touch, she sucks in a deep breath. The sound sends a rush of heat through me. I struggle not to kiss her. This is pure torture. I wonder if I should just make a move. What's the worst that can happen?

"I had a great time today," she says, a sincere smile lingering on her face as her eyelashes flutter.

"So did I. Thank you for showing me around. Are you free tomorrow?"

"Of course, I took tomorrow off. I offered to be your tour guide, and I'm determined to show you everything I love about Portland. Tomorrow, you'll need your hiking boots."

I beam. Can't help myself. "Thanks for taking time from your schedule for me."

She shrugs, claiming it's no big deal and she's due for a break. She pushes up to her feet, ready to make her exit. "I should probably get going so you can get some sleep. What time did you arrive today, anyway?"

She doesn't know my meeting took place in Seattle, and I

only came down here to spend time with her. At first, hesitation fills me, but it's the truth, and I'm not going to tiptoe around her any longer. I'm not in control of how she'll react to this. I hope it doesn't freak her out, but I've got to be honest if we're going to work.

"I flew into Seattle on Tuesday night. Had a meeting there this morning, then drove to Portland today. I got in around two o'clock."

"Do you have work to do in Portland, too?" Her voice, her gaze, her posture—everything about her is passive, giving nothing away.

"Nope. I came here to see you. Get that tour you promised me."

She strolls over to the railing that overlooks the river. I'm not sure what to make of her response, so I walk up behind her and patiently wait for her to speak.

She's gripping the railing like it's a rescue buoy and she's adrift in the sea without a piece of land in sight. You would've thought I had told her I want to impregnate her and elope. As I inspect her more closely, I see what's going on. Shit, her mouth is open, her chest heaving as she sucks in air.

My throat tightens. "Are you okay?" I manage to choke out, while my body goes hot with fear.

She doesn't say anything, just stands there. Her eyes remain fixed on the river while she slows her breathing.

Her silence is killing me, a slow, torturous death. It's too much to bear. I break, reaching down to touch her hand. "I didn't mean to freak you out. We had such a great time when you were in San Diego, and since I was in Seattle, I wanted to see you again. I like you, Beverly. I can't get you out of my head."

Okay, Gavin, you should probably stop there. But I don't.

"When I'm with you, it just feels right." I clasp her hand a little tighter.

Seriously. Stop. Now.

"And I had to take the opportunity to come here and explore those feelings. I believe everyone holds the key to his or her happiness, but too many people live in fear and don't open the door."

All right, that's it. No more. Shut up now.

When her eyes meet mine again, they're moist with unshed tears. Man, I thought I was good at reading people, but I'm failing here. Was Evelyn right? She stands there, staring at me for what seems like forever, but I know it's only been seconds.

Mental note, never play poker with Beverly.

"Kiss me," she whispers so gently, I'm not sure I hear her correctly.

I seize this opportunity, lifting her hand to my mouth and planting a gentle kiss on her palm. She puckers her lips and narrows her eyes at me, and she looks adorable.

"Not there?" I ask, feigning innocence.

She shakes her head. "Uh-uh."

So I lean over and kiss her right cheek. Before I can straighten, she brackets my face with her hands, holds me still and finds my lips.

Her kiss is urgent, passionate, and better than I could've imagined. I wrap my arms around her so tightly, I'm not sure she can breathe. Her small body feels strong and in control as she presses into me. It's like we're puzzle pieces designed to connect.

I never want this moment to end. I want to live right here. In Portland. With Beverly. Forever . . . And that's how I know I've found my home. She's what I've been searching for. In her arms, I have found my heart's home.

Too soon, Beverly pulls away. The kiss ends. She leans into me, breathing hard, and I kiss the top of her head, then hold her in silence.

"What are you doing to me?" she whispers against my chest. "You're making me break my rules."

"You're not breaking them, just making necessary adjustments. I'm learning that rules need to ebb and flow, the same way life does. You're making me reevaluate the rules I set for myself years ago, too." I rub my hands soothingly up and down her back.

She moves out of my arms and faces the calm river, only a couple of boats left in sight. "I don't change my rules." She shakes her head. "At least, I didn't. Not until I met you."

She likes me, but she's afraid of something. I can only hope our connection drives out her fear.

Beverly turns back to me, face contorted in distress, brows drawn in, and the usual light in her eyes replaced with fear. "I need to tell you more about myself. Before you start to develop feelings for me. I shouldn't have kissed you, that was selfish of me, but I can't help that I'm attracted to you. And not just your looks, but your intelligence, kindness, and mostly the respect you've shown every person I've seen you interact with, including me." She says in a rush.

I lean over and whisper in her ear, "You're too late." Then, I kiss her again. This time I lift her off her feet and kiss her tenderly, trying to show her what I already feel for her.

It doesn't matter what she needs to tell me. I'll listen, because it's important to her, but my heart and mind won't change. I want to be with her. And now that I've kissed her, I won't let her go.

Still in my arms, she breaks the connection of our lips and presses her forehead against mine. "Give me this weekend. I'll

tell you everything you need to know before you fly home, but give me this weekend to spend time with you, without you knowing my dark cloud. I promise you'll know my whole story. I know this is selfish for me to ask of you, but it's something I want more than I've wanted anything in a long time."

My throat tightens. I sense she thinks we only have this one weekend together. Once she confides in me, she expects me to be gone. She doesn't understand that, whatever she says, I'm not going anywhere.

Maybe she's the one who's planning to run.

I shake off my pessimistic thoughts. "Let's enjoy our weekend and, before I leave, you can tell me your story. But, I have one condition."

God, I hope this doesn't backfire.

She blinks in quick succession, but her eyes remain locked on mine. She clears her throat. "Okay. What is it?"

What's this big secret she's hiding, anyway? It can't be *that* bad. Surely, if it were, I would've heard about it already.

Here goes nothing, I really hope I'm not going to regret what I'm about to say.

"We can't sleep together until you tell me. I don't want you to ever regret being with me. Also, I want to show you that your past doesn't change how I feel about you. I already have feelings for you, Beverly. My fate was sealed that first day I met you in my office, and you arched your beautiful, perfect eyebrow at me."

A small, sad smile crosses her face, her eyes shift, and she focuses on the river again.

As I await her response, my heartbeat thunders in my ears and my shoulders tighten with tension. Did I just make the biggest mistake of my life?

"Okay . . ." She gnaws on her bottom lip. "Deal." She grins, nudging me with her elbow, "You know, I think this is our thing."

"What?"

"Making deals. That's our thing. I've made more deals with you than a drug dealer does during Mardi Gras."

"Whoa. How do you know about drug dealers during Mardi Gras?" I chuckle at her comparison.

"I saw a documentary on it. It was kind of crazy. Dealers even sold fake drugs to tourists. It was very educating," she says matter-of-factly.

I tap my lips with my index finger, "Hmm, I'll keep that in mind in case I ever go and decide to buy drugs while I'm there."

"Very funny. Anyway, I should let you get some sleep. Well, unless . . ." She stops herself and looks back out at the river.

Unless? Woman, don't leave me hanging. I chew on the inside of my bottom lip, and I wait and wait, and then wait some more for her to continue. She doesn't.

Lowering my mouth to her ear, I murmur, "Unless what, Beverly?" A shiver runs through her body.

"Unless you want to come to my house. We could watch a movie or something."

I picture Beverly and me curled up on a comfy couch together, my arms holding her close. "I'd like that." There's nothing I'd like more. I want to spend every minute with her.

"Okay. I'll wait here for you to grab your stuff."

Grab my stuff? What stuff? Does she want me to stay the night? We just made a deal not to sleep together. If I stay the night at her house and can only kiss her, I would be in absolute agony.

She twists her hair in one hand and pulls it over her shoulder. "Er. Sorry. I mean, if you want, it might just be easier

to crash at my place." Then she quickly adds, "Don't worry. I have a guest room for you."

The phrase *like a moth to a flame* comes to mind.

"Phew. I was worried you were going to throw yourself at me," I joke. My hands tremble at my sides. I shove them into my pockets, hoping she doesn't notice.

Am I really considering this? Moreover, is she really offering this?

Beverly purses her lips at me. "You're not my type," she says and crosses her arms.

"Damn, woman, how do you kiss when someone *is* your type?"

She covers her face and laughs. When she brings her hands back down, I swoop in and give her a quick peck on the lips.

"Are you sure about this? Won't it make our deal more challenging?"

She sucks in a steadying breath. "If it becomes too difficult, you can always come back here."

"Deal." I grin at her, then turn and hustle up to my room.

Luckily, I hadn't unpacked anything. I just need to grab my toiletries from the bathroom. Suddenly, I pause. I feel a little off balance. Like sophomore year in college, when I was picked as team captain for baseball. I was terrified of screwing it up. Spending more time with Beverly doesn't scare me, nor staying the night at her house. I'm nervous that the deal we just made will be broken.

I never thought it would be possible for me to have such strong feelings for a woman in such a short amount of time. If she does throw herself at me, there's like a one percent chance I'll be capable of resisting her.

I hesitate, one hand gripping the hotel room door and the

other my luggage. I inhale a few times and roll my neck, then I head back downstairs to my future.

— 27 —

Gavin

A long private drive leads up to Beverly's home, which is perched on a hillside. Shadows of towering trees hang over her home in every direction, offering complete privacy from any neighbors. The location is perfect, only about twenty-five minutes from the hotel and fifteen minutes to downtown.

She leads me inside. I'm overwhelmed by the dozens of windows featuring stunning views. Like an unexplained gravitational pull, the nearest window summons me, and I'm lost as I gaze at the sparkling city below.

Beverly joins me. "In the morning, I'll show you my favorite view. You can see Mt. Hood from my back deck."

"This is incredible."

"I thought you'd appreciate it. Since you have that amazing view of the ocean."

"You know, that's the only reason I bought my home. Well, that and the pool."

Beverly's home has a calm, tranquil aura to it. The walls are painted a soft gray, and her furniture is natural wood. Cream and tan colors dominate with hints of pale blue and gray.

It's decorated more like a beach house than a home nestled against a forest. I feel at home. It's more than a little depressing that after only five minutes, I feel more comfortable here than in any house I've ever lived in.

I shift my feet as the realization of how unhappy I've truly been settles into my bones. I've been functioning on autopilot in San Diego, accepting average and allowing complacency to hold me back. I run my hand through my hair. I live more like my grandfather than I want to admit.

I turn to tell Beverly how happy I am she invited me over, but she isn't next to me any longer. I roam around in search of her. Following the sound of a door opening, I find her in the linen closet, standing on her tiptoes as she reaches for some blankets.

"Let me help," I say.

"Thanks."

She steps out of the way, and I grab the blankets. When I turn back around to hand them to her, she's gone again. Dang, that little woman moves fast. I wander around some more and find another living room. Beverly is there, rolling out a giant foam mattress topper thing.

"What are you doing?" I ask, amused.

"Getting ready to watch a movie. I want us to be comfortable, and the couch is rock hard. Unless you prefer my bed?" She raises her eyebrows and swipes the tip of her tongue across her lower lip, taunting me.

My saliva gets stuck in my throat, and I swallow hard just to get it down. Her bed, my bed, the guest bed—shoot, any bed— is entirely off limits with her. I'm not sure how I'll even manage to lie on the floor with her.

"Do you have pajamas with you?"

"Sweats." I'm not going to share with her that I sleep in boxers. Given her playful mood, she might encourage that.

"Let's change and meet back here in a few. I'll show you the guest room." Without waiting for a response, she sashays down the hall.

I trail behind her, similar to the way a dog chases its owner. Walking into the guest bedroom, I'm overwhelmed by its enormity; two of my master bedrooms could fit in here. In the center of the room, Beverly sets a fresh towel on a king bed, two abnormally massive nightstands adorn each side. To the left of the door, I spot a reading chair with a side table facing the fireplace. A couch sits near the oversized windows.

Geez, how big is this place? I wonder.

"I'll leave you to it," Beverly brushes her body against my arm as she heads for the door, but I place my hand on her stomach, stopping her. I caress her cheek, then I lean over, planting a feather-light kiss on her lips.

When neither of us pulls away, our kiss blooms into something deeper. Unlike our kisses at the hotel, which were a frantic indication of our hunger for each other, this kiss is unhurried and gentle. The need to savor the feel of her soft lips pressed against mine courses through me. Trying to memorize the curves of her body, which fit perfectly against me, I want to remember every stroke of her tongue and the sound she makes when I nip at her full bottom lip.

Ending our kiss with a sigh, she says nothing and turns to leave, clicking the door shut behind her. For a moment, once she's gone, I'm paralyzed, stranded, rooted in the spot she left me.

My brain resets, permitting my limbs to function again. I pull on a black T-shirt and black sweats, brush my teeth, and splash some crisp, fresh, Oregon water on my face.

Before stepping out of my room, I close my eyes and inhale, attempting to summon every ounce of self-control in my body. I hope it will be enough to prevent my other brain from taking over. I know better than to sleep with Beverly before she shares the secrets of her past. All my rational thoughts slip away when I kiss her. I'm diving in headfirst and spinning out of control.

Just three days, I remind myself.

I only need to hold back for three more days. Hopefully, after she spills her secrets, we can move forward and lose ourselves in each other. I want to unfold her layer by layer.

I stroll down the long hallway, my feet gliding over the smooth hardwood floors. Once I step into the living room, I stop dead in my tracks. Beverly's already here, with her hair still flowing down her back. She's wearing black-rimmed glasses, a tank top without a bra underneath, and tiny pajama shorts.

Like a siren daring me to resist her, she looks so damn hot, I can't help but stare. My eyes settle on her toned legs, and I picture those legs wrapped around my waist.

She's a savage who knows exactly what she's doing.

"There you are. Sit down." Her eyes sparkle with a teenager's excitement. "I'll grab the rest of our chocolate. What do you want to drink?"

My mouth is void of all moisture. I stay rooted in place, afraid to move any closer to her. "Water, please."

"You got it. Be right back, get comfortable."

My eyes follow her. I admire the grace of her body, which makes me regret the deal we made.

Idiot.

Opting for a safer alternative, I sit down on a pile of blankets, prop a pillow against the couch and lean back. I review the reasons I made that deal with her. As long as she's

emotionally blocked off, an intimate relationship with her isn't possible—not a rule I can alter. She needs to reveal her cards before we have sex. Otherwise, we're just a hookup without a meaningful connection. Not what I want.

Beverly struts back in, carrying glasses of water and our chocolates. Gracefully lowering herself to sit beside me, she leans back against the couch. She stretches out her legs, taunting me, yet I resist the itch to touch them.

"What kind of movies do you like?" she asks while turning on the TV.

"I'm not much of a movie person. You pick."

"Really? Me, either!" She laughs. "We can watch TV instead and just chill. I can't remember the last time I sat in front of the TV and zoned-out for a bit."

"I'd like that," I say, examining her cute glasses. "You look good in these." I tap the black frames. "Do you wear contacts?"

"Yeah, it rains so much, it's easier to wear contacts. When I'm at home, I prefer my glasses."

She selects two pieces of chocolate from the boxes beside her. "This one is my favorite. It was the first piece I ever tried from Sal's wife, Dolly."

She places the promising treat in my mouth, her fingertip stroking my lower lip before she withdraws her hand.

Distracted by the vibration her touch zipped through my body, I briefly delay biting into the flavorful chocolate, with its hints of vanilla. I moan as it melts on my tongue.

"Right? So delicious. I was sold after that first bite."

She slides a piece into her mouth, and I don't miss the opportunity to watch her enjoy it. I would love to feed her all day long.

I've never realized it until now, but my exes rarely ate in

front of me. Maybe it's a California woman thing, or they were cautious of their diets. No matter the reason, I love that Beverly appreciates food. I hope she never changes.

"Tell me something about yourself." She lowers the volume on the old game show she settled on a moment ago. It reminds me of my childhood. My grandma and I would watch them, shooting out wrong answers more often than not.

"What do you want to know?"

"Anything you're willing to share," she answers, looking back at the TV.

With a gentle hand, I guide her head back to face me, I need to see the reaction in her eyes at this confession. "I wish we would've met sooner. My head of PR has been urging me to connect with your company for months. I regret not contacting you sooner."

Her eyes light up, and the sweetest smile I've ever seen sets her aglow. Then she trails her fingers down my jawline until she reaches my chin. She turns my head to the side, scooting her body closer to mine, and presses kisses from my jaw down to my neck.

The sensation of her mouth on my skin is glorious. I lose myself in the feeling. My control disappears, and I guide her onto her back. Stroking my tongue over her bottom lip, she rewards me with a throaty moan.

Just seconds later, she is caught between me and the floor, our kiss becomes desperate, and she's clawing at my back and wrapping her legs around me. I slide my right hand down her body, reaching her smooth legs. I remember our deal at the worst possible moment. My willpower returns, and I slow our kiss until I break our connection.

"I've never been kissed like that before." Her chest heaves as

she struggles to pull in more oxygen. Once she's breathing more evenly, she tugs me closer and peppers my face with quick kisses.

I chuckle at her playfulness. "You unlock a hunger I didn't know I had."

"The feeling's mutual. But why do you want to stop us from going further, when we both feel this gravitational pull? You sure you want to wait?" She purses her lips.

"Are you sure you want to wait until Sunday to tell me what you need to tell me?" I counter with sincerity.

Beverly scoots her way out from under me to sit upright. "You don't understand. Remembering my past turns me into a different person. And truthfully, I'm enjoying who I am with you right now. I want to savor this time with you, Gavin. I'm afraid everything will change once I tell you."

Her gaze falls to her twisting hands. "Do you think you can wait until tomorrow? I know it's unfair to you."

I cradle her face in my hands and wait for her to make eye contact. "Beverly, you can wait as long as you want. Whatever you share with me, it won't change what I feel for you. I want to be with you."

She frowns, pressing a hand to her chest. "But, reliving it will change *me*. Can we make another deal?" Her wide eyes plead with me to say yes.

"Sure, but do you have a notepad? I think I need to start writing these down," I tease, trying to lighten her mood. I know I'm successful when her forehead unfurrows and she smiles.

"This one is kind of a one-sided deal." She gnaws on her lower lip. I wish she'd stop. It makes me nervous.

"You can't fall in love with me."

I flinch, thrown off by her demand, and I take a few moments to process her words.

I blow out a breath, unsure how she'll take my response. "That's a deal I'm not willing to make. Even if I could control my feelings for you, I wouldn't want to." I decide it's best to leave out the part that I'm already falling, the ember in my heart burning strong.

Her shoulders slump, yet she doesn't seem all that surprised by my response, and like most times, I sense she already knew I wouldn't agree. She nods once. "That's your choice, but you should know I'm not looking for anything serious."

Okay, I get it, she's afraid of commitment. I already had a hunch that was the case. Now she's confirmed it. It's not like I'm asking her to marry me next week.

"That's fine. We'll take our time and get to know each other. There's no rush." I place my hand atop hers.

She withdraws her hand, placing it in her lap. "No," she argues. "You don't understand, I'm *never* going to be looking for a serious relationship. Any relationship we have will always be casual. I don't ever want anything more. It's only fair that I manage your expectations upfront."

My pulse quickens, and my stomach turns sour, imagining all the possibilities. What the hell happened to her? Who hurt her so badly, she's sworn off relationships? I want to find the asshole who did this to her.

Tension builds in my neck and shoulders. "Expectations are managed," I say. I have no other choice. For now, I'll take Beverly anyway I can get her, but my ego is confident that our chemistry will win her heart.

Eager to change the subject, I draw her hand to my lips and kiss each finger. My heart is filled with more reassurance when

it doesn't take long before we're making out like teenagers again. I had almost forgotten how much fun kissing could be.

—

BEVERLY'S HEAD IS RESTING on my chest. We've been talking for hours, learning more about each other. She's told me about her younger brother. They're close, but grew apart a little bit when she moved to Portland a few years ago. I'm shocked to learn she's originally from Carlsbad. Her dad and brother both still live there. She hates peas, prefers the forest over the beach, loves to fish, is an avid hiker, and loves to read.

After she shares about her life, I offer her parts of mine. I've been rambling for a while now about Sports Management and that I enjoy it, but feel it's missing something. That I could be doing more with the company. I realize she hasn't spoken in a while. Shifting a little so I can see her face, I understand her silence. She's out cold.

Warmth spreads in my chest at the sight of her pouty lips slightly open and sucking in little puffs of air.

Wonder when I lost her?

I slide my fingers through her silky hair. Even though I love having her in my arms, I can't sleep here on the floor with her by my side all night. I carefully lift her up in my arms. The moment I stand up, her eyes pop open.

"I can walk," she insists. "How long have I been asleep?" Her voice is alert, and it's as if she hadn't slept.

I approach the stairs with her slightly struggling in my arms. I tell her, "I want to carry you."

She doesn't protest any further. Instead, she snuggles up in my arms as I climb the stairs. I'm thankful she doesn't fight me. Some strong women like Beverly would be a royal pain in the

ass right now, insisting they aren't a child and can walk on their own damn two legs.

"Which room is yours?" I ask when we reach the top step.

"That one on the right." She nuzzles her nose into my chest and inhales.

That's right, baby, get comfortable.

I pull back the sheets on her bed, lower her to the mattress, cover her, lean down and kiss her forehead. As I turn to leave, she grabs my wrist.

"Stay with me. Just until I fall asleep," she whispers.

Giving the middle finger to doubt, I slip in beside her, wrap her in my arms, and inhale the sweet scent of vanilla, wildflowers, and Beverly.

Afraid I'll fall asleep with her, I force my eyes open and repeat in my head, *stay awake.*

Stay. Awake.

— 28 —

Gavin

SLAP!

Ouch.

My eyes spring open.

Beverly stands above me with a huge grin plastered on her face. Did she just spank me?

"Come on, get up! We don't have time to waste." She rushes out of her room and disappears down the hallway.

I groan. So much for not falling asleep in her bed.

Rolling onto my right side, I notice a huge window I didn't see last night. I'm overwhelmed by endless green trees towering everywhere, with a snow-covered mountain poking between them. I climb out of her bed, rub the sleep from my eyes, and amble over to the window to admire the beauty before me. It's difficult to take it all in, the amount of green, all different shades, covering everything.

The rich aroma of coffee floods my nostrils, and it's enough to draw me downstairs. In the kitchen Beverly's hauling stuff out of the fridge and pantry. She reaches into the cabinet closest to the refrigerator, pulling out two glasses. She pours

water to the top of each, squeezes lemon into both, and places one in front of me.

Did Jenny provide her a file on me? Or is this really how we both start our mornings?

"I didn't poison it." She nods to the glass.

"Why did you give me this?"

She looks at me with a don't-be-stupid kind of look. "We're going on a hike, you need to be hydrated. Besides, you should start every morning with a glass of water."

"Actually, that is how I start every morning. Thanks." I lift the glass to my lips, and it's gone in seconds.

"No problem." She tilts her head to the side, wanting to say more. I can feel it, but she doesn't. Instead, she asks me to hand her the bananas from the counter behind me.

Her gourmet kitchen is my mom and grandma's dream kitchen. The stove has ten burners and two ovens—didn't even know that was possible—and a gigantic glass door refrigerator. The cabinets are distressed white and complement the soft gray quartz countertops with an enormous center island. There are windows everywhere, offering spectacular views of the city, mountains, and trees.

"Do you need help?" I ask.

Her hands are full, and she bumps shut the door of her fridge with her hip.

"Sure. Will you peel and slice the bananas? Then place them on the bottom of this dish." She sets a square glass baking dish in front of me.

"What are we making?"

"An oatmeal recipe. It's easy, tasty, and filling, which we'll need for our hike." She peeks up at me. "But if you're not into oatmeal, I have eggs, bread, and avocado. You can make a sandwich, instead."

"No, this sounds great."

"Good. Will you hand me the cinnamon, please?"

After putting all the other ingredients together, she scatters blueberries on top, then slides our breakfast into the oven.

Beverly pours two cups of steaming coffee. I watch her put a splash of creamer in one mug. "Want some?" she asks.

"No, thank you." I take my coffee black, the stronger the better.

She smiles and slides my mug over to me.

"Do you want to sit outside on the back deck while we wait for breakfast?"

I bring my mug to my lips and inhale before taking a sip. "Yeah, I want to see that amazing view you told me about."

"Grab your sweatshirt. The sun might be out, but this is still Portland."

With coffee in hand, she doesn't lead me to the doors located just off her kitchen. Instead, we walk through a sitting room boasting colossal glass sliding doors, nearly as tall and wide as the wall they're sitting in.

I need to find out who the architect was on this place.

When we step outside, I don't even notice the cold bite in the air because, instantly, that snow-hooded mountain I only got a peek of from her bedroom captures my attention. The sky-scraping mountain takes my breath away, yet breathes life into me at the same time. Unable to ignore its pull, I walk across the deck, trying any way I can to get closer.

"This view right here is why I bought this house. The trees and city views I have are beautiful, but nothing compares to being able to see Mount Hood or, Wy'east, as the Multnomah tribe named it, proud and erect every single day. It's such a gift. All I'll ever need. Sometimes, I just sit out here with coffee and

a blanket, and stare at it for hours, thinking about the legend of Wy'east and how the Multnomah people believe it was formed."

I didn't even know which mountain I was looking at until Beverly said the name, let alone that there was another name for it. But the wonder oozing from her voice when she talks about Mt. Hood is alluring, and she makes me want to learn more.

"How do they believe it was formed?" I ask.

"I've heard a couple different versions of the legend. My personal favorite, and the one I contemplate most, is the one about the two brave sons of the Great Spirit Sahale, who both fell in love with the same beautiful woman, Loowit. Basically, jealousy caused them to fight over her. Their fighting became destructive, forest and villages were burned down, and many warriors killed.

"The Great Spirit was enraged by their evil behavior. He killed them, and where they each died, he rose a mountain in their place. Wy'east is Mount Hood, Pahto, the other son, is Mount Adams, and the beautiful Loowit is Mount St. Helens. A painful reminder of how disastrous love can be."

"You must have googled all this."

"I did, but only after I met a man, maybe a year after I moved to Oregon. He was probably in his seventies. His name is Awan, and he's Native American. We met in a small coffee shop in Corbett, and I saw him there many times before we ever said a word to each other.

"One day, I sat at the table next to him and said good morning. He took it as an invitation to talk to me for the next thirty minutes straight, which I'm so happy he did. It became routine. Every Saturday that I was in town, we'd meet at the coffee shop and he'd share his wisdom and all the stories that were passed down to him.

"We never exchanged last names or phone numbers, and that's something that's been weighing on me because almost six months ago, Awan stopped showing up. I've asked everyone in that shop if they know what happened to him, including the owner who's there almost daily. Everyone claims the only person Awan ever spoke to was me."

Turning to face me again, I can see Beverly's embarrassed. "Sorry! You made a simple comment, and I've been rambling on and on about stuff you probably don't want to hear."

"Of course, I want to hear it. I'm sorry you don't know what happened to your friend. I wish I could help you find him."

"Thanks." She sips her coffee. "Enough of that. We're supposed to be having a fun day. Let me go top off our coffees and we'll enjoy the view until breakfast is ready."

I get cozy on the outdoor couch that's tucked underneath the large patio cover on her deck to protect the furniture from the frequent Oregon rain. Beverly slips back outside with coffee in hand and lowers herself next to me. We sit there for the next twenty minutes, neither of us pressured to fill the silence surrounding us, just enjoying the peace of this glorious view.

Beverly breaks the silence and bounces up to her feet. "Breakfast is probably ready."

Her enthusiasm is infectious, and I follow her to the kitchen.

When she pulls breakfast from the oven, a sweet aroma sweeps through the kitchen and my stomach responds with a loud growl. "That smells delicious."

"It was my mom's favorite," she responds absentmindedly.

Last night, she talked about her brother, dad, friends Nell and Aubrey, but she didn't mention her mom. I didn't want to

pressure her, so I let her lead the conversation, figuring she and her mom weren't close. Just now, though, she spoke about her mom in the past tense.

I force down the curiosity expanding inside me, unwilling to ruin the energy in the room. I sit at the kitchen island. Beverly places a bowl of her oatmeal concoction before me, and I dig in.

The breakfast gods smile down from heaven! The warm fruit melts in my mouth. This is so damn good. I'm a sucker for homemade food.

Wishing I paid more attention to how she made it, I take a mental note of the ingredients I can clearly see and the ones I remember her adding. Beverly doesn't seem to notice me dissecting my food. Her mood appears to be shifting. She's growing uneasy and distant. I think she's searching for her mask.

After a brief mental debate, I figure letting her eat breakfast and sort out whatever she's feeling is the best approach. Acknowledging her pulling away from me might prompt her to throw her wall back up and pack on the body armor.

When we finish eating, I stand and grab our plates, heading to the sink. I'm ready to wash up, but I feel Beverly's gentle touch on my back.

"Leave those." She smiles and reaches up to plant a soft kiss on my cheek. "Let's get changed. Make sure you have a warm jacket and wear your hiking boots."

Before I can speak, she's out of the kitchen. I hear her rapid footsteps as she darts upstairs.

Twenty minutes later, after changing into hiking gear, we meet back in the kitchen. Beverly's dressed in tight black yoga pants and a pale yellow, long-sleeved shirt that looks amazing

with her dark hair and honey eyes. Yellow might be my new favorite color.

My eyes linger over her curves. As my gaze meets hers, she flushes a deep scarlet and dips her head to avoid my stare.

Yeah, I'm checking you out, and I don't care if you know.

"You're gorgeous."

Like the flip of a switch, her head pops up and her sensual lips turn up into a sexy smile as she saunters toward me. "You know, if you want to break our deal," she says, placing both hands on my chest and leaning into me, "I'm okay with that."

I groan in response. Damn, how can she read my thoughts? Did I go from Peyton the psycho to Beverly the psychic?

Gripping the back of my neck, Beverly yanks me forward and kisses me before I can respond.

Little seductress.

Her hands move to my hair, she twists and tugs hard. I make a conscious effort to try and keep my hands anchored on her back, but right now they're gliding down her hips, making their way to her backside. Somewhere inside me, I find the strength to stop and gently pull away from her.

I rest my chin on her head. "Trust me, more than anything I want to sweep you upstairs and take you right now, but we should wait."

At first, she doesn't say anything, and I think I've offended her. Then she reaches a hand behind me and grabs some fruit that's on the counter.

"It was worth a shot. Can't blame a girl for trying." She grins at me.

I cannot believe I just turned down sex with Beverly Morgan. If Trevor ever finds out, he'll check me into the psych ward.

Beverly tosses the fruit into a small ice chest.

"You ready?" she asks.

"You're enjoying this, aren't you?"

"Enjoying what?"

"Torturing me."

"Hey, you're the one torturing both of us. But, yeah, I do find it entertaining. Now, let's go." In typical Beverly fashion, she doesn't wait for my response and heads to the door.

— 29 —

Gavin

I'm scrolling through Beverly's music playlists on her phone. I thumb through The Fray, Lord Huron, Bebe Rexha, Elvis, Johnny Cash, Usher, Snow Patrol, Ed Sheeran, John Mayer, James Bay. Jeez, so random. Her taste is eccentric.

She's patient while I search for a first song. We need something fun, light, and I've just landed on the perfect one. Pressing play, I turn up the speakers and *Happy* by Pharrell pulses through the speakers. Her face erupts into the biggest smile. Mentally, I high five myself.

Beverly belts out every word unashamed, in the most terrible voice I've ever heard, and I fall even harder for her. When the song's over, we're both cracking up over her awful performance.

Now that I've caught my breath and a calm John Mayer is cooing in the background, I want to find out where we're headed. We're on the highway. Beverly grips the steering wheel and focuses on the road. I peer out the window, noting that the tall Douglas firs line everything here. I could never tire of looking at Oregon's strikingly vibrant trees. "Where are we going hiking?"

"Appropriately enough, given our morning conversation about the Multnomah tribe, we're going to Multnomah Falls. It's a tourist favorite, but even as a local, I can't deny the allure of this hike. It's on my top five list for Oregon." Her eyes remain glued on the road.

"What do you love about it?"

"Well, for starters the legend of how it formed. I won't bore you with all the details, but it formed after a great sacrifice of a chief's daughter, who saved her people from illness and death."

"Another story your friend Awan shared with you?"

"Yup, he was filled with priceless knowledge and stories. I miss talking with him." She grips the steering wheel even tighter, looking uneasy. "I still go to the same coffee shop every Saturday I'm free, just in case he shows up."

I don't know what to say. I want to give her hope, but I don't have a clue what happened to him, or if she'll ever see him again. So, I return to my original question.

"Okay, so what are your other reasons for loving it?"

"No matter what's going on with me or in my life, I find peace there. It's like my burdens, regrets, and pain are absorbed into the mist of the waterfall."

I can't help but wonder what burdens she carries, and I wish I could take away some of her pain. Zoned out and immersed in my thoughts, I look up and see that we've pulled into a parking lot situated in the middle of the highway. Beverly hops out of the car and pulls a backpack from the backseat.

I climb out, walk around to her, and reach for the backpack. "Let me hold it." She looks down at the bag, then up at me and smiles.

"Purple and yellow are your colors." Playful Beverly is back, and she hands me the tiny girly backpack. Even with the straps

stretched out all the way, it barely squeezes onto me.

From the parking lot I follow my dream girl through a tunnel, then under some railroad tracks. The closer we get, the more the temperature drops. I zip up my jacket, grateful Beverly made sure I dressed warmly enough. As we walk closer, and the waterfall comes into view, I catch my breath at the force of nature thundering down the mountain before me.

"This is amazing," I manage to whisper.

"Just wait until we're on the trail. If you have enough left in you, afterwards we can check out some of the other falls, too."

"There's more than one?" I ask in disbelief that this much beauty can be in more than one place.

She laughs. "Oh, yeah. There's a bunch in the Gorge." She grabs my arm. "Oh! Oh! If you've got enough in you, we'll hit up Devil's Rest."

"That doesn't sound pleasant." I chuckle, remembering Torrey Pines. I'm a bit terrified for her to lead this hike.

"Oh, it's not too bad for a fit guy like yourself." She squeezes my bicep as if to prove her point. "Plus, the scenery on the way up is extraordinary."

Within minutes, we're at the bridge that overlooks the base of the waterfall. Knowing this is only the beginning and that Beverly is a machine, I don't get too excited that this first part is a breeze.

We admire the view from the Benson Footbridge, the cool spray of the fall misting our faces. Beverly shocks me when she pulls out her phone and snaps a quick selfie of us. With the thought that she wants to capture us in this moment and remember this day every time she looks at that photo, endorphins surge through me. I'm fueled up, ready to take on any trail she leads me up.

As we climb the path, we're assaulted with switchback after switchback and throngs of visitors making our trek slower than Beverly seems to prefer. She weaves past people at every opportunity. As for me, I'm savoring the climb, taking in the beauty.

Being in the middle of these towering trees, a peaceful calm swells in my chest. The vegetation thrives, covering every inch of the ground off the paved path. Moss clings to rocks and trees, and I catch glimpses of the Columbia River Gorge, which provides this trail with more beauty than my brain can filter. Between the clean air and exquisite backdrop, I barely notice the burning in my lungs. I can now understand how this place is able to clear Beverly's mind. Being surrounded by this much natural glory, the outside world ceases to exist.

We've made it to the top of the mountain and the stream that flows to the waterfall's drop-off point. The stream moves slower than I imagined, given the intensity of the water's fall from the sheer mountain. Beverly and I walk down to the stream, balancing on some rocks so I can reach down and feel the cold water traveling to its six-hundred-foot plummet. The water jolts me awake and provides a renewed sense of energy to my body.

Beverly leads me toward the formidable observation deck, where a handful of people cautiously lean over the edge to watch the water hurtle to the ground below. Others hang their phones or cameras over the edge to catch the action for them. Then there are people like me, who'd much rather enjoy the view from the ground than up above. Unfortunately, Beverly and I are not in sync this once. She's pressed against the railing, waving me over.

I take a few hesitant steps forward. When she hangs a little too far over the side, I surge forward and plant my hands on her waist.

She twists and looks up at me, "Isn't it stunning?"

"Yes . . ." *you are*, I say in my head.

After we've had our terrifying fill of peering over the sheer face of the cliff, we find a couple of rocks near the stream to rest on and eat some trail mix and fruit.

As we sit there, I can see my ducks lined up, my life coming together in the way I always hoped it would. In the past month, I've found the place I want to live, the woman I want to spend my life with, and recognized that I want more out of the company I'm running.

How can I leave on Sunday morning? Just two days away. Is that enough time to win her over? I can't go until she's agreed to at least date me. I can take it slow for her, but I can't leave with us being nothing. Plus, how can I leave her right after she shares some huge secretive part of her past?

No. I can't do it.

I'm going to reschedule my flight home.

"You have a hot pensive look," Beverly teases, running her index finger along my furrowed brow, and bringing me back to her. "What has you all tied up in knots?"

"So much," I reply, uncertain how much I should share with her before we spend more quality time together.

"Oh goodness, a taciturn Mr. Reed. Oh, how our roles have reversed," she teases.

I frame her soft cheeks with my hands, my eyes imploring her not to break me because, without forethought, I gave my heart to her. For once, I pray she reads my thoughts as she presses her lips against mine.

When we break apart, there's a group of people near us. An insanely fit older woman asks Beverly, "Would you like me to take a picture of you and your boyfriend?"

Not giving Beverly an opportunity to correct or turn down the woman, I step forward and hand her my phone. "Yes, we'd love that."

Beverly seems to think I'm playing a game, because she turns to me with a mischievous grin. "Babe, a picture of you holding me would be cute." She jumps into my arms and the lady taking our picture must think it's adorable, because she's smiling ear to ear.

"Thank you," Beverly and I say in unison to the kind woman.

"You're very welcome. Cherish your young love. It's the sweetest time of your life. And *always* stay active together. Adventures will keep you together forever. I've been with this old coot for nearly forty years." She points to the fit gray-haired man standing on the trail and waiting for her with a broad smile spread across his bearded face.

I offer to take a picture of her and her "old coot," and they're appreciative. While the woman, whose name I learn is Joann, talks to us, I notice Beverly's posture stiffen at the mention of love.

You've got your work cut out for you, my subconscious reminds me.

Once we say our goodbyes, Beverly's body relaxes again. "So do you have enough in you to go farther?" she asks.

"Let's do it!" I place my hand on her lower back, pointing her toward the trail. When she sharply inhales at my touch, I know I have a chance, but I'll need to get over the hurdles she will place in the way.

Beverly guides us back the way we came, but then turns off the paved path, following along a fast-flowing creek. We cross a narrow, weathered wood and metal grate bridge. I spot a few small birds diving beneath the water. As we hike deeper into

the valley, everything becomes even greener. A green I thought only existed in the fairy tales grandma used to read to me. We pass several small waterfalls that are as breathtaking as the giant one at the beginning of our journey.

Once we reach a small intersection in the trail, Beverly turns back and points behind me. "Look."

Turning around, I'm speechless. I take in the towering, moss-covered firs that populate the narrow valley we just climbed through.

"Amazing, right?" Wonder drips from her voice.

Glancing over at her, I fall in love with the way she appreciates the view—as if it's the first time her eyes have landed on it. Here in nature is where Beverly belongs. She's in her element.

"Here, let's have some water," she suggests, reaching into her backpack.

"Good idea."

As we drink, I feel a burst of exhilaration so profound, my heart races. "You know, I think you might have made this place impossible to beat. I've had a blast with you today."

I grab her by the hips and tug her toward me, tangling my fingers in her ponytail as I tip her head up. My lips fuse with hers. She drops her water and her hands clutch at me. My body reacts instantly to her. I jerk back, my breathing ragged.

"Okay. Now *you've* made this place impossible to beat," she says, her bashful smile enhancing her gorgeous mouth.

Bending down, I pick up her half-empty water container and apologize for making her drop it.

She shakes her head. "Never apologize for a kiss like that. Not. Ever. Now come on, we should be able to get to the top in about thirty more minutes."

We approach a sign that says 1.6 miles remain to the summit, and I think Beverly's estimated time frame might be a bit low unless she intends to whip me the rest of the way up.

"This trail is all about the hike up. Once we reach the summit, it's not as impressive as everything else we've seen. It's more about the accomplishment and the journey upward," she shouts back to me.

I lag about ten feet behind her insane pace, sucking in quick breaths and struggling not to allow more distance between us.

"That's okay," I huff.

The first part of the trail was much steeper. As this stretch flattens out, Beverly kicks into overdrive, speeding the rest of the way.

When I reach the summit, I collapse near some grim-looking rocks reminiscent of the name Devil's Rest. Crouching down next to me, Beverly slips free the backpack. She takes out water, fruit, granola bars, and sandwiches.

Thankful for the fuel, I dig into the lunch she packed. "I hope I haven't worn you out too much for the rest of our weekend together," Beverly says, nudging my arm.

"No, I'll be good. I just haven't gone on this hard of a hike in a long time, and I think my lungs aren't used to such clean air." I chuckle.

After a long, grueling, but well-worth-it day, we arrive back at Beverly's Jeep. I can't remember the last time I've been this exhausted. My legs feel heavy, my feet ache and my shoulders are knotted from lugging around her too-tight-for-my-body backpack. I offer to drive us back to her house. Beverly refuses, indicating I look like I could use some rest.

Not surprisingly, Beverly appears to be fine. As I drag myself into the passenger seat, she bounces behind the wheel

and pulls her shiny hair down from her ponytail.
I can't help but wonder, what happens next?

— 30 —

Gavin

As I stand under the steady stream of hot water, every muscle in my body howls in protest. I've been in Beverly's guest room shower for at least twenty minutes. While it pains me to think about the amount of water I've wasted, it pains me even more to consider getting out.

I've always believed myself to be in excellent physical shape. I swim daily, run, hike and strength-train weekly. But apparently, I'm not in as good of shape as I thought, because a tiny yet strong woman with endless energy put me in check today.

After another few minutes, I force myself to limp out of the shower. Despite fatigued limbs, I dress. In my exhausted state, the bed tempts me to climb in, but my stomach objects with an angry rumble.

Opening the guest bedroom door in search of Beverly, I inhale the delicious aroma of garlic and butter. Speeding up at the promise of a meal, I find a completely put-together Beverly wrestling around in the kitchen. Dressed in tight, ripped jeans and a fitted long-sleeved black scooped neck shirt, her clothes flatter her curves. How can this woman possibly be cooking after this morning?

She sees me in her peripheral, and a beautiful smile spreads across her face. "Hey! Are you hungry?"

I stare at her, stupefied. I can't get over her endless energy. I am barely capable of walking, and she's zooming around the kitchen.

I inch closer and examine her appearance. Her wet hair is tied in a knot atop her head, and her face is free of makeup. Well, thank God, if her hair and makeup were done, I'd seriously consider having her tested for being an alien life-form.

She stops and is now staring at me staring at her in wonder; I clear my throat. "Starving. How's it possible that you're cooking right now?"

"Excellent. So am I." Her eyes travel down my body. When she licks her lips, I feel my pulse quicken in response. "It'll be ready in fifteen minutes," she says, her gaze still roaming my body.

Desperate to get my mind off the way she's eyeing me, I ask, "Seriously, when did you have time to do all this?" My eyes scan the stove where quinoa simmers and spinach is sautéing.

She shrugs. "Before I woke you up this morning, I prepared the salmon and put it in the fridge. I figured after our hike, we'd be too tired to go out to eat."

"Always prepared," I say.

"Ha! My dad would be damn proud to hear you say that." She snorts. I think I'm missing something, but before I can question her, she asks if I want something to drink.

"Sure. Whatever you're having."

"I was thinking of a glass of wine tonight." She pauses and looks up at me. "If that's okay with you? If we decide to go anywhere tonight, we'll call a cab," she quickly adds.

"Wine sounds great. I'm okay staying in the rest of the night if you are." I glance at the clock. It's only a little after

4:30 p.m., but I'm worn out and would love to take it easy with her tonight. Also, I'm hopeful her drinking wine with me is a sign she trusts me and feels comfortable.

"Staying in sounds perfect. I have an amazing Pinot Noir from a winery here in Oregon. It'll go great with the salmon, but if you're not a fan, you can choose something else." She points behind me to her built-in wine rack.

"That's great." I've actually heard phenomenal things about Oregon's Pinot Noir. Plus, she's right, it should pair nicely with the salmon. "Do you need any help?" I ask.

"No, sir. You're my guest, sit down and let me pour you a glass of wine." She gestures to a cross-backed barstool at the center island. I settle onto it with no small amount of relief.

Beverly places two large red wine glasses down in front of me. She leans into me, brushing my arm as she pours our wine. With me seated on the barstool, we're eye-level with each other. I can't resist the impulse to snake my arm around her waist and pull her into my lap for a simmering kiss.

Once our kiss becomes incendiary, Beverly let's out a frustrated growl and slowly peels herself away from me. "Sorry. I haven't kissed someone so often in years. You're making me a little crazy with temptation," she says, making her way over to the oven.

An insane surge of jealousy shoots through me at the thought of Beverly's mouth on any other man. To make sure her thoughts aren't anywhere but with us, I walk up behind her after she places the salmon on the stove. I wrap my arms around her body, nibbling at her ear and trailing kisses down her neck.

"Never. Apologize. For. A. Kiss. Like. That. Not. Ever." I mimic her words from earlier.

Dinner is delicious and our conversation flows. Once I

finish eating, I feel Beverly's energy start to shift. She's slipping back into the ugly habit of closing herself off again. My chest tightens with concern. The more detached and quieter she becomes, the more I fear her slipping through my fingers.

Dude, cut her some slack, I tell myself. We did have a long and exhausting day. Perhaps she's just tired, but I wish she'd say something.

The silence becomes too much for me to bear. I decide to clear our plates and give her a few minutes to herself. I understand how wearing entertaining for long periods can be. I look forward to my alone time. It's how I recharge. Maybe Beverly is the same.

When I place our dishes in the sink, I notice our plates from this morning are gone.

What the hell is she? A ninja?

I snatch the pots and pans from the stovetop, motivated to show her my appreciation. I begin my task of washing the dishes and cleaning the kitchen.

Only a few minutes into cleaning, Beverly walks in and leans up against the counter to watch me. Neither of us says a word. I like that she hasn't asked what I'm doing or told me not to worry about the mess.

Instead, she accepts my appreciation and allows me to continue. Though, eventually, she tires of watching me and picks up a kitchen towel to dry the dishes. She'd probably like to speed up the process because I'm a slow cleaner. I'm spoiled with a housekeeper who comes daily, which allows me to be lazy in the cleaning department.

Now that the kitchen is returned to its former immaculate condition, I turn to Beverly, needing to ask her a question that's been nagging at me since we got back to her house.

"Should I head back to the hotel? I can call a cab if you're too tired to take me."

"Do you want to go back to the hotel?" she asks just above a whisper, stepping closer to me.

"Answer my question first." I grin.

"Gavin, if I wanted you to leave, you would already be gone. We only have *one* weekend, and I'd like it if you stay here with me. Of course, only if you want to . . . I understand you paid for a nice hotel room."

"Hmm . . . you're right. Tough decision." I rub my chin. "I don't know. On one hand, I can stay at a hotel all alone, or I can spend the night again with an alluring woman."

With a sweet smile playing on her lips, she steps forward, reaches up and with a gentle hand cups my cheek. I clasp her arm like it's my lifeline, then plant a soft kiss on her lips, careful not to jumpstart the heated episode from earlier.

"Do you want to make dessert together?" When she sees my startled expression, she adds, "I mean that literally, like bake a chocolate cake or something."

"Come on, we both know what you really want," I tease, and her cheeks turn bright red as she shuffles her feet.

"Well, yeah, but for now, I'll settle for some cake. A woman needs something sweet in her life," she fires back.

With the cake cooling in the kitchen, Beverly and I step out onto her back deck. It's freezing, but I am happy to snuggle up under blankets with her.

We sip hot chocolate topped with marshmallows, the way my mom would make it when I was a boy. I want to ask Beverly deep questions. We've been hovering over safe topics all night, which I suppose is better than an awkward silence.

"I still can't believe you knew about Jenny and Trevor, and

I didn't," I grumble.

Snickering, Beverly argues, "They weren't trying to hide it from me. You're the one who forbade them to date."

I still resent just learning about the secret Trevor kept from me for nearly two years. TWO YEARS! It all poured out of him after I saw the photo of Jenny blowing a kiss at the camera on his phone.

When Trevor's eyes shifted from his phone to me, he looked trapped and guilty. My intention that day was to withdraw my objection to a personal relationship between him and Jenny. But his phone rang and the truth of the last two years exploded in my face. My plan went sideways. I was pissed they'd both lied to me, so I threw him out of my truck. We haven't spoken since.

Beverly's gentle touch on my forearm brings me out of my head. "You know Jenny and Trevor feel horrible for deceiving you, right? But come on, they did it to protect their love for each other. Fear can make people, even the most loyal people or the ones we love the most, do funny things. You need to forgive them."

"I do. I'm not one to hold a grudge, but I'd be lying if I said it doesn't sting being lied to for that long. Did you know there were even times he was in San Diego visiting her, but he didn't tell me he was in town because he didn't want to lie about what he was doing there?"

"Isn't it good that he didn't want to lie to you?"

"I wish I hadn't created an environment where he felt he couldn't be honest with me."

"Okay, stop right there. While I said I understood why they lied, I didn't say you caused them to do it. They're both grown adults and chose dishonesty."

Not wanting to waste any more of our night talking about

them, I change the subject. "Is that cake cool enough yet?"

A grinning Beverly taps my thigh. "Let's go check."

The cake is ready. And it is delicious.

"Ah, no more," I say, pushing aside my dish after my second slice. "You're an incredible cook; breakfast, dinner, this cake. Hell, even lunch on our hike was delicious."

"Well, thanks." She glows with every compliment I give her.

"Are you tired?" she asks.

"You kicked my butt today, I've been tired since 2 p.m."

She giggles. "Come on, let's go upstairs."

Oh, no. She wants me to sleep in her bed again, but I don't have the self-control to sleep with her a second time and keep my hands, along with other body parts, to myself. Under any other circumstance, I'd be racing up to her room. I made our deal knowing deep down it is what she needs. What *we* need for us to work.

"I'm not sure that's a good idea. I think I should sleep in the guest room tonight," I say cautiously, not wanting to offend her, but needing to be honest with her.

Beverly releases a heavy sigh. "I get it. It's difficult for me, too. I'm just lonely. I haven't been with anyone on an intimate level in a really long time. Last night, I slept so peacefully. I was selfishly hoping for the same thing tonight." She looks up at me through her lashes. Something in her voice makes my heart ache, and I long to give her what she wants.

"Well, let's give it a shot. If it's too difficult, or we can't control ourselves, I'll come downstairs."

"Deal," she responds too quickly.

— 31 —

Gavin

I'm the first awake the next morning. Surprisingly, I managed to keep my hands to myself last night. Well, mostly to myself. As I gaze down at Beverly sleeping, stretched out on her stomach with her face turned toward me, her hair fanned out across her pillow, and her mouth slightly open, I feel my heart swell.

Each hour I'm with her, my feelings grow stronger. I never knew falling in love could happen so quickly, or that it would feel so encompassing. For someone to wield power over my emotions isn't a concept easy for me to grasp. I've always been a firm believer that we're all in control of our own emotions, and no one holds the power to make us happy, sad, or angry. Those are choices we make.

However, now that I feel my heart is tied to another person, confusion invades and rearranges my thinking. Top that off with the need to keep a leash on my feelings in order to not scare her away. It's a burden I never expected to bear. All the rules in the world could not have kept me from Beverly.

When I set my standards—no one more than two years younger, can't work together, tall, an open book, and shares my

desire for a family—my goal was to create order and to mold a life that would make sense. I thought this would make love smoother and easier. I know now that love isn't always easy, it isn't always fair, and sometimes only one person's heart is willing to give and to receive it.

Beverly's walls remain up. They're not coming down as freely as I hoped, yet sometimes, she surprises me with her vulnerability. In my bones, I know she aches to be loved. Once I determine what's holding her back, I will launch a campaign to persuade her that she deserves love, too. Thank God today is Saturday, because it means I must wait only one more day to learn about her past and what still causes her so much pain.

No matter how hard I try to stop myself, I keep obsessing over what she intends to share. She implies we will have no shared future because of her past. Multiple times she's said, "We only have this weekend."

There's almost nothing she could tell me that would make me not want to be with her. I'll need to figure out how to navigate and ease her insecurities so we can be together.

Beverly stirs next to me. Her eyes flutter open, her long eyelashes perfectly framing those big beautiful brown eyes. She greets me with an adorable smile.

"Good morning, Miss Morgan."

"You stayed," she says with a beautiful shade of pink flushing her cheeks.

"I think I fell asleep before you. That hike took everything out of me," I confess with a chuckle.

"I didn't realize how tired I was. I don't think I woke up once last night. What time is it, anyway?"

"Almost eight."

Her eyes grow wide in disbelief. "I haven't slept this long in years."

"I'm shocked I woke up before you." I press a kiss to her forehead. "So, what are our plans for today?" I ask.

"I thought we'd hit up Angel's Rest today since you were too tired after Devil's Rest yesterday," she says deadpan.

Please be kidding. Please be joking.

Finally, she cracks a smile.

"Very funny. Maybe I should make the plans today."

"Okay, deal. What do you want to do?"

"My mom visited Portland a few years ago. She raved about the Japanese Garden."

"Perfect. Let's get moving. We can go out for breakfast." She jumps from the bed.

When I hear the shower turn on, I know I need to leave. And fast. Seeing Beverly naked would guarantee a broken deal.

Heading downstairs, I grab my phone from the charger and call the airlines. Fifteen minutes later, my flight is changed to Monday. Then I type out a quick text to Jenny, letting her know I won't be back in the office until Tuesday afternoon.

After I finish showering and dressing, I wait for Beverly outside on the back deck. Leaning into the railing as the morning moisture surrounds me, I'm thankful for the new routine I've adopted here in her home. I'm eager to make the Pacific Northwest my home. Will I open a new office branch up here? Should I work from home?

Lots of questions fill my mind.

"There you are," Beverly's sweet voice sounds behind me. She walks over to me and slips her hand into mine.

My heart beats erratically.

"Here I am," I say, looking down into her warm honey brown eyes.

Her long straight hair frames her face. Taking in the rest of her, I scan her signature tight jeans, a loose white cable-knit sweater, and tan half boot things that all the hipsters seem to wear. She's perfect for me.

"You're going to miss this view, aren't you?"

"How do you do that?"

"Do what?" She scrunches her nose in confusion.

"Read my mind. All. The. Time."

"Oh, that. I have an explanation; my dad was a detective for nearly twenty years, and he's been a private investigator for the last ten years. I grew up with him drilling me on how to read people's voices, habits, body language, all of it. He never wanted anyone to be able to take advantage of me, and he was always afraid I'd get scammed. He's a huge worrier. I don't blame him, considering everything he's seen during his career." She shrugs.

"Here I thought our connection was something special." I can hear the disappointment in my voice.

Suck it up!

"It is. You are special." She squeezes my hand. "You're unlike anyone I've ever met. In fact, I rarely need those skills to know what you're thinking. You wear your emotions loud and proud. Being so transparent takes real courage. I admire that about you, and I hope one day I can be that confident and strong."

Her praise startles me. "You disarm me. I'm not usually as forthcoming, at least not with other businesspeople. But being with you makes me want to share every thought and experience with you. It's your energy. It draws people—in particular, me—to you."

She twists her hair in her hand. "Let's get going. I'm

starving," she says, effectively ending our conversation.

When we pull up to my hotel, my mind races with what went wrong, why are we here? Beverly sees the confusion on my face and grabs my hand. "We're eating breakfast here."

I shift, uncomfortable with how easily she reads me and my reactions.

"The food here is delish. Since you haven't spent any time at the hotel, I thought it was a good idea."

"Yeah, sounds great," I manage.

This isn't a place where I expect people to recognize Beverly. Our other stops have been little mom and pop shops, yet the energetic young brunette hostess who seats us is on a first-name basis with her. The only difference as she seats us next to a window overlooking the river is she doesn't make a fuss that Beverly brought a guest with her.

I read the menu while Beverly's phone rings and dings messages. I wonder who it is? Should I encourage her to take the calls?

"You're awfully quiet," she says as I fail to actually read the items listed on the breakfast menu.

"Just trying to figure out what I want. It all looks so good," I lie.

Her phone rings again. "I'll just turn it off." She does, then tosses it in her purse.

I open my mouth to ask about her persistent caller, and our waitress pops over to take our drink order.

"What do you recommend?" I hope she gives me a few options.

My wish is her command as she once again applies her psychic powers. "The pancakes are always good, but I normally get the two-egg any style, with an English muffin, and I always

ask for extra of their homemade and freaking amazeballs Elderberry Jam. I've also had the Chilaquiles Rojos, which was delicious too, but I've got to be in the mood for it."

Yum. Chilaquiles it is. I haven't had Mexican food since I left San Diego. I feel deprived.

The food is delicious. Beverly is extra chatty this morning, but I'm still stuck on who kept calling her as we arrived. Was it one person? Because, if so, he must've called at least four times in a row.

Back in Beverly's Jeep, we drive to the *Japanese Garden*. Wanting to get out of my own head, I snatch Beverly's phone and scroll through her music. It doesn't take long for me to locate the perfect song to lift my mood. While I turn up the stereo, I keep my eyes glued to her as Sir Mix-a-Lot's *Baby Got Back* starts streaming through the speakers.

She turns and squints at me. For a split-second, I think I've insulted her, but then she smirks and starts spitting out the lyrics. I mean she seriously doesn't miss one word. I never realized how many words were in that song, until now. The whole time she's singing—rapping—whatever, she's bouncing around in her seat. I'm floored, because after her crummy performance yesterday, I never would've thought she could actually be any good at rapping.

"You're a nut!" I crack up as the song ends and she gives me a smug smile with the sweet victory of surprising me.

She parks near some tennis courts. "We're here," Beverly announces before climbing out of the car.

I look around for some sort of entrance or sign for the garden. This isn't what I expect, but I follow Beverly up the road, only to be greeted by a water garden of flowing ponds.

"Wow, this is new," Beverly says. "I guess it helps lead

visitors to the entrance, because it's slightly hidden up the hill there." She points in the direction we're heading.

The dense native forest showcasing towering firs and cedars surrounds us on the path to the entrance of the *Japanese Garden,* which is tucked into Washington Park. Once we're inside, I feel a sense of renewal. The Japanese culture truly knows how to restore one's soul and create a space to attain a feeling of peace.

As we move from garden to garden, I'm in awe of each garden's elegance and uniqueness. Here it's a different beautiful than Multnomah Falls. The falls are wholly natural, while these were planted and are maintained, yet done in such a brilliant way you forget you're in a garden planted and organized by man.

The *Strolling Pond Garden* is my favorite, so far. It features two ponds, filled with Koi fish and connected by a flowing stream. Stunning Japanese irises are everywhere, and behind the lower pond I spy a small cascading waterfall surrounded by lush plants.

We take our time wandering through each garden. I love that Beverly, just like yesterday, possesses the enthusiasm of a first-timer. We stroll to the last garden, *The Natural Garden.* Beverly admires the vibrant moss that covers the ground, rocks, and trees. I imagine it would cover us if we stand here long enough.

As we exit, I feel anxiety slowly rooting itself deep in my gut. Questions start to float around in my head. I try to grasp how I could allow the peacefulness I was just experiencing to slip away.

Am I anxious about what Beverly will tell me?

Is the thought of returning to San Diego and leaving her here the cause of my unease?

Then, like a swift kick to the nuts, it hits me. I'm terrified Beverly will break my heart. Someday, maybe not tomorrow or even weeks from now, but eventually, this woman could rip out my heart and break me in a way I've never experienced at the hands of any woman.

As we approach the *International Rose Garden*, I try to force down my unwelcome realization. I feel Beverly's sixth sense homing in on me, ready to pounce at any moment.

I scan the vast array of roses lined up in every direction. I never knew there were so many kinds of roses, over six hundred varieties, according to the sign. Beyond the garden is a view of downtown and Mount Hood.

While I try to admire the view, the fragrance of fresh roses fills my senses as Beverly tucks firmly into my side. I know that nothing, not even fear, will stop me from falling in love with her, but will I be enough to open her heart and keep her at my side?

— 32 —

Beverly

I can't do it anymore!

Today something shifted inside of me. Keeping my past from Gavin is draining me. I felt a change in him, too, ever since my brother started blowing up my phone at breakfast. Stress was pulsing off of Gavin, and he didn't finish his meal.

I should've told him it was just my brother calling, but something stopped me. During our drive back to my house from the *Japanese Garden*, he gripped the handle on the passenger-side door until his knuckles went white, barely saying a word or glancing my way.

I think he feels what's about to come. Even though he's made it clear he likes me, I've also made it apparent I'm not available in a girlfriend capacity. I also know I've been teasing him these past couple of days, but my mind is chaotic, my emotions evershifting, and Gavin Reed tempts me to want things I know would screw up our lives.

I should've never allowed any of this to happen. I let him see a side of me I thought died years ago, a side no one else has

seen since before the accident. I pray my instincts are wrong, and I didn't give him hope for something more.

Even though this is the first time I've ever wanted to share this part of my life before, and I'll miss the fun we've shared, Reed needs to understand and accept why my heart will never beat again.

Okay, Beverly, it's go time.

Time to rip open my past and get this over with.

I rub my forehead and try to slow my heartbeat, which is thumping in my ears. My only hope is that he won't give me that damn look of forced sympathy I've come to know so well. The look that says "no I don't know what you went through, but here is my pity."

I hate pity.

I drag myself back into the living room to find Gavin and bring him a glass of water, but he isn't on the couch where I left him. I place the glass on the table in front of me and sit on my uncomfortably firm couch to wait.

I should search for him so I can rip off this Band-Aid. Instead, I wait. On the wall to the left of my fireplace is a large, rustic clock I bought last year at downtown a thrift shop. It's one of my favorite pieces in my house. I love this clock, but right now it's tormenting me as the seconds tick down. It's like watching a bomb ready to detonate as my time with Gavin Reed comes to a close.

"Hey."

I nearly jump off the couch at the sound of his husky voice next to me.

I scan his frame one last time. He has changed into a black, long-sleeved T-shirt. The man is too damn hot for his own good. Casting my eyes downward, I say, "It's probably time I talk."

When I'm met with only silence, I glance up at him to make sure he heard me. I'm met with his warm eyes, which possess the power to pierce my damaged soul.

Tell him, a voice whispers somewhere deep inside me.

"Beverly, tell me only if you want to. I won't dig up your past. It doesn't matter to me, anyway. I mean, it matters because it's part of you, but it won't change my feelings for you."

God, why does he have to be so perfect? Maybe I can stick to only being friends with him, because I want him in my life. But the intensity of our attraction to each other would prevent friendship from working. Can't ignore reality.

"I appreciate that, but I need to tell you. Otherwise, you'll hear it from someone else, and it's a rare opportunity for me to actually be the one to share my story. Plus—" The doorbell interrupts me.

Gavin straightens up beside me. "Are you expecting someone?"

I shake my head. "No."

"Here. I'll get it for you." He stands and heads for the front door.

I scurry to catch up with him. "Gavin, it's fine. I'll get it."

He frowns, full of concern. "What if it's Jeremy or someone you don't want to see?"

What? Seriously, Jeremy?

"Jeremy doesn't know where I live." I narrow my eyes at him. "It's probably UPS or something. Please just wait here."

"Beverly, it isn't hard to get someone's address. I'm not waiting here."

"You are waiting here." I cross my arms and stare him down. His eyes lock with mine, challenging me until the doorbell rings again. I hold up my hand, ordering him to stay.

I swing open my door to find Ian standing on my porch, his hair wild and dark circles under his eyes. "Hey. What are you doing here? Are you okay?" I ask, unable to keep the worry from my voice as I take a step toward him.

He throws his arms up in the air. "Finally! I've been calling you since yesterday morning. We need to talk."

My first thought jumps to Dad and my chest tightens. Ian peers over my shoulder and jerks his head back as I feel a strong arm slip around my waist.

I ignore Gavin and take a step closer to Ian, pressing my hand to my chest and waiting for him to speak.

Ian backs up a few steps. "You have company." He shakes his head. "I shouldn't have stopped by unannounced."

"Ian, is it Dad?" My voice cracks, and I feel Gavin's hand on my back again.

My brother clutches his stomach. "Oh, God. No. Beverly, no. Dad is fine."

My shoulders sag. I let out the breath I've been holding since first seeing Ian's distraught face.

"Beverly, I'm so sorry. I didn't mean to scare you."

"Then what's wrong?" I ask.

Ian looks from me to Gavin, and back to me. Whatever he needs to tell me, I don't think he's going to do it in front of a man he's never met before.

"Just come in." I step out of the way and Gavin follows.

Once Ian clicks the door shut behind him, I start to make introductions. "Ian, this is—"

"Gavin Reed, I know. It's nice to meet you, man." He shoves his hand forward to shake Gavin's.

I feel my rogue eyebrow twitching. "How do you know who he is?" I ask.

"C'mon, B, I'm trying to be a sports photographer. You think I don't know one of the biggest behind-the-scenes names in the sports industry? The man who was a baseball one-year wonder, rookie of the year, and who walked away from it all to start an insanely successful Management and PR company. Also, are you forgetting that I talk to Aubrey, and she's friends with Jenny?"

I roll my eyes at him. "Whatever. Gavin, this is my younger brother, Ian."

"It's good to meet you. I've heard a lot about you," Gavin says.

"Nice to meet you, too. Sorry to drop by, I just got into town and needed to see my sis."

Did he fly here to see me? Or did he make the mistake of trying to see Aubrey again?

"But I can see now that you're busy and probably have other plans."

As Ian talks to Gavin, I examine him more closely. He looks like he hasn't showered or slept in days. I need to get Ian alone and figure out what's going on. Maybe it's time Gavin heads back to the hotel.

"We're just heading out to dinner, so you should join us," Gavin says. My head snaps up, and he smiles at me, oblivious of my irritation.

"Are you sure?" Ian looks over at me for permission.

I plaster on a fake smile. "Of course. This is Gavin's first time to Portland, and I offered to be his tour guide for the weekend."

Ian fidgets with his jacket. "I'm kinda gross from the plane. Is it cool if I hop in the shower real quick?"

"Of course. Use the spare one upstairs."

He tilts his head to one side, reminding me of Dad. "Why not the one in your guest bedroom down here?"

I chew on the inside of my cheek and try to remain composed. "Gavin's staying in that room."

Ian laughs, certain I'm joking, then does a double take looking from me to Gavin. "Oh." His mouth splits into a knowing grin.

I interlock my hands together in front of me to stop myself from punching him in the throat.

He grabs a blue duffle bag I hadn't noticed he brought in, then bounds up the stairs. Once he's out of sight, I march into the living room in search of my phone. Once I find it, I tap out a quick text to Aubrey.

> Me: Bre, Ian is here and he looks a wreck. Do you know what's going on?

Pacing my living room floor with my hand clutched around my phone, my mind starts to fill with all kinds of possibilities.

"Beverly, what's wrong?" Gavin asks.

I shake my head. "I don't know. But something is up with my brother, and I need to find out what. Before you came to the front door, he was going to tell me something." My stomach is heavy, even though I haven't eaten in hours.

"I'm glad your dad is all right," he says.

"But is my brother?"

— 33 —

Gavin

Now that Beverly's brother is showered and seems in much better shape than when he showed up, we all head out the door. I fight off my disappointment. I had come so close, just seconds away from learning more about Beverly. Now, I don't know where I'll be sleeping tonight.

"Ugh. I forgot my jacket. Here, get in." Beverly presses the button to unlock her Jeep and darts back inside the house.

The moment Ian and I shut the car doors, he cuts to the chase and shifts from a fan of mine to the protective brother in a second. "Are you dating my sister?" He narrows his tired eyes at me, and for a pretty boy, he can be a little intimidating. After all, his disapproval of me could sway Beverly's feelings.

"I would like to, but that's up to her."

He cocks his head to the side in an eerily familiar way as his sister. "But you're sleeping at her house?"

I rub my clammy hands on my jeans to dry them. "In her guest bedroom, yes."

"Hmm," is all he says as Beverly emerges and scampers toward us.

The drive into downtown is epic in its awkwardness. Beverly asks question after question, trying to get to the bottom of her brother's visit. Ian dances round every one of them. Evading in-depth conversation seems to be another Morgan family trait. I remain mostly quiet in the backseat, my ears open and seeking any clues hidden in their conversation.

There's no discussion on dinner. Beverly simply drives through the city and we wind up in front of a pub. As we climb out of the car, she explains this is where she and Ian go whenever he's in town. Explaining her reasons for anything isn't typical Beverly behavior. She's clearly shaken up by her brother's visit.

After we order our drinks, Beverly excuses herself from the table to use the restroom. The moment she disappears from sight, Ian closes back in on me.

"How'd you guys meet?" he asks, taking a swig of his beer.

The difference between the Morgan siblings and me is that I won't avoid answering anyone's questions. "I hired her company to work on a project with me."

Choking on his drink, he snags a napkin and wipes his mouth. "You're working together?" His eyes go wide.

"Your sister's company is very reputable, and she's a talented businesswoman," I snap, offended by his reaction.

"I know that. That isn't why I'm surprised."

I'm irritated with his obscure response. Is he implying that my business isn't good enough to work with her? I fold my hands on the table and wait for him to continue. However, he isn't as perceptive as his sister, because it takes him a few moments to realize I'm waiting for an explanation.

"Isn't it obvious? My sister doesn't date. Especially not someone she's working with." He's already halfway through his

beer, and I'm starting to wonder why he showed up in Portland unannounced.

"Like I said, I want to date her. She's still undecided."

He dismissively waves his hand. "Yeah. Yeah. Yeah." He slams back the rest of his drink, then scans the pub for our waitress. He shifts, his back straightens, and he puts on a smile.

Glancing over my shoulder, I see Beverly approaching our table. She slides in next to me, probably able to pick up on our energy because she gives me a curious look.

By the time our food is served, Ian's on his third beer. Beverly's keeping a watchful eye on him. She seems to have given up on the interrogation. I'm able to relax some through their banter.

Ian and Beverly have wicked senses of humor together and mostly bash on each other. It's apparent they're close and would do anything for each other. They remind me of Trevor, and I feel a pang of guilt for the tension between my cousin and me right now.

I hate that we got into it over his decision to date my assistant. Ultimately, my close relationship with Trevor is worth the risk of losing Jenny as an assistant. It would suck, but it wouldn't be the end of the world. Losing my cousin, however, would be.

I slip my arm behind Beverly and rest it on the booth. As she slides a little closer to me, a grin forms on Ian's face.

"Aw, sis. It's 'bout time you moved on. You know I was worried and stuff, and rushed up here, but for what?" The alcohol is kicking in, and Ian is getting sloppy.

Beverly goes pale. "Ian, don't."

"What? It's okay. It's okay to talk about things, ya know, get them out in the open. I came here to tell you something important."

"Then let's talk about Aubrey, because I know what's going on," Beverly counters.

I feel her body stiffen. At the sight of Ian's shoulders slumping and his head dropping into his hands, I feel like I'm intruding on something personal.

"N-no. That's not right," Ian slurs.

I shift in my seat. Pretending my phone is vibrating with a call, I excuse myself and walk outside. As curious as I am to hear what Ian and Beverly speak about, it's best I give them some privacy. Ian is on the verge of tears, and if it were me, I wouldn't want some stranger seeing me like that.

From the street, I can see Beverly holding her brother's hand across the table. His shoulders are still slumped over, and he's shaking his head. I keep up my act for a few minutes, watching Beverly comfort her brother. When Ian gets up to use the restroom, I walk back in.

"Thanks for that," Beverly says when I slide into the booth next to her.

"For what?" I kiss the top of her head and play dumb.

"Come on. There wasn't anyone on the phone."

"Is your brother okay?" I ask, because he still hasn't come back to the table.

"Not really. The woman he's in love with, who doesn't know that he's in love with her, is engaged to another man, and her fiancé doesn't want them to talk anymore. Apparently, he also drank a bunch on the plane, so he's pretty buzzed. But it feels like he's still holding something back from me. Some of the things he said don't add up."

"You said it yourself. He's drunk, so not everything he says will make sense. Why hasn't he told this woman he's in love with her?"

"Yeah, I guess." She toys with her earrings. "He stays quiet, because he doesn't want to hurt her."

"How would that hurt her?"

Beverly arches an eyebrow at me.

"I'm just saying he should express his feelings before it's too late and she's married. She's already cutting him out, so if she doesn't have feelings for him, then it will only solidify her terminating all communication. If she does have feelings for him, maybe the realization will hit that she's with the wrong man or, at the very least, not ready to get married yet."

"I know she does have feelings for him, but she always says her fiancé is perfect for her."

"Oh, so you know her. Are you friends?"

"Best. It's Aubrey."

"Don't you think you're doing them a disservice as two people you love by not telling them about each other's feelings, or at least encouraging them to share it with each other?"

Ian plops down at the table, startling both of us and suspending our conversation until a later time. I hate unfinished things, but it seems to be a theme today.

"Drink this." Beverly shoves a tall glass of ice water at Ian.

He picks it up and starts gulping, then he looks over at me. "Hey, Gavin, I'm sorry for crashing your evening. Let's head out and I'll grab my bag, then get a car to a hotel."

"Where are you staying?" I ask.

"I need to see what's available online," he says.

I glance over at Beverly, "If you want, I have a room at the RiverPlace you're welcome to take." Beverly gently squeezes my knee. I reach down and cradle her hand.

Ian's eyes bounce from me to Beverly. "Yeah, that would be cool. I can pay you for the night."

I wave my hand through the air. "Don't worry about it. I'm just happy someone's going to use it."

My chest warms as Beverly leans into my side, and Ian smiles at his sister.

"Since we're in town, we can drop you off at the hotel now, so you can get some rest. I'll swing by later to drop off your bag at the front desk, and if you feel up to it tomorrow, you can join us at the farmers market," Beverly encourages.

"Sure. Sounds good." Ian tips back the rest of his water.

We're in the hotel lobby of the RiverPlace. I'm waiting in line at the front desk counter to get a new key for Ian since I left mine at Beverly's. Ian and Beverly are behind me to the side of the elevators, but still in hearing distance. I unintentionally overhear every word they say.

"It's so great to see a smile on your face. You two seem good together."

"We're just friends, Ian."

"You gotta stop doing this to yourself. It's okay to be happy again."

"Can we not do this right now?"

"Fine. But hey, seriously, before I leave town can we talk again?"

"I knew there was more."

"Of course, you did. You're worse than Dad. Look, it isn't life or death, but I want to talk to you soon, and it should be in private."

"Ian, you're worrying me. Are you in some kind of trouble?"

"Excuse me, sir. How may I help you?" the lady behind the counter asks, ripping me out of Beverly and Ian's conversation.

— 34 —

Beverly

Gavin and I finally head back to my house after dropping off Ian's bag at the hotel. I peek over at him as I turn right, heading up the tree-lined road to my home. "Thanks for letting my brother take your room."

"No problem. Honestly, it wasn't only for him. I didn't want you to offer him a place to crash and not have a chance to continue the conversation we started earlier." He clears his throat and shifts in his seat. "That is, if you're still up to sharing."

I force down a swallow. After witnessing Gavin's kindness with my foolish brother, not to mention the way he excused himself from the table when Ian's filter malfunctioned, I want to tell Gavin now more than before.

"I want you to hear it from me." I put the Jeep in park and reach over to squeeze his hand, wishing my life were different. Wishing I could be the woman he wants and needs.

Gavin strokes the back of my hand with his thumb when my phone rings and startles both us from our trance. "It's my dad," I say. "He might be calling about Ian, I should probably answer." I hand Gavin my keys. "Do you mind letting yourself in?"

"Sure." He kisses the back of my hand before he climbs out of the Jeep.

I suck in a deep breath and roll out my shoulders. "Hi, Dad," I say into the phone.

"Hey, kid," is all he says in response. I wait a few beats before I decide to continue speaking and ask him how he's doing.

"I talked to your brother," he says, ignoring my question.

"He'll be okay, Dad. He just needs to figure out what he's going to do about his feelings for her."

"I'm not calling because of his feelings for Aubrey, kid."

I grip the back of my neck and twist. He's more taciturn than usual. I hear him blow out a breath on the other end of the line.

"Dad, what's going on? You and Ian are acting weird. Do you know what else he needs to tell me?"

"I don't. Believe it or not, my children don't tell me everything. But I guess I taught you both that particular habit, so I can only blame myself."

The chili cheese fries I ate at the pub earlier churn in my stomach. Feeling confined, I climb out of my Jeep. It's dark outside, and my driveway is dimly lit by the coach lights hanging on each side of my garage.

"Dad, what are you talking about?"

"Honey, I need to tell you a couple of things. Do you have a few minutes alone? I know you have a friend over."

I'm going to kill Ian for telling Dad about Gavin.

"Before you decide to rip into your brother, just know he cares about you. He wants to see you happy, and so do I."

I walk around the side of my driveway, following one of my large planters, to the privacy of my side yard, careful not to trip on any tree roots. "I'm alone right now. Please just tell me what's going on."

"Now, I've let this go on for far too long, Beverly." He clears his throat, but it doesn't help. His voice is still hoarse with emotions, causing my eyes to tear up. "I thought it was your grieving process, because I have no clue what you went through on that day. I can't imagine what you had to see . . ." His voice cracks.

"Dad." I squeeze my eyes shut in a failed attempt to clear the image in my head of Mom's bloody face.

"Let me finish," he says between sniffles.

"When you moved away, stopped dating, quit your dream, and started your mother's company . . ."

I gasp and clap my hand over my mouth. How does he know I'm doing this for Mom?

"Yeah, kid, I know what you've been up to. I knew all about your mom's plans. She was gearing up to start the business. I know I haven't been the best father, but I loved your mom with every ounce of me. I wanted every one of her dreams to come true."

Tears slide down my cheeks.

"But I've failed her, kid. I've allowed my heartache to shut me down, and make excuses about you throwing your own talents away."

I swipe at the tears streaming down my cheeks. "I'm not throwing anything away. I'm bringing her dreams to life," I argue.

"Beverly. My little wolf . . ."

My lip quivers at the sound of my nickname.

"Let me ask you one question. Are you happy?"

I bite down on my lip to stop myself from yelling. How can I be happy when Mom isn't alive to feel joy? My eyes wander to my house, and I think about the man waiting for me inside. I'm

happy when I'm around him, but that's different. He's just a distraction from a past that still haunts me. Surely, I can't feel true, blissful happiness again?

My dad's deep voice cuts into my thoughts. "If your answer isn't immediately 'yes', then I've let your mother down. I've let her down with both of our children, because her number-one dream, and reason for living, was to make sure her kids were fulfilled and happy. If you really want to do something for your mom, do that."

I hear footsteps behind me, mushing in the wet grass, and my heartbeat speeds up. "You can't just throw all this at me over the phone. I have a business guest right now. I have to go."

"We need to talk about this."

Why now? Why years after it happened? I wrap my sweater tighter around my body. "I can't. I have to go."

"Just think about everything I've said. You deserve happiness, Beverly. I love you."

My throat constricts, yet I'm able to say, "Love you, too." I end the call, and turn back toward my home. I only take a few steps before seeing Gavin. His concerned big blue eyes and furrowed brow spike my heart rate further.

He stops in his tracks and shoves his hands in his pockets. "Hey, sorry. I wanted to check on you, and I followed the sound of your voice over here." His worried eyes scan my face.

Like a dam that's old and worn, with several patches from holes over the years, I burst. I can't hold it together in front of him any longer. Tears spill from my eyes, streaming down my face and adding to the moisture of the damp grass below my feet.

Gavin reaches me in two large strides and pulls me into his arms. "Beverly, what's wrong?"

I sag against his body, the tears continuing while I gulp for more air. Have I really thrown everything away? Would Mom be ashamed of the empty shell I am now? Or would she understand, would she know the perfect things to say and respect my choices?

Gavin carries me inside and sets me down on my couch then disappears down the hall, likely terrified by my outburst. I focus on his feet slapping against the hardwood. When he reappears, he's holding a box of tissues.

"Here," he says, pulling one from the box and handing it to me.

I wipe my cheeks and eyes, covering the white paper with black mascara. I grab a clump and try to mop up the best I can.

"I'm sorry," I say.

He scoots closer to me and tucks my hair behind my ear. "Tell me what's wrong."

I pull the sleeves of my sweater over my hands, attempting to protect myself as much as I can as I prepare my heart to tell him everything.

Gavin interprets my pause as hesitation, and he extends his hand. "I'm here when you're ready. But can you at least tell me if you're okay?"

I shake my head, reaching one hand out of its safe cocoon and pulling his hand into my lap. "I'm so grateful our paths crossed." I lift his hand to my mouth and press my lips to it, his eyes follow my every move.

"These past few days you've helped me to forget and to feel joy again. For that, I'll always be indebted to you."

The beautiful skin on his face pales. He grips my hand and squeezes.

In that simple touch, I can feel how much he already cares for me, which is going to make it harder to hurt him.

"You deserve to be happy every day," he says as his eyes search mine.

I shrink back at his statement. I don't deserve happiness. But his comment hurls me into my darkest memories. To the part of my life I wish I could erase. Without another thought, my mouth starts to move, and I start seeing my past played before me as if on a movie screen.

"I'm a runner, or rather, I was a runner. Short distance, sprints mostly. I was good, too, and I loved it." Releasing his hand, I stand and walk over to the window, needing space. That, and I don't want to see the pity that always follows my confessions.

"My mom noticed at a young age how much I enjoyed running. She'd watch me from the kitchen window, sprinting back and forth on the grass in our backyard. She used to have to come out and tell me to take a break and hydrate. Something was freeing about running, like I was pushing the limits, and I was the only one in control."

I can't help but smile, recalling my mom coming into the backyard and forcing me to sit in the shade. She'd always have water and frozen grapes with her. Then a slow burn creeps into my chest as my dad's words from earlier echo in my head.

Could I be happy again? What about Patrick? His dreams were lost, too.

Gavin walks over to me and places his hand on my lower back. "Look at me," he whispers in my ear.

Turning around, I analyze his eyes. They're filled with the same warmth that now fills his voice. "You don't have to do this right now. It's been a long day."

Doing something that I know I shouldn't, I stand on tiptoes and kiss his sexy soft lips. In another life, I could have

fallen hard for this man. In another life, he might have even been my happily-ever-after.

But this isn't a fairytale, and Dad was right about one thing. He will never know what it was like to see Mom's lifeless and bloody body pulled from the wreckage. He doesn't know how painful it was to see her arm, the arm she used to try to shield me, with bones sticking out of it because it was shattered. No, I need to lay this out now, so I can curl up and lick my wounds later tonight.

Straightening my back, I muster the courage to continue. "My mom encouraged me to run, and she'd always tell me how lucky I was to have a passion so young in life. She said many people went their whole lives without finding their calling." The image of my mom is one that, if I think about it for too long, sends me down a rabbit hole of depression and self-loathing.

Just keep going, a voice in my head urges.

"When I was seven, she found a local running group for kids and signed me up." That's where I met Patrick, but I keep that memory to myself. "It was the best thing she ever did for me; I felt happy and it's my first memory of feeling physically strong. She told me I was never too young to follow a dream, but she made sure I knew that if I ever found a new dream I wanted to follow, it would be okay to let the old one go. She'd say 'it ran its course, it served its purpose, and it led you somewhere new.' She always cheered me on."

I attempt to calm the pain that's crawling up my throat, tightening its hold, making it difficult to speak. Before I'm able to continue, Gavin fills in the silence. "Do you still run?"

"Sometimes," I say with a sad smile. It makes me sick that I still miss running, but I don't think the passion that dwells deep inside me for the sport could ever fully die.

"I used to run every day. Mom would take us—my brother and me—to all the local high school track meets. She did everything she could to nurture my dream. Our dedication paid off and, as the years passed, I got better and better.

"Freshman year of high school, I made varsity and broke my school's record in the 400-meter race. By the time I was a junior, I was competing nationally. I was on cloud nine, achieving everything I worked my ass off for. A few weeks after I graduated high school, I went to the Olympic Trials . . ."

My throat becomes too tight with emotion to continue speaking. This is where I normally break. This is the rabbit hole I hate traveling into. Reliving that day, thinking about all of the people I disappointed in the weeks after. Hearing my brother's voice haunts me. "Mom would never want you to quit now." But one of the hardest memories to revisit—I've only talked to my therapist about it in any great detail—involves Patrick. He wasn't able to look me in the eye when he asked me to leave him alone, because we both lost everything that day.

Just when I'm ready to lose it again, Gavin's fingers tilt my face up. "Let's go outside. Some fresh air will help."

I want to resist, but he's already leading me to the backyard deck. He pulls out one of my patio chairs, sits down and draws me into his lap, facing him. I inhale. He is right. The fresh air helps. I tell myself it's the pine-scented trees filling my nose, but I know it's his strong arms that calm me and make me want to forget my past, to focus solely on the present.

Gavin rubs his hand up and down my back. "So you went to the Olympic Trials." He drags me back into the dark.

"Yes. We all went, my parents, brother, and my boyfriend." Gavin's grip around me tightens at the mention of a boyfriend, but I can't let his feelings distract me. "They were all there to

cheer me on. That day, I ran the best time of my life on the 400."

"Did you make the Olympics?"

I can hear the excitement in his voice. It feels like a knife to my heart, slowly twisting, then is jerked out and repositioned multiple times. Soon, his excitement will fizzle out. Like always, one of two reactions will occur. Either pity for the girl who lost it all, or confusion for the girl who gave it all up.

The next part I say in a rush, worried that if I don't, I won't be able to spit it out at all. "Yes. I broke the world record in that event. But none of that matters." A small sob escapes my mouth.

Gavin pulls me tight to his chest, gently cradling me like one would a helpless infant. This man is making my world come undone, everything he does is unique from others. He doesn't say a word, but he doesn't need to, because I can feel the compassion pumping out of his every pore.

I ease away from him. I need to look at his face. I need to see his gentle blue eyes, and I need to finish this story before I'm sucked back into the dark vortex that has enslaved me for too long.

"Since I did so well, the day was a lot more hectic than I expected. I had agents, coaches, colleges, and advertising companies fighting over a chance to talk to me. But once the realization sank in that I broke the record, and possibly peaked my career at only seventeen, I felt overwhelmed.

"My dad and brother had already left for the airport because Dad needed to work, and Ian had a Fourth of July Football Party the next day. But Mom, Patrick and I made a road trip out of it, and we planned to stay another two nights at the hotel. So being the mom she was, she encouraged me to mingle and talk to people. Patrick was so proud of me that day and also wanted to stay longer, bask in the glory with me and celebrate.

"But it was all too much, even though it's what I had been working for since I was a little girl. Once it all came true, the enormity of the experience felt like a building collapsed on my chest. I convinced them to leave, but I tried to play it off as exhaustion. My pride was in the way, I didn't want to tell them I was scared and having a mini panic attack.

"It was Fourth of July weekend, and the roads were busy . . ." I can't breathe. My heart pounds, and a wrenching pain is twisting in my stomach. I need space.

I leap free of Gavin and move over to the railing. Sucking in a few deep breaths, I remind myself to keep breathing and to finish this so my life can go back to dull and lonely. After all, it's what I deserve. No, it's better than I deserve.

It should've been me.

"Then what happened, Beverly?"

I look over at him, and his eyes still overflow with compassion. It feels like he already knows my story's ending.

"I was reckless, driving on adrenaline and fear. I didn't see the drunk driver until it was too late. He rammed into the passenger-side door." I clutch at the burning in my chest, remembering my sobs when I tried to fight off the paramedics because they weren't helping Mom. They pronounced her dead at the scene, and their focus turned to Patrick and me.

She isn't dead! Help her! Please help her! I still cry those words in my nightmares.

I don't know when Gavin got up and came to my side, but he's cupping my face with both of his hands. Before I can react, he gently pulls me to him and kisses my forehead.

"I lost them both that day," I choke out.

That's all it takes for my tears to flow again, and I bury my face in his chest, too pained to explain what happened next.

Too mentally exhausted to relive how Patrick survived the accident but was no longer the same.

"It wasn't your fault," he says, stroking my hair.

This is when I would normally shout, "Tell it to them!" It terrifies me when his words bring comfort to me and draw me to him even more. If I'm not careful, my feelings for him will be my undoing. I need to stay on course and keep the promise I made myself never to love again.

Love would only prevent all of my mom's dreams from being fulfilled. Plus, with Patrick miserable and with crushed dreams of his own, how can I ever move on?

I don't deserve living a happily-ever-after when I robbed Patrick and my mom of theirs. My hands have blood on them, and this fantastic man who stands before me was made for someone who will love him the way he deserves. Even with all this awareness, I still doubt if I'm strong enough to let him go—especially since I already know he's going to put up one hell of a fight.

He gently lifts me away from his chest, and his eyes are filled with sympathy and understanding. Before I consider the pain I'm going to cause him, my desire takes hold of me. I kiss him with more passion than I knew could live within me. Devouring him with my lips, I'm desperate to forget the pain. Selfishly, I want Gavin to sweep away my internal turmoil and take my mind and body to another place.

Can I really do this to him?

Lead him down a path I know will end in hurt?

Gavin lifts me up. I wrap my legs around his waist, and he carries me into the house, never losing our connection. Then, he places me on the couch and sits next to me.

Wait.

What?

I cross my arms over my body like a sullen teenager. I thought this was going to get good right now, but I guess I should be grateful one of us has willpower. Plus, he probably wants to hear every detail because he's one of those men who *actually* cares.

Hormones are still firing through every centimeter of my body. All I want is to give in to the sexual tension, take him to my bed, get lost in each other, and forget all the pain. But as he stares at me with concern and compassion, I know that's not what's going to happen.

First, he needs to make sure I'm better because he doesn't want anything tainting our experience together. I appreciate that about him. The world needs more Gavin Reeds in it, but right now I need an insensitive ass who will let me use his body to drown my sorrows.

Preferably a six-foot-three and sexy-as-hell Gavin Reed.

After a few more minutes of our silent staring contest, Reed is the first to break. "I'm hungry. How would you feel about going back to La Bottega for dinner?"

Hmm? Come again?

I was preparing myself for a lecture on why he couldn't let things go any further or him probing into my past with questions. Forcing me to talk about it in more detail and telling me what everyone always says, that I'll feel better if I get it off my chest.

What a crock of shit, too, by the way. I never feel better after talking about it. If anything, I feel ten times worse. My throat closes, my stomach twists, and my chest aches. Another reason his question startles me is he doesn't have a clue that I go to that restaurant every week because of Mom. My sole purpose in moving to Portland was to feel close to her again.

She and I vacationed here for two weeks when I was sixteen. It was just the two of us, a mother-daughter getaway. One of my favorite things from my trip to Portland with Mom was La Bottega. She would order tons of food, and we would sit for hours laughing and eating. La Bottega is one of the few places I go when I need comfort.

Even though we only came to Portland a few times during my childhood, I feel my mother's presence everywhere. Portland was where her soul belonged. She only moved from this city because she fell in love with Dad and he's a stubborn man. If he said he was moving somewhere, that's what he was doing. There were never any negotiations in his house.

I love my dad, he's a good man, but the connection I had with my mother was different. She could read my every emotion. I would never have to tell her if I was sad, angry, happy, or even hungry. She just knew.

Nobody but her could ever know what I was thinking or feeling. People make fun of me, saying I have a poker face and that it's creepy I don't show any emotions. Nobody else could read me like Mom could, not until now.

Now, I'm staring into the eyes of a man who can read my mind, but he doesn't even know it. I don't plan on ever telling him.

"Beverly?" Gavin says gently after God only knows how many minutes have passed.

"Yeah. I'd like that."

— 35 —

Beverly

After reliving the accident, dinner's going better than I thought it could. I usually go into shutdown mode, curl into myself, and hide under my covers for an extended amount of time. But this time is different—I'm different.

Gavin's acting like his usual self, making me laugh, and relentlessly flirting, yet not making me feel awkward like he's avoiding the topic. Though in the back of my mind, I keep waiting for him to bring it up, anticipating the typical questions to ensue.

Did you go to the Olympics?

How do you get over something like that?

What's your relationship like with your dad and brother now?

Are you in therapy?

But now we're almost finished with our dinner, and since the questions haven't come, I begin to relax.

"What time is your flight tomorrow night?"

He looks down at his almost empty plate of pasta and pushes the last few noodles around.

"Ah, I hope you don't mind, but I...I decided to make a change. I knew we were going to have an important conversation, and it didn't feel right leaving immediately after. So, I pushed my flight out a couple of days."

My jaw may have just slammed into my half-eaten plate of penne. The ability to speak abandons me, there are literally no words coming out, no coherent thoughts. Zip. Nada.

He mistakes my reaction with panic. "I can change it back! I just thought it would be nice to stay. I know it was presumptuous. I should've asked you first..."

My brain and mouth sync up again, and I interrupt his babbling. "I'm happy you're staying, just surprised."

His chest deflates as the breath he was holding gusts out of him, and a small smile pulls at his lips. "That's a relief. I understand if you can't take more time off from work. Maybe we can have an early dinner on Monday? My flight is late on that night."

"Work can wait." I feel a twinge of guilt, and it's not because I'll be missing more work. It's because I haven't reminded him that this won't go anywhere past this weekend.

Maybe I can casually date him? We could see each other once a month or something. Is it even possible for me to casually date Gavin Reed? No doubt he's the full package, everything I could and would ever want in a man. But he's determined. If he wants a serious relationship with me, he might jump at the opportunity to date me, just to win me over.

A new knot twists in my stomach as I realize I'm getting in too deep. I'm the one feeling too much for him, unfamiliar feelings that unnerve me. A tremor rattles through my body, I'm doing the one thing I promised myself I wouldn't do; I'm falling for Gavin Reed.

"What are you thinking about?" he asks.

Before I can respond, our waitress walks up beside our table to deliver our desserts.

After she serves our Crème Brûlée and walks away, I respond, "Can I tell you when we're alone?"

"I'm going to hold you to that."

I offer a small smile in return.

We're fifteen minutes into our drive home, and he hasn't asked me again what I was thinking about in the restaurant. I'm a coward for not telling him of my own accord. I know I need to talk, but I'm afraid of losing his friendship, and I'm scared of hurting him.

Which is more of a reason for me to tell him now before I take this too far, because I can't live with any more guilt. He deserves to understand that my heart isn't available and won't ever be.

Listen to yourself, Beverly. You don't even know for sure he wants a serious relationship. Maybe this can be casual. Just ask, I try to convince myself.

But deep down, I know it's bullcrap. Gavin looks at me like nobody else ever has, and he treats me like I'm his own personal treasure. He wouldn't have driven down here from Seattle after a business meeting, stayed for multiple days, if he was looking for a hookup. And he wouldn't have stopped me from throwing myself at him earlier, that's for sure.

We both stay in our heads on the car ride home, but the moment we walk through my front door, he pushes me up against the wall and kisses me with purpose.

"You're so beautiful," Gavin whispers, his voice so low and sensual it causes a new knot to form in my stomach. I push away from him and search his ocean-blue eyes. I don't know what I'm looking for until I see it, and I'm not happy with what I find.

Affection and passion are staring right at me, both precursors of love. I can't do this. It's time for me to make him fully aware of where I stand. If it messes up the rest of our night, so be it. I owe him this much.

"Earlier... at dinner when you asked me what I was thinking..."

Gavin reaches up and places two fingers over my mouth. "I don't want to know, not yet." He glides his hand down my cheek, then cupping my chin, he draws me in for another kiss.

Does he know what I was going to say? Instead of arguing with him and forcing him to listen to me, my doubts slip from my mind and I give in to my hunger for him.

"Reed." My voice is husky and unfamiliar as his last name falls from my lips.

He tangles his hands in my hair and trails kisses down my neck. "Say it again."

Unable to concentrate on anything other than the feel of his mouth on me, I don't say anything until he stops, waiting for my response. "Reed?" I say more as a question, unsure if that's what he wants to hear.

"Yes. I love it. You sound in control and hot calling me by my last name."

Years of fear vanish or hide somewhere deep in the back of my mind. I'm grateful because I need this—I need him. Now.

Tugging on his shirt I pull him back against my body. I start my assault, kissing him and then sliding my lips down the side of his neck. Then in one fluid swoop, he bends his knees and lifts me up, cradling me in his arms as he climbs the stairs two at a time.

Reaching my room, he lowers me onto my bed. When he grabs hold of the hem of his shirt, I reach out and stop him.

"Let me." I'm rewarded with an adorable, shy smile. I wriggle my way to my knees and tug off his shirt, exposing his tanned, toned chest and hard belly.

I shamelessly stare at every inch of his glory.

He's flawless, and I feel like I hit the lottery with him. I plant a few kisses across his chest, and a deep moan escapes his lips.

"It's been so long," I whimper in between applying kisses to his glorious body.

"Since?" He pulls my chin up for me to look at him, and I feel my face turning bright red under his scrutiny.

"Since I've been with a man," I say, embarrassed and avoiding his penetrating eyes.

"Well, we're not going to be together."

Like hell, we're not, the vixen Beverly in her lace teddy screams in my head.

"I'm going to make love to you. I'll make sure you never want anyone but me ever again."

Oh, crap! Code red! Code red! The responsible part of my brain is waving her surrender flag in the air with sirens blaring and alarm bells screaming.

But it all goes silent when his soft lips claim mine.

—

GAVIN'S PASSED OUT NEXT to me and has been asleep for at least thirty minutes. I'm resting on his chest, listening to the steady rhythm of his breathing while replaying our night in my head.

My body feels light, and the tension, which normally invades my shoulders, is nowhere to be felt. I think Gavin just ruined me. How can I ever forget the connection we just

experienced together? His tender touches, soft lips, instinctive sensuality and adoring looks will be seared into my mind until the day I die.

I scan his handsome face one more time before slipping out of his arms. I quietly pad my way to my bathroom. Desperate to stop myself from hurtling down a treacherous path, I splash cold water on my face. I hope to wash away these new desires blooming inside me after this weekend.

I dry my face and stare at myself in the mirror.

Who am I?

My mind takes me back to my spikes digging into the track. My heart thumps in my ears. My lungs burn. My desire to win explodes. Ambition drives me. Sammy closes in.

Kick! Kick! Kick!

I yelp when I feel Gavin's hand on my waist.

"Whoa. Sorry. Didn't mean to startle you."

I glance up in the mirror at him. His hair is tousled, his features satisfied, and he's even hotter than before. "It's okay. I just didn't hear you," I say, trying to calm my racing heartbeat. *Do I really have to let him go?*

"You okay?" he asks, running his hand up and down my back.

"Sit," I order, pulling the stool out from beneath my vanity. I am desperate to clear my mind of whatever just happened.

"I love that you're direct," he says as he lowers himself to the stool.

There's that word again. It's the second time tonight he's used it. With that one word, I'm now in full-blown panic mode inside.

I've made a mistake. I saw the signs and slept with him anyway. *What have I done?*

Relax, crazy, it's not like he's told me he loves me.

When I start to walk away, Gavin reaches for my hips and turns me to face him. "Hey, where are you going?" he asks with a cautious voice.

As soon as my eyes meet his, I see anxiety reflected back at me. He's too perceptive. I need to get my act together, to preserve the fantastic night we just had. If I tell him now, he'll only feel used, and that's the last thing I want. This isn't how I wanted things to play out. So instead of ruining our special night, I'll wait until Monday when he leaves.

It's a low blow, but Gavin won't let go without a fight. It's not like I plan on cutting him off entirely, but with our chemistry, maintaining anything other than friendship is too dangerous to my future goals.

"I'm going to fill the bath for us," I answer with the most cheerful voice I can summon.

He pulls my body against his, and I inhale his tantalizing scent. "Let me do it," he says as he places feather light kisses on my cheek. And like magic, by the time he's done kissing me, my nerves have quieted.

"But I want to do something nice for you. I feel like earlier was all about me. It's my turn to take care of you," I argue.

"Okay, I'll sit back and enjoy my view, then." He smirks and slaps my bottom.

"Now you're gonna get it." I laugh.

Padding over to the bathtub, I turn on the faucet. As it fills, I put a few drops of lavender oil in the water, light a few candles surrounding the tub. All while completely aware that Gavin's watching my every move.

"Will you grab me a hair tie? They're right behind you on the sink."

He picks one up and walks it over to me. Once my hair is up in a messy bun, he signals for me to turn around. I'm skeptical but comply. Carefully, he slides his hands over my shoulders and starts massaging. His firm grip melts away my knots. The sweet gesture warms my heart, yet scares the pants off me at the same time.

Gavin climbs into the bath first, then holds out a hand to help me in. Since I know he's being a gentleman, I bite my tongue and accept his kindness.

— 36 —

Beverly

My tender, aching muscles welcome the burning water. We sit in silence for several minutes. As much as I'd like to convince myself it's because we're both tired, I sense he's chewing on something.

Hey, maybe he's trying to have "the talk" with me. You know, to make sure I realize this is a casual fling and he doesn't want anything serious.

At least, that's what I hope for.

Tired of my curiosity nagging at me, I end the silence. "What are you thinking about?"

He rests his head on the back lip of the tub and looks up at the ceiling. "Too many things. Normally my thoughts are organized and calm, predictable even, but since you walked into my office, my mind's been a jumbled mess."

I roll my eyes, knowing he can't see me. Yeah, I know the feeling. The only difference is, he had no idea who I was, but I, on the other hand, was already infatuated well before meeting him.

Now that we've met and been intimate...the thought of

saying goodbye sucks every ounce of energy from my body.

"Beverly, what happened to the Olympics?" he blurts out before I can confess my sins for the night.

"Whoa, change of direction." I force out an uncomfortable laugh, but I knew it was only a matter of time before he'd need to finish this conversation. We might as well continue, so we can stop digging up my past, and I can go back to pretending it doesn't still haunt my every waking hour.

"Sorry. I told you my thoughts are frantic, and that question keeps popping up in my head since you told me you broke the world record."

"I didn't go," I state matter-of-factly.

His head pops off the rim of the tub and he searches my face with intense blue eyes. "Why? I-I mean, I know why, but I want to hear your explanation," he stammers.

Repositioning myself in the tub, I wish we were having this conversation dry and preferably dressed. I close my eyes, count to three inside my head, and then go for it.

"I couldn't go without my mom. Track wasn't just my thing, it was *our* thing. We were a team. I fell into a deep depression after it happened. I stopped seeing my friends and family, stopped talking, stopped eating and stopped running. Especially, once Patrick cut me out . . ."

Gavin abruptly sits up, sloshing water out of the bathtub. "He's alive?"

I nod. He might be alive, but he isn't the same Patrick I once knew. "I felt like I couldn't breathe anymore. Right after it happened, family and friends kept saying things like: 'Your mom would want you to keep going,' 'She wouldn't want you to stop living your life,' 'Do it for your mom,' or 'You will regret it if you quit now.'

"I felt like nobody cared what I wanted to do. They all thought they knew what was right for me . . ." I bite down hard on my lip to stop myself from talking. I've only ever told this part to my therapist, Stan. Yet here I am with a man I feel like I've known forever, spilling my heart out to him.

You're in too deep, the annoying voice in my head reminds me, adding that I need to keep Gavin at a distance.

It's a little late for that, don't you think?

Ugh! I rub my temples. *When did I start talking to myself so much?*

"I thought you said you lost both of them that day?"

"I did. Just in different ways."

Gavin slowly nods. "Okay. So, you felt like nobody understood you. What else?"

"I don't normally talk to people about all of this," I say, breaking eye contact.

"If you're willing to tell me, I'd like to hear."

Of course, I want to tell him. I feel an intense pull to tell him. As if he'll be able to wipe away the pain of my last few years.

Sweetie, let him in. I shudder when I think I hear Mom's voice in my head.

Gavin looks into me with his deep blue eyes, eyes so filled with sincerity. All these years I've done well hiding my fears and scars from everyone. He sees through the illusion I've created.

"What are you doing to me?" I whisper under my breath, feeling like I'm beginning to lose control.

"I'm sorry. I don't mean to push you too far. I only want to help you, Beverly. I want you to set yourself free of this prison you've created for yourself. You don't deserve to be punished.

Here," he says and climbs out of the tub, wrapping a towel around his waist and then holding one up for me.

For a moment, I stare at him. Then I clamber out and let him bundle me up. As he rubs my arms, it feels like those big ocean-blue eyes are stripping another layer of armor from me.

"I felt like nobody understood that running was a constant reminder of my mom's death, of the accident, of losing Patrick. I couldn't even look at my running shoes anymore without bursting into tears.

"How could I ever get the same pleasure out of that dream? I was struggling to just get out of bed. I couldn't strap on my spikes and sprint around a track as if I didn't just lose two people I loved.

"People told me I needed to do what used to make me happy. That I needed to continue living my life. I know my friends and family had good intentions, but without meaning to, they added to the guilt, shame, and heartache I already felt. It wasn't until I met Aubrey that I began the journey to sorta piece my life back together."

"Are you still in love with him?"

I flinch at his question. He closes his eyes, waiting for my answer. I could easily lie right now. It would release me from this Gavin dilemma, but the tugging in my chest stops me. I search for the right words to explain my feelings.

Gavin opens his eyes and takes a small step backward, his face stark with pain. "Is this why you won't let me in?"

I clench my towel around my body. I need to put on clothes. I brush past him and into my room, because I can't stand in that bathroom any longer, staring at his shattered face. All I want to do is hold him, reassure him it's not what he thinks. But, I can't. I must maintain his expectations—it's like

a balancing act I need to perform, spooning him just the right amount of truth, but leaving him no hope.

My legs don't carry me to my dresser. Instead, I collapse into my favorite chair and drop my head into my hands. Why was I intimate with Gavin? It muddled our relationship even more.

Gavin kneels down beside me and gently unwraps my left hand from my face. "Beverly, I'm sorry, but I need to know. Are you still in love with him?"

My eyes are damp, my pulse erratic, and renewed guilt slices through me. Not because I'm going to hurt Gavin, though. It's because I realize I'm not sure if I know the meaning of true love. Patrick was my childhood comfort. We were ambitious kids chasing crazy dreams. Yes, he was my best friend. And, yes, I loved him, but what kind of love was it?

"It's complicated. I don't know how to explain it. I've never had to before."

Getting off the chair, I head for my dresser and pull out sweats. Although once I'm in them, they're not as comfortable or protective as I expect. Instead, I feel confined, and the room is burning up. Gavin patiently stares at me, waiting for me to elaborate.

I dart into my walk-in closet, throw off my sweatshirt and yank down a T-shirt, instead. Then head back into my bedroom where Gavin is now hunched over in my chair, his hands hanging between his knees.

I twist at my shirt, then sit on the floor next to him, bringing my knees to my chest and wrapping my arms around my legs, effectively putting myself into a safe ball while I search for the right words. "For a long time after the accident, and after Patrick decided it was too difficult to be around me anymore, I

still loved him. Once he was gone, depression gripped me and pulled me lower than I even knew possible.

"I felt like my world crumbled, and I lost everything. My mom was dead, I abandoned my dream of being an Olympic runner, and my boyfriend, my best friend from childhood, couldn't even stand to be in the same room with me."

Gavin slides off the chair and sits next to me. "How could he leave you at a time like that?"

He doesn't understand what Patrick went through. What I put him through. "How could he stay with me? He lost everything that day." A chill runs through my body, and I wish I had kept my sweater on. I pull my legs tighter to my chest. "Patrick had a full-ride soccer scholarship, his ticket to a four-year college."

I stare at my toes, too worn out to watch Gavin's reactions. "In the accident, Patrick's feet, ankles and shins were crushed in the small backseat of my Jetta. Twenty-two bones broken in his right foot alone."

As I squeeze my eyes closed, tears slide down my face. I remember Patrick in his hospital bed, the bottom half of his legs wrapped up and metal pins sticking out of his feet in every direction. "If it weren't for Aubrey, I don't know what would've become of me."

Gavin scoots closer to me, resting his back against my bed, and slides his gentle hand up and down my back.

"How did Aubrey help you?" Gavin asks in a soothing voice.

Grateful to change the subject, I grab hold of the memories when I first met Aubrey. I felt like she was a gift I didn't deserve, but I was so desperate for something to help dull the stabbing pain, I accepted the gift. "Five weeks after the accident happened

I came to Portland, searching for a way to feel closer to my mom. Aubrey didn't know it then, but I was only here visiting.

"I was in dire need to connect with happier times, and I remembered how much fun my mom and I had on our trip here. How she'd constantly say that Portland would always be her home.

"On our vacation, my mom took me around to places she loved from her childhood, as well as the new places she fell in love with on her yearly trips to visit her sister, who lives in the Greater Portland area. We went to Multnomah Falls, the Japanese Gardens, her favorite restaurants, Mt. Hood, her high school, and a bunch of other spots around town.

"While I was on this quest to reconnect with my dead mother, I found myself sitting on her high school bleachers. As it turned out, Aubrey went to the same high school my mom had attended. It was a Saturday, so there wasn't anyone around as I sat there in my running clothes, wallowing in self-loathing, obsessing over the 'what-ifs' and unable to summon the courage to run.

"Trapped in my misery, I didn't notice the tall, redheaded girl zooming around, training on the track. But she saw me, and I probably looked pathetic, because she marched up to me and said, 'Just stop!' I practically jumped out of my skin, looking behind me for someone else she must've been talking to. But, we were the only two there.

"'Excuse me?' I said with more attitude than I felt. The reality was, it felt good to have someone be direct with me. It felt right, like more people should be doing the same thing. It also felt freeing to be around someone who wasn't afraid of damaging me further. For that split second, I forgot about everything painful."

I glance over at Gavin, who's sitting still and waiting for me to continue. "Sorry, I'm babbling. I'll give you the short version."

"No." He shakes his head. "I want to hear every detail."

Of course, Mr. Perfect does.

"Okay. My attitude spurred Aubrey on and she told me, 'Whatever you're thinking about, stop it! You look like you're ready to walk in front of a train. Your life isn't that bad. Come run with me.' She looked me up and down and added that sprints would be good for my current moping energy.

"My first thought was, who's this chick? She doesn't know anything about my life, and guess what? It *is* that depressing. I've been living in hell for weeks. If she hadn't mentioned sprints, I might've cussed her out. But running—sprints, in particular—was my life. Even though I wasn't willing to admit it, I missed the rush.

"She crossed her arms, and with an I-dare-you kind of look, she told me to stop yelling at her in my head and to get up. I wanted to tell her she had no clue what I was going through, but I didn't. Instead, I gazed out at the track and felt an ambition building in me that I hadn't felt since before my last race. Plus, it would be fun smoking this girl on the track a few times, and putting the sassy redhead in her place." A little smile flashes on my mouth.

"Since I wasn't moving yet, Aubrey thought she needed to sweeten the agreement. 'Tell you what, if you win, I'll let you tell me your sorrows, and if I win, I'll let you tell me your sorrows. See, you win no matter what! Come on, best out of three, hundred-yard dash.' As she coaxed, I felt the competitor inside me take over.

"It was such a relief to be around someone who didn't have pity in their eyes when they looked at me. This stranger could

only judge me from this moment forward. She knew nothing about the records I broke, nothing about the Olympics, and nothing about the accident or the life I lost.

"It was all quite liberating. I followed her onto the track, and we started with a warm-up lap. While Aubrey and I were jogging around the track, I felt in my gut that my mom had sent Aubrey to me. My mom thought red hair was gorgeous and unique. Whenever she saw someone with red hair, she'd stop to compliment them. Also, she had that brassy attitude, which was exactly how Mom was when I needed to be put in check.

"My mom was amazing, but when either my brother or I, hell, even my dad, acted like a baby, she'd put her foot down and call us out on it. Plus, my mom knew I wasn't like her. Even before the accident I didn't let a lot of people in or have a lot of friends, and she knew exactly who I'd respond to." I uncurl from my ball and join Gavin, leaning back against the foot of my bed.

"After our lap and a quick stretch, I still felt tight, so I told myself to take the first one in stride. Aubrey, with a cocky little attitude, asked if I was ready.

"I told her sure, and I felt a healthy dose of anxiety move through my belly. I wondered if I would feel the same rush that I did before? We lined up and she yelled, 'Okay. On your mark. Set. Go!' We took off together. She was sprinting, I was striding, and she beat me by a hair. Her eyes were mixed with surprise and suspicion, and she told me I was pretty quick. I didn't reply, and we walked back to the line to do it again. I pushed myself harder, and that time I barely beat her.

"Again her skeptical eyes roamed over me, and she said, 'You look like you're already feeling better. But you're not

going to beat me again. I must be off my game today.' I remember every detail of that day. I stayed quiet as we walked back to the starting line.

"'On your mark. Set. Go!' she yelled. I didn't hold back on the third sprint and smoked her. I felt the warmth and tingle from my head to my toes, and I didn't want it to end. Aubrey was in shock. She asked, 'What the hell was that?'"

The tension in my shoulders loosens as I share my story with Gavin. "It felt good. I had a runner's high, but there was something different about it that time. There was something different about me.

"Aubrey was pissed at losing to some random, depressed girl from the bleachers. She questioned me about my speed, but I kept my mouth shut, protecting my secrets because I didn't want to explain anything to her. I was enjoying the competition, and I didn't want to ruin it with my grief.

"She demanded a rematch, and I was happy about that because she didn't give me a chance to think. That was the first tolerable day since the accident. Finally, I felt like maybe, I could keep living. I never told Aubrey—actually I haven't told anyone this except my therapist—but I was contemplating suicide that day.

"For the longest time, Aubrey didn't ask questions about me. We just kept meeting every day at the track for the following two weeks to run. Eventually, she asked for my name, and I told her. Then, I ended up telling her my story and, much to my surprise, she didn't pity me. She knew most of it once I told her my last name. The story was fresh at the time, but she never said a word and waited for me to share in my own time.

"I was still a whole person in Aubrey's eyes, and that was exactly what I needed. She didn't avoid specific topics or feel

awkward talking about Track & Field with me. She saw me for who I was, and we became best friends after that. She was the best therapy for me, at least that's what my therapist told me."

I sag and blow out a breath, thankful to be done. He knows everything now. This was rougher than a session with Stan. Unlike with Stan, I care how Gavin feels now that he knows the truth.

"Why did you want to kill yourself, Beverly?"

Gavin's question is like a fist to my gut, knocking the air out of me. It's probably not an unusual question for someone to ask, given what I shared with him, but it still startles me. Not even Stan asks that question. He probably thought the answer was obvious, or maybe he didn't think it mattered anymore. Stan is all about moving forward and focusing on how we feel in the moment.

Should I be honest? Uncomfortable with his question, I remain silent and look down, twisting my fingers together.

"It wasn't only because your mom died? Or because your boyfriend left you, was it?" he asks.

I'm exposed and raw. Gavin's keen eyes study my every move. Today's already been emotionally and physically taxing. Why is he pushing this? And more importantly, how does he know?

He's patient. Waiting. Staring.

Argh! I can't take it anymore.

"What do you want from me?" I throw up my hands.

Remaining calm and gentle, he says, "I want to hear you say it, Beverly."

I won't.

I refuse.

"Why did you want to kill yourself? Please tell me."

"Because I don't deserve to live! She's dead, and he's ruined, and it's my fault!" I shout.

"You were drunk that day?" he asks calmly, unaffected by my outburst.

When I don't respond, he continues. "Then you drove a car while drunk?"

I still don't respond. "And while you were drunk driving, you caused a car accident that killed an innocent woman and injured others?"

"I made them leave!" I slam my hand on my chest. "Me! Nobody else!" I jump to my feet, itching to flee. "It is my fault, and I don't have to listen to this shit." I dart out of my room and down the stairs, desperate for air.

— 37 —

Gavin

Beverly storms out of her bedroom. My gut churns. I wasn't trying to push her. I only wanted to help. Her guilt is so obvious. She blames herself for her mother's death and her ex-boyfriend's injuries. But she is not the person who made the horrible mistake that day.

The blame falls on the person who got drunk and decided to get behind the wheel. He's the person who's guilty, not her. Yet, here she is, years later and still punishing herself. It's painful and heartbreaking to witness. Somehow, I must help her to forgive herself, but maybe with a more careful approach. She's had years to construct her walls, and I tried to knock them down in a few minutes.

I was a fool.

I push myself off her carpeted floor and go in search of Beverly. As I descend the stairs, I hear the backdoor click shut. Before I head outside, I jog down to the guest bedroom and toss on a shirt, hoodie, and pants.

From the glow of the light on her backyard deck, I see her pressed up against the railing, gripping it like she's trying to rip

it off with her bare hands. She probably wants to whack me over the head with it. I swallow the lump in my throat and approach her.

"I'm sorry, Beverly. I never should've forced you to admit those things to me. I promise you I had no ill intent." I wish she would look at me, but she keeps her gaze fixed out on the green trees.

"Gavin, what exactly was the point of all that?"

Afraid that my answer might hurt her, I don't respond immediately.

"Please," she whimpers.

"Ever since our first dinner together in San Diego, I felt connected to you, and I could feel this burden that you were carrying. Earlier today, while you were telling me about the accident, I saw the guilt and shame you feel. I just sort of... lost it." I glance over at her shivering body, clad in a thin T-shirt. I unzip my sweatshirt and drape it around her narrow shoulders. "It breaks my heart to see someone as kind and good as you, torturing yourself because you believe you don't deserve happiness. That you believe you should suffer."

Beverly pushes off the railing and turns, walking a few feet away from me. With her back still turned to me, she pulls my hoodie tighter around her body. I follow her, immediately closing the distance she created. She begged to know why, and I refuse to let her run from it.

"Tell me if I got it all wrong," I persist. "Because I don't think I do. But if you look me in the eyes and tell me I'm wrong, and tell me you're not persecuting yourself, I'll believe you. I'll leave it alone."

She wraps her arms around her waist, still refusing to face me. I'm beginning to regret ruining the glorious night we had.

Why couldn't I keep my stupid questions to myself? Beverly's been on a roller coaster today, from her brother, whatever happened on the phone with her dad, to sharing the darkest time of her life. Then sleeping with me, plus the feelings she has for me, feelings she's clearly struggling with. Top it off with me bombarding her with personal questions I have no right to ask.

I know my desperation to help her is coming from a good place, but fear is also a driving force, because I'm falling in love with her. I'm afraid if she doesn't forgive herself, or if she still loves her ex, her walls will never come down to let me in.

Without facing me, Beverly breaks the painful silence with a whisper. "You're not wrong." Slowly, she turns to me and adds, "You're just the first person I've admitted it to out loud."

A heavy ache settles in my chest at her admission.

"It's cold out here, let's go back inside," she says with her head bowed, already moving toward the door.

I know I can't push her any further tonight. I'm sure admitting she blames herself was a massive step for her. The last thing I want to do is lose her.

Once we're inside, I attempt to bring our conversation back to safe territory. "Tell me something, what made you decide to start the modeling company?"

Beverly swallows before she speaks. "My mom's actually the reason. Two weeks before I met Aubrey, I was going through mom's computer and found a folder titled *Dream*. It was filled with plans for a company she wanted to start.

"She must have been working on the idea for years, because there were so many details in that folder. I mean, step-by-step strategies on who her clients would be, where she'd get business, and what her mission would be. At first, I was devastated, realizing my mom had put all of her dreams on hold to help me

follow mine. The day after I met Aubrey, I felt inspired to do something worthwhile. That was the day I promised myself I'd fulfill my mom's goals. That's another reason I moved to Portland. I decided if I was going to take on my mom's idea as my own, I needed to feel connected to her."

"Did moving help?"

"Eventually. When Aubrey and I were meeting up every day, she was getting pissed that I kept beating her. At that time she still had no idea who I was, but she asked me to coach her. I agreed. The next day I flew back to Carlsbad, loaded up my car, and moved to Portland.

"I lived at the RiverPlace for a few weeks until I found a little place to rent. My mom had accidental life insurance, and my brother and I were her beneficiaries, so I had more than enough funds to start the company."

"What a beautiful way to honor your mom," I say.

Beverly shifts in her chair. "Yeah, I thought it was, but I guess my dad disagrees."

"Why?"

Shifting in her chair again, she doesn't respond. She stares at her hands, twisting them in her lap. Deciding it's best not to push her, I shove a life raft her way. "It's okay." I pull her delicate hand into mine.

"Thanks for listening to me and for not judging me. You're much easier to talk to than my therapist. I should pay you, instead."

"I'm always here to listen." I stand and give her a chaste kiss on her forehead. "I'm also exhausted. Are you ready to go to sleep?" Without a word, Beverly stands. We climb the stairs together in silence.

— 38 —

Beverly

Finally, after not moving a muscle for the past twenty minutes, Gavin's breathing levels out. He's asleep. Considering I've talked more about my past than during all of my appointments with Stan combined, I should be exhausted. But I'm not normal, and my sleeping habits are less than satisfactory.

I think Gavin would've pushed me harder if I hadn't run out of the room like a child. His questions were a lot, but the part I couldn't handle was the desire raging inside of me to share everything with him. I wanted him to take away all of my pain. I also wanted to hand over my shame to someone else.

Stan will have his work cut out for him when I see him next, and I know to expect that same dreaded question. *"Beverly, why are you avoiding love? Is it more than punishing yourself for the accident and what happened to your mom and Patrick?"*

I explode upright in my bed. Gavin stirs next to me. Not wanting to wake him, especially not right now, I ease off my bed, grab my phone, and sneak out of my room.

"Stan, you're a real piece," I say aloud as if he's in front of me.

Then, in the safety of my office downstairs, I punch out a text to Stan with shaking hands.

> Me: 3 years. 3 damn years of seeing you, and you knew the answer to your stupid question. You knew why I couldn't, why I wouldn't love again. Why didn't you tell me?! I thought you were supposed to HELP me!

It's almost one in the morning, and I doubt I'll hear back from him until tomorrow. He'll probably want to make an appointment to discuss this. But I'm so freaking pissed, I don't think I can face him.

My phone rings in my hand. It's Stan.

"You better be calling with an explanation." I disregard any hellos in search of answers.

"Beverly, I do have reasons, but before we get into that, I need to know what happened and if you're okay?"

"What do you think, *Stan?*" I spit out. "I just pieced together that my therapist has withheld information pertinent to my life for the past three years!"

I'm yelling, and I know I need to calm down, because this isn't something I want to explain to Gavin.

"I wasn't withholding anything from you, Beverly. Part of therapy is allowing my patients to draw their own conclusions in their own time. I can't and I won't rush anyone's healing process. Please tell me what triggered your realization?"

His calm voice brings my fury down a notch.

"Stan, it's late, and your wife is probably pissed you're on a work call right now. Do you want to handle this tomorrow?"

"If I didn't want to deal with this now, I wouldn't have called. What's going on?"

All right, Stan, I gave you a way out. "Do you remember our session when I got back from San Diego, and we talked about Gavin Reed?"

"Yes."

"Well, he's here."

"In Portland?"

"In my bed."

"Okay. And how do you feel about that?"

"Please don't play therapist right now. You know I pay you to talk like a friend."

"Well, I am your friend, Beverly."

"Yeah, because I pay you to be," I counter, and continue before he argues again. "We slept together, and he's all kinds of amazing. He never ended up googling me, but he could tell I was hiding something. He told me he wouldn't sleep with me until I opened up to him."

"He gave you an ultimatum?" Stan sounds agitated.

"No!" I look over at my closed office door and cup my hand over my mouth. "It wasn't like that. Look, do you want to hear the rest of this? I'm giving you the short version, because I don't want him to wake up and find me on the phone in the middle of the night."

"Sorry. Please continue."

"Anyway, I ended up sharing *everything* with him. He was a pain in the ass about it, all intuitive and asking the hard questions nobody else dares to ask. I was just lying in bed next to him while he slept, thinking about how much I need to sort out. Then your damned question popped into my head. I jumped out of bed, really pissed and needing answers."

"Did you get a different answer this time?"

He's such a know-it-all prick sometimes.

"Yes."

"Would you like to share it with me?"

I sink down into my leather office chair behind my desk. "I'm scared."

"Of what, Beverly?"

"Of someone leaving me again. The way Patrick did." My voice breaks.

"Thank you for sharing with me, Beverly. Now, how do you plan to tackle this fear?"

"Not so fast. How could you have kept this from me for all this time? It's such a simple answer. Constantly, I was wracking my brain for some deep dark secret I was withholding from myself. Wouldn't it have helped me to know this? I mean, every session you've asked this question, and every time I answered, you'd ask if I was certain nothing else was holding me back."

"There's no other reason other than what I've already told you. You weren't ready to admit to yourself that Patrick abandoned you during the hardest part of your life. You wanted all of the blame on your shoulders. And I believe you had to start having feelings for someone else so the fear could come out from hiding in your subconscious mind.

"Beverly, you're a strong-willed young woman. You don't allow anyone to tell you how you feel. Even if I agreed with pointing this out to you, I don't believe it would've been received well. It's good that you're at this point now. I can help you overcome this fear. You'll be able to move forward with your life."

"I'm not moving anywhere. This has to end." What I don't

share with Stan is my other fear, that maybe I know nothing about love, that the feelings bubbling inside my heart for Gavin are unlike anything I've experienced before.

"It doesn't have to stop, Beverly. If you end things, it's because you're scared and allowing fear to control your choices."

"I don't care. This isn't going anywhere, because you know what I'm more afraid of?"

"Please share."

"I'm terrified of hurting him, too. He's the sweetest man I've ever met, and I'm not going to be responsible for breaking him." I press my fingertips to my lips, steady myself, and then say, "Look, I need to go."

"I think we should talk more about this."

"We can during the week. I'll schedule an appointment."

"Beverly, please don't do anything until we talk again."

"It's too late, Stan. I've made up my mind."

"You can't run from love forever. If you break things off now, before giving your brain and heart a chance to open again, you might just hurt both you and Gavin."

"Goodbye, Stan."

He doesn't argue. Instead, he says, "Think about it," then hangs up.

Sneaking back upstairs, I gently place my phone on the nightstand and crawl back into bed, next to the man who blurs my life's finish line and makes it impossible to know the right path to choose anymore.

— 39 —

Gavin

After a sound night's sleep, I awake before Beverly. She's nestled against my side, and I can't help but feel protective of her. I am still struggling to wrap my head around how her ex could ever leave her. What kind of man dumps someone right after their mom dies?

Beverly stirs next to me. Not wanting to wake her, I remain as still as possible. It's too late. My stiffening actually wakens her, and it's not long before I'm greeted with her stunning, golden brown eyes.

"Good morning, gorgeous. How'd you sleep?"

She stretches her legs and yawns. "Hi. Shockingly well, once I finally fell asleep. I slept so well, I don't know what I'm going to do without you in my bed."

"I know the feeling." I pull her close and kiss the top of her head.

Her stomach grumbles. "I'm hungry. Let's go downstairs."

"Not so fast." I pull her to me, closing my mouth over hers, then moving down to plant soft kisses on her neck.

She runs her hands through my hair. "Breakfast can wait."

An hour later we finally make our way downstairs. Sitting outside on her backyard deck, we devour the pancakes I made. It didn't take much convincing for me to make her breakfast this morning. I enjoy taking care of her, and she seems to enjoy being taken care of.

"It's crazy. You couldn't have visited Portland at a better time. We've had hardly any rain since you've been here. It's unusual." She stabs a slice of pancake and a raspberry with her fork, then swirls it around in syrup.

"Yeah, it's been beautiful, and I love the cool weather, but I was kind of hoping for a lot of rain. We never get good storms in San Diego. I like the rain. Something about it is calming. The best part is when the skies clear, and the air is clean and fresh."

She's smiling at me with a look that I swear is filled with something more than like. A feeling of certainty washes over me. We're going to be okay. I've broken through one of the barriers she built, and our connection will be able to overcome her walls.

"I know what you mean. I love it, too. I love walking around downtown, listening to car tires on the wet asphalt, my face and hair soaked. I look like a crazy person." She pops her last raspberry into her mouth. "I'm just doing my part to keep Portland weird." She chuckles.

Laughing, I picture a playful Beverly jumping around in the streets of Portland.

"Hello?" Our conversation is interrupted when a voice shouts over the fence from the side yard. I stand, ready to investigate.

"Gavin, it's just Ian. Will you open the side gate for him?"

My shoulders relax, and I walk over to let him in.

"Hey, man." Ian pats my back. "I was ringing the doorbell, but nobody answered."

"Yeah, we're eating breakfast outside," I say as we walk back to Beverly.

"Morning, Princess," Beverly says to her brother. "You look much better today."

Ian rolls his eyes and plops down on the chair next to Beverly.

"You hungry?" she asks.

"Naw, I ate at the hotel." He narrows his eyes at Beverly, then looks down at her pale pink sweats. "Why aren't you dressed yet? I was worried you guys would've already left. I called your phone like five times."

Beverly blushes. Only I notice.

"I'll get ready now. Leave in twenty-five?" She stands and starts to clear the table.

I reach for the plates in her hands. "I'll get it. Go get dressed."

Beverly brushes her hair back with her hand and smiles. "Okay."

As I bustle around picking up our mess, Ian grabs the syrup and butter from the table and follows me inside. He puts the items away then leans against the fridge, crosses his arms and stares me down.

"She likes you." He narrows his hazel eyes at me all protective-brother-like, trying to determine if I'm worthy. Only thing is, he's much more intimidating sober.

I turn away from his stare and place the last dish into the sink. "Is it enough, though?" I half say to him and half to myself. Are her feelings strong enough for me to release her from her past? From her self-imposed emotional imprisonment? From Patrick?

"Are you patient?" Ian asks.

I face Ian. He lifts his eyebrows at me, waiting for my

answer. "I'd never stop waiting for her." And I mean that. The day she strutted into my office, she imprinted on my soul. Now, after these past few days with her, I know I never want to be without her.

Ian nods once, satisfied with my answer. "Just don't hurt her. She's had enough pain in her life."

Rapid footsteps slap against the hardwood stairs. "I won't," I say just as Beverly bounds into the kitchen with reusable grocery bags hanging on her arms.

"Ready?" Her smile spreads across her face but falls slightly when her eyes land on my sweats.

"Five minutes. That's all I need." I trot down the hall to the guest bedroom.

The drive to the market is entertaining. I get to witness more of Beverly and Ian's sibling jokes. They're funny to watch, and it's obvious they're connected on a deep level.

As soon as we arrive, Beverly busies herself around the tables, while Ian chats me up. "It's nice to see her smiling again. I told my dad about you." Ian takes a gulp of his water.

I don't flinch. "Is that why he called her yesterday?"

Choking on his water, he asks, "He called her?"

I nod, deciding to withhold the part about how upset Beverly was after she hung up. I don't tell him how her eyes were puffy and red, her mascara smeared across her face.

"Great. I'm going to have to deal with that now, too." He runs a hand through his dirty-blonde hair.

I scan the crowd. Searching for Beverly, I spot her picking out a container of blueberries.

"You know, you're only her second boyfriend, ever."

She never dated again after Patrick left? Or did she just hide that from her brother? "Well, she hasn't given me that

title, yet." I wish she would, but I'm not going to shoot myself in the foot by not correcting him and having Beverly thinking I'm calling her my girlfriend.

Then I ask Ian something that's been driving me crazy, something that I should be asking Beverly about, but I'm a coward. "How long were they together?"

He blows air out of his nose and scoffs at me. "They were inseparable since they were eight."

I tense. My gut burns upon hearing how long Beverly was with another guy. Will she let me be her second chance at love? As fear churns inside my body, I again search for Beverly. I spot her shiny dark hair. She's talking animatedly to a woman, maybe in her sixties, and a handsome young man standing beside her, staring at Beverly with wonder. I tap Ian's arm and point at Beverly. "Hey, who is that?"

He looks over to where Beverly, the woman and the guy stand. "That's Dolly." He sounds pleased to see her, and the name sounds familiar. Although I'm more curious about the man hovering too close to Beverly.

"From the chocolate shop, Sal's wife? And what about the guy?"

Ian looks back at me like I just told him I own a leprechaun who rides around on a unicorn and steals puppies. "You met Sal? Beverly took you to the shop?" He shakes his head in disbelief. "Whoa. How serious are you guys?" Our conversation stops when Beverly calls us over with a wave and a broad smile.

Stuck on Ian's reaction, I replay his words in my head.

How does a chocolate shop equal serious in his head?

As we approach, Dolly shoos away the man standing with them, and Beverly's sweet voice draws my attention. "Dolly, I want you to meet my brother, Ian." My eyes jump to Ian's face,

and he reads my confusion. He blinks, then flashes me a pleading look that begs me to stay quiet.

Dolly engulfs Ian in a huge hug. She gushes about how nice it is to meet him and how handsome he is. As I watch their encounter, I notice Dolly winks at Ian. I look over at Beverly to see if she caught it, but her attention is focused on me.

She smiles sweetly at me, and I exhale my relief.

I love you, I admit in my head while she stares at me like I'm her whole world.

It's stupid to try and deny it to myself any longer. But, it's just too soon to tell her. If I did, I'm positive I'd scare her away.

Beverly focuses her attention back on Dolly. "And this is my friend, Gavin."

Dolly grabs me in a tight embrace. "Sal was so excited to tell me our sweet Gemma brought a man to the store. Though, he didn't tell me you were this handsome."

Dolly's English is much better than her Sal's. She has the slightest of Italian accents, and she isn't what I imagined. She has light brown hair, and pretty light-blue eyes. She's a beautiful older woman. Damn, Sal did well.

"It's wonderful to meet you."

Dolly homes in on Beverly again, speaking in rushed Italian. Beverly's face reddens. When Ian roars with laughter behind Dolly, Beverly glares at him. He lifts his hands in the air like he's surrendering and backs up a couple of steps, still chuckling.

I curse myself for not learning more Italian from my grandparents. I did manage to catch marito, which I think means husband, and amore, I'm confident that translates to love, but uova—isn't that eggs? Maybe they're talking about what Sal had for breakfast this morning?

Doubt it, Gavin.

I'm downloading one of the language apps on my phone as soon as we get back to Beverly's.

Beverly becomes animated as she talks to Dolly, her hands moving, her brows arching, and her feet shifting. She can't remain still. Ian chimes in and points in my direction, then all of their eyes are on me. The ignorant fool that I am, I thought Dolly switched to Italian because it's easier for her. Instead, she changed to talk about me.

To test my theory, I say in the most severe, CEO voice I can muster, "I speak Italian."

Dolly's mouth falls open, Ian cracks up all over again, and Beverly looks like she could die from embarrassment. But she quickly recovers and narrows her eyes at me.

"No, you don't," she accuses.

"You're right, but now that I know you're all talking about me, someone is going to translate."

"Oh look, I have a customer," Dolly says, snatching someone walking nearby to come to her table.

"We need spaghetti squash. I'll be back," Ian excuses himself.

Like mice, they scatter, and Beverly and I are left alone. I cross my arms and wait.

"I'm not going to tell you." She pops out her hip and places her hand on it.

"Oh yes, you are. I have my ways, Miss Morgan."

"Is that a threat, Mr. Reed?"

"You take it however you want, but if you tell me now, you'll save yourself a lot of discomfort later on."

Pursing her lips, she seems to debate my words in her head and calculate the risk. Her intense eyes scrutinize me, no doubt trying to see how serious I am.

Somehow I manage to keep my poker face intact. As a reward, she tosses a morsel of information my way. "Dolly thinks you're a sexy man and that I'm getting too old to be alone."

"Now was that so hard?" With one hand, I tickle her side.

"Stop." She slaps away my hand, but she can't keep herself from laughing, and the sweet sound encourages my other hand to join in on the fun. She tries to wriggle away, but I tighten my hold.

But as the clouds above us decide to drench us, I grab her hand instead and pull. Forgetting about her brother, I lead her out onto the street to the left of the tents that cover the vendors and their goods at the market. When I'm satisfied with our spot, I stop, turn to take both of her hands in mine and tilt my head up to the sky.

"Gavin, what are we doing?"

"Enjoying the rain and keeping Portland weird... together." I pull her into a kiss, running my fingers through her already drenched hair.

Before I can catch my breath, a man behind us clears his throat. "Uh, guys?"

Beverly lurches away from me. "Did you get the rest of the stuff we needed?"

"Yeah." Ian looks mortified.

I don't blame the guy. He witnessed his sister's tongue down my throat and her hands clawing at me like a lost kitten.

"Let's go," Beverly orders, straightening her wet shirt.

— 40 —

Gavin

We're back in the car and awkwardness strangles the air. Ian and Beverly avoid eye contact. For fifteen minutes they ignore what Ian just witnessed. All while I sit in the back seat, feeling better than ever, my hands tapping to the rhythm of the music, and replaying the delicious scene over and over again in my head.

Before we head to lunch and explore downtown, Beverly wants to stop at her house to drop off the groceries and change out of her soaked long-sleeve shirt.

I'm itching to get a moment alone with Ian. He knew Dolly before we walked over to them. I need to know why he's deceiving his sister. I'm not going to lie to Beverly, but if Ian has a good enough explanation, I won't go out of my way to mention it to her.

"Hey, when we get to your place, why don't you run inside and change while Ian and I unload for you?"

She glances at me in the rearview mirror, lifting one eyebrow at me in question. "Okay," she says with a cautious voice.

Ian shifts in his seat, but he remains silent.

The second the front door clicks shut behind Beverly, Ian

releases a huge sigh. "Thanks, man, for not blowing my cover back there. B wouldn't be too happy if she found out I already knew Dolly."

I snag the last bag from the backseat. "What's that all about? And why doesn't Beverly know?"

He anxiously looks around the driveway, as if Beverly might pop out from behind a bush. "Will this be in confidence?"

"My loyalty's with Beverly, but I might be more inclined to keep your secret if your explanation is worthy."

Ian hangs his head in defeat. "There are some things my sister doesn't know."

Yeah, I kind of already caught that.

He sets his bags down on the porch and takes a deep breath. "About two months after Beverly moved to Portland, almost all of our communication stopped. I was worried about her, and so was my dad, so I hopped on a plane to make sure she was okay. I didn't tell her I was here, at least not at first. I sort of followed her around for a week. She kept going into that chocolate store. Well, one day after she left the shop, I went in and Dolly and Sal were there. I overheard them talking about what a blessing my sister was to them . . ."

The front door suddenly swings open.

"What's taking you guys so long?" Beverly's already changed her top and is looking down at her bags on the floor then up at Ian's colorless face.

"Oh-uh, I-I'm, we were just talking." Ian sweeps up the bags and darts into the house.

She crosses her arms and glares at me.

What did I do?

"What embarrassing story was he telling you about me?"

A wide grin spreads across my face. "Oh, so there are

embarrassing stories, huh? Just how embarrassing are we talking?" I nudge her, hoping to distract her from investigating our conversation any further.

"Hopefully-you'll-never-find-out embarrassing," she says over her shoulder as she walks into the kitchen.

Ian is staring at his phone as we walk in, then he shoves it into his back pocket and starts frantically yanking items from the bags.

"Hey, Gavin, did Bev end up telling you what Dolly said?" Ian's mischievous smile makes me realize Beverly definitely only gave me a morsel.

"Don't you dare." Beverly points her finger at him and snatches the bags from across the island.

"Oh, come on, Sis. I just saw you two swapping spit. Nothing's gonna scare this guy off." The shift in Ian's energy makes it tough to tell if he's messing with Beverly or not.

"I will kick your ass, Ian."

"Eh, might be worth it."

As much as I'm dying to know what Ian wants to tell me, the bright red flush of humiliation across Beverly's face stops me in my tracks. Nothing is worth putting a strain on our new relationship.

"I'm going to use the restroom before we leave." I head down the hallway to the guest bedroom, leaving Beverly and Ian to squabble.

I take my time, splashing cold water on my face while debating if I should continue digging for more information from Ian. What will happen if I learn things that Beverly should know? If I tell her, it could create a rift between her and her brother, or she could get upset with me for talking about her to Ian behind her back.

No matter how I look at the equation, in every outcome someone gets hurt. And yet, the desire to know more is impossible to ignore. I want to find out why the people closest to her are hiding things from her. After everything she's been through, she should at least be able to count on her family to be honest with her. It's no wonder she has her walls up. Who can she trust?

I hear a knock on my door. It cracks open, and Beverly peeks inside. "Gavin?"

"Yeah, come in."

"I need to make a phone call for work. Having a little bit of a modeling meltdown. I should only be about twenty minutes, then we can leave for lunch. Sound okay?"

"Yeah, of course. I'll hang out with your brother."

She kisses my cheek. "Okay, you both better behave."

Ian and I are left alone again.

As soon as I hear Beverly shut her office door, I lay in. "All right, we're at the part where you were spying on your sister."

"Shh." Ian pops up from his barstool and jams his phone into his pocket again. "She's right in the other room. Come on, let's go out back. I can't risk her overhearing any of this. She'd freak out and blame my dad."

Her dad? Is he freakishly overprotective of his adult daughter, too? I follow Ian outside, across the back deck and to the side yard. Once we're a reasonable distance from the house, he starts to open up.

"Look, I know it seems odd that I'm keeping this from her, but I'm only doing it because I'm afraid of losing her again. After our mom died, my relationship with my sister changed. When she moved to Portland, I was terrified I'd never see her again. It turned out the move was good for her and our

relationship. She still isn't the same person she once was, and I know she won't ever be. At least she doesn't look like she's on the verge of death." He checks behind him to make sure his sister isn't lurking nearby.

"We might not have much time before she starts looking for us. Tell me how you know Dolly?" I demand.

"Right. Like I said, I was worried about my sister and flew up here to make sure she was okay. If I had showed up on her doorstep and told her I was concerned, she wouldn't have opened up and told me the truth. Beverly's always been strong, but that strength can make her too proud to ask for help.

"I decided to observe her from a distance. After following her to the same chocolate shop day after day, I went inside. Dolly and Sal were in a conversation about Beverly. They called her their guardian angel. Dolly kept saying she seemed sad.

"After listening to them for a few minutes, I interrupted and asked in Italian why they thought so highly of her. I startled them, and they didn't answer my question. I pressed the matter, but they still refused. I finally told them I was her brother, and I was worried about her.

"The loyal Italians that they are, they remained tight-lipped. I was so desperate to know what was going on in my sister's life, I turned to Dolly and told her about the accident and that our mom died. I promised I'd never reveal anything they shared with me.

"I was truthful with them, although I still feel like I manipulated them to get what I wanted." He closes his eyes and hangs his head, his shame evident.

"Don't feel guilty about caring about your sister's well-being."

He nods in response. "I stayed at their shop for more than

two hours. They explained meeting my sister at the farmer's market, where they had a table with their organic dark-chocolate-covered strawberries. Each week Beverly visited with them at their table. Before she'd leave, she would purchase all of their remaining strawberries.

"One day Dolly followed her after she bought pounds of chocolate-covered strawberries. Beverly was passing out everything she'd purchased to homeless people. Dolly approached her, praising her kindness, and they talked for hours down by the river.

"Beverly admitted she'd been watching Dolly and Sal, and noticed Sal gave homeless people free food, and Dolly would give children treats." Pausing again, Ian scans the yard.

"Look, I'm leaving a lot out here, but I'm trying to be quick. At the end of their conversation, my sister offered to rent a location for Dolly and her family to run their business until they were established enough to cover the overhead. Her only stipulation, no one ever could know she helped them. Dolly swore me to secrecy. I've kept that secret until just now."

I consider why all of this needs to remain a secret, then ask Ian. "Why wouldn't Beverly want people to know?" Being generous can get you far in business. It would've been great publicity for her to advertise what she did to help Dolly and her family.

"My sister believes if she does a good deed and makes it public, it's no longer good. It becomes a selfish one. She's helped countless charities and people, but you'll never see her name mentioned. Though I believe her helping Dolly goes deeper than charity. She and I have a lot of happy memories of our mom taking us to buy chocolate bars. For years I've been trying to figure out why she'd keep this from me." He sighs and falls silent.

After listening to Ian's explanation, it's clear as day to me why Beverly didn't tell anyone, especially her family. She's trying to redeem herself, so if she believes sharing her good deeds makes her selfish, then her brother is the last person she'd share this with. Does he really not see the bigger picture here?

The pain in her eyes from yesterday haunts me. Does Ian not understand she still blames herself for her mom's death? She's been torturing herself for years. Has anyone ever told her it wasn't her fault?

"There you are!"

Ian and I jump at the sound of Beverly's voice.

"Whoa. It's just me." She lifts her hands up in the air and gives us a suspicious look.

Ian smiles at his sister. "Well, it's time I head out. My Uber is almost here." He leans down and gives Beverly a quick kiss on her forehead.

"I thought we were going to lunch together. You don't need to leave," Beverly says.

"I think I do." He smiles at Beverly. "I'm in town for another week. We'll grab lunch another day." He turns and pats me on the back. "Gavin, great to meet you. Be good to my sis, and we won't have any problems."

"We'll walk you to the front," Beverly says.

— 41 —

Beverly

As much as I love my brother and he's always welcome to stay, I'm grateful he's heading out. Gavin is only in town a little longer, and I want to spend every second with him—alone. After talking to my dad, I feel a tiny ember of hope blossoming inside of my heart.

If he's right, if my happiness is what Mom would ultimately want, which I know deep down it is, then don't I owe it to her to at least try? *But, what about Patrick?*

I chew on the inside of my cheek, trying for the first time not to dwell on my past. Instead, as we walk back through my house to the front door, I listen to Gavin and Ian. They are trailing a few feet behind me, animatedly chatting about baseball. The lightness in their voices and the comfort of their presence calms my doubt. In this moment everything feels right, and I welcome happiness back into my life.

I grip the smooth metal doorknob, pulling open the front door. I am eager to be alone with Gavin again.

Shock startles a yelp out of me and robs me of air. I clap a hand over my mouth. I am paralyzed.

I stop moving, speaking, thinking—hell, I don't even know if I'm breathing anymore. Ian and Gavin rush forward to my side as I gasp for air.

Gavin's hand settles against my back. "What's wrong? Talk to me, Beverly."

"Oh, shit!" Ian steps outside, heading for the ghost seated on my porch swing.

Goosebumps rise all over my body. Even the minuscule hairs on my neck are rigid. Patrick stands and steps forward, his eyes never leaving mine.

Ian places a hand on Patrick's chest, stopping him from coming any closer. "How'd you find her?" he asks in a hushed tone.

Find me? What does he mean by that? Has he been looking for me? Does Ian still talk to him?

I stumble back a step, still not believing what I'm seeing. Gavin protectively grips my hip, stabilizing me.

"Beverly, are you okay?" Gavin asks.

I look up into those deep ocean-blue eyes, the corners creased with concern. My stomach clenches. I don't want him to see me like this. Talking about Patrick was one thing, communicating with my ex-boyfriend in front of my brother and Gavin is another ballgame altogether. I haven't laid eyes on Patrick since that day in his hospital room when he asked me to never come back.

Less than twenty-two hours after Mom's funeral, he told me he couldn't look at me. He said my face served as a painful reminder to him of the worst day of his life. Through my sobbing, I begged him not to leave me, too. I told him I couldn't survive without him, and that I was sorry and wished I could change everything.

He looked at me with tears in his eyes, but the rest of his features remained hard, determined. "But you can't, Beverly. You made your choice, and now we must suffer the consequences."

My eyelids burn with unshed tears I fight to hold back as the pain of his final words that day rip through me as if I'm hearing them for the very first time.

Patrick moves Ian's hand from his chest, his eyes locked on Gavin as he speaks to my brother. "Don't worry about it, Ian. I asked you for help, and you made it clear how you felt about me. I figured out another way." Patrick shrugs.

Ian's driver beeps his horn at the end of my driveway, jolting all of us. Ian looks back at me with a pained expression. "What do you want me to do?"

I bite the inside of my cheek. Desperation takes hold as I attempt to stay in control of my emotions. I'm raw and vulnerable, and all I want to do is reverse time. Hit rewind to before I opened the front door. I was a heartbeat away from getting a second chance.

But maybe this is the world's way of correcting me. Letting me know I was right all along to believe people like me don't get second chances. Once you've had it all, you should just be appreciative to have had it once in your life.

"Beverly, I need to talk to you. Please give me ten minutes." Patrick pushes past Ian and inches closer to me, clasping his hands together out in front of his chest, begging me.

My gaze falls to his feet. There's still a limp in his step. The tears I am holding back select this moment to betray me. They slowly roll down my cheeks as all of the agony from my past burrows deep in my gut, reminding me to never forget the misery I caused.

"Patrick..." His name spills past my trembling lips in a

whisper. I don't know what to do. Gavin stays put at my side.

I look from Gavin's loving, anxiety-filled eyes to Patrick, and then back to Gavin. On shaking legs, I step away from Gavin. He looks stricken, his reaction like a knife savaging my heart. "Gavin, I need you to leave with Ian."

He shakes his head and reaches for me. I step out the door. If I feel his touch, I won't want him to leave, but he must. I need to be strong for Patrick. This is only the second thing he's asked of me since the accident, the first I've honored since the day I stepped foot out of the hospital. Yet, the obligation to repent still weighs heavily in my chest.

"Please," I say to Gavin as he rakes his fingers through his hair.

I turn to my brother, searching for support, for a life raft, for anything before my tears drown us all. "Ian, take Gavin with you. I need to deal with this. I'll call you when I'm done."

Ian steps forward and pats Gavin's back. "Come on, man. Let's give them some time."

Gavin sucks in short quick breaths before he springs forward and wraps me in a tight hug, burying his face in my hair. Slowly he peels himself away, his eyes scanning my face. I feel as though he's memorizing my every feature. His Adam's apple bobs as he forces down a swallow, his broad shoulders slump, and he gives in. He follows Ian to the waiting car.

Something I didn't believe possible happens. The sound of the slamming car door shatters my heart a little bit more.

—

LEANING OVER MY kitchen sink, I count the trees in my window, trying to calm my shaking hands. I've fantasized about this day for so long. I've rehearsed scenarios in my head: Patrick

wrapping his arms around me and saying he made a mistake and he still loves me. All those fantasies stopped the day I met Gavin Reed.

I finally rally enough nerve to walk back into the living room to face the man who haunts my memories.

I can do this. I will be fine.

I blow out a long breath. Whatever he needs to say can't hurt as bad as the day he ripped out the remains of my heart.

"Here you go." I place a glass of ice water on the coffee table in front of Patrick.

"Thank you."

I sit on the opposite side of the couch and press my hands together in my lap, bracing for whatever's coming my way.

When nothing happens, I look up and lock eyes with familiar emerald ones. Every drop of moisture evaporates from my mouth. When we were kids, I used to tell him it wasn't fair he had such pretty eyes as a boy, and that mine were the color of poop. We were eight at the time. He fell off the swing, rolling in the dirt of his backyard as laughter consumed him. That entire summer he called me poop-B, thinking he was clever.

"You look good, B." A sad, pathetic smile touches his lips.

This isn't why he's here, and I wish he wouldn't delay with pleasantries.

He rubs his palms against his jeans. "Looks like Ian beat me here, huh?"

My left eyebrow twitches. "What're you talking about?" This must be the big secret Ian needed to share.

"I just figured since he was here, he must've told you I went to see him last week." He leans forward, grabbing his water from the table and bringing it to his lips.

"I didn't know you were coming." It's all I can think of to say as I remember Ian asking Patrick how he found me. Patrick stands and moves closer to me on the couch.

"And the other guy? Is he your boyfriend?"

My heartbeat speeds up. The burning urge to defend our relationship courses through me. "You lost the right to ask personal questions like that long ago."

Patrick rubs his hands on his jeans again. "Right." His voice sounds choked with unspoken emotion.

"B, I'm sorry for dropping by like this, especially after all this time. I tracked down your brother and begged him for your address. He shut me down and said he had to talk with you before giving out your information. Along with cussing me out for leaving you, and other things." He pulls on his left earlobe, the same way he always does when he's anxious.

"*Why* are you here?"

Moisture fills his eyes, and he pulls my hand into his, but his touch feels foreign. All those years I spent wishing, praying I could change life, that he could hold me one more time. Now, here he is and my body no longer recognizes his touch.

"I'm here to apologize." A strangled noise escapes his mouth. I pull my hand from his grip, bolting upright on my feet, preparing to run.

"Don't. You have nothing to apologize for."

I don't want to hear this. I don't want to live through our tragedy bit by bit or listen to him utter those words. I've never wanted that. We all know who forced us to leave that day.

"Please sit down. I need to do this, Beverly. We both need this."

"Wait." I spin around and face him. "If my brother didn't tell you where I am, how'd you find me?"

He tugs on that damned earlobe again, and I have a feeling I won't like the answer.

Not my dad.

Just not my dad.

"Nell. And you know how painful it was for me to turn to her, but there was no way I could face your father. Although she wasn't much easier. I think she wanted to throw me off her balcony. But once she let me get in a few words, and explain why I had to see you, she relented."

My scalp prickles as I try to imagine what he could have said to sway Nell. She's my fiercest protector, my loyal friend, the only person I could count on after I lost Mom and Patrick.

"Will you sit?" he asks. "You're making me more nervous than I already am."

With a stiff back, I cautiously lower myself back down, leaving extra space between us.

"Thank you. All right, I'm just gonna go ahead and say this."

I remain quiet, my eyes locked on his face.

"I've given everything that happened between us, the crash, the weeks that followed, and even the years prior when things were good, a lot of thought. And I know if I want to ever truly move on from all of this, to live any sort of happy life again, I must talk to you."

Patrick lifts his hand to his neck, his index finger and thumb rubbing each side of his throat, pinching the skin together in the middle. I watch and try to sync my breath with his movements until he stops and continues his speech.

"I'm sorry."

My eyes pinch closed, and I wish I could close my ears because I can't bear to hear these words from him.

"I'm sorry for the resentment I had for you. I blamed you when none of what happened was your fault, Beverly."

He reaches for my hand again, but this time I bunch it into a fist and pull it tight to my belly.

A sigh escapes him. "I was angry about how my life was going to change, and I didn't have the tools to cope. Then, the day after the crash when you strolled into my hospital room with only bandages on your wrists and head, resentment surged through me."

He dips his chin to his chest and avoids eye contact, but he can't hide what he's feeling from me. I know it all too well. I've worn guilt every day since the crash. It's practically a second layer of skin. I can't stand seeing him this way. "Please stop," I whisper.

He ignores my plea. "I felt robbed and like everything was unfair. I was angry and immature. I was a mess, B. I took everything out on you." A strangled sob escapes him.

"Beverly, I never even said I was sorry about your mom dying. She was like a second mother to me. I loved her, and I didn't even acknowledge her death." He swipes at the tears wetting his face. "Through my anguish, I hurt myself more. I pushed you away, the best thing in my life. I also lost Ian, who was like my only brother."

Unable to remain silent, I grab his knee. "But if I would've listened to you and my mom, we wouldn't have been on the road. Or if I had let you drive, everything could be different."

He covers my hand with his and squeezes. "I used to dwell on that all of the time. Then when I was in an AA meeting, a girl said to me 'If you were driving, you could be the one in your poor ex-girlfriend's shoes,' I stormed out that day—at the time, I wheeled myself out. But she was at the next meeting,

and the one after that and after that. We eventually talked again, and she opened my eyes to so much.

"What I did to you was cruel. You were my best friend, my first love, my first everything, and I stomped on your already wounded heart. I made you go through everything alone. I blamed you, and worse, I told you I blamed you." His voice cracks. "Roadrunner . . ."

Hearing my nickname slip from his lips, I collapse forward. My eyes blur with tears. When Patrick wraps his arms around me, I fall apart, emptying every sorrow, regret, and heartache that's been burned into my body and burdens my soul.

— 42 —

Gavin

I wave my hand in the air, begging for the attention of the small punk-rocker Asian chick behind the bar. "Another, please!"

She nods her head in response and the bright yellow plugs in her earlobes, which I have an urge to try and fit a dime through, sway even after her head stops moving.

"Maybe you should slow down, buddy," Ian says and pushes a glass of water in front of me.

"Pshh." Buddy. I hate when people call me that, but I say nothing. The moment my shot is in front of me, I toss it back. The hot, amber liquid slides down my throat, but it does nothing to ease the vice crushing my chest and making each breath more labored than the last.

"Look, don't jump to any conclusions. We don't know what he's doing here. Trust me, I tried to find out, but he wouldn't say a word."

Slowly I turn my head to glare at Ian. He flinches away from my stare. "You knew he was coming?"

He holds his hands up by his shoulders with his palms facing me and shakes his head. "I didn't know he was coming

now. I thought I had more time, I didn't think he'd be able to track her down so fast."

"What do you mean track her down?"

"Last week, he came to me and asked where she lived."

I rub my face with my hands. I'm not buzzed enough to forget the look on Beverly's face when Patrick stood up and pleaded with her. "And you didn't tell him?" I want to hear him say it out loud.

"God, no! I'd never do that to my sister. When Patrick broke up with her, every ounce of the Beverly I knew crumbled. Then, once she crawled out of her hole, a new hardened and distant Beverly emerged. I told Patrick I had to talk with her before giving him her contact info."

He looks down at his beer and slides one finger through the condensation on the glass. "I tried calling, over and over again. Then I called Aubrey, hoping she could help me get hold of Beverly, but her fiancé answered, cussed me out and hung up on me. I didn't know what else to do, so I got on the first flight I could."

Ian's gaze remains fixed on the beer in front of him. "Then when I showed up and saw you guys together, I couldn't bring myself to ruin her weekend."

A warm tingle slowly buzzes its way through my body as the alcohol starts to do its job. It's not enough. I want to numb every feeling that's flooding my body and stop each doubt from mocking me. My eyes connect with the bartender's. When she walks over, I downgrade from liquor to a beer this time.

"So it'd spin her out that bad just to hear his name, huh?" I clench my jaw, imagining Beverly with Patrick. Do I even stand a chance? They share a history, so who am I to think a few dates could be enough to erase years of love?

"No, that's not what I meant, not entirely, anyway. Sure it would've upset her, but I didn't want anything to stop the happiness that was pouring out of her." He rubs the top of his right shoulder, slowing rolling his head from side to side.

"Maybe it was selfish of me, but this weekend was the first time I saw a glimpse of my sister's true nature again. She was joking around, bantering with me like we used to growing up, her big goofy grin was on her face almost every time I looked at her. She giggled more times in the last couple of days than she has in the last few years. I wanted to savor every moment." A small smile tugs at the corners of his mouth. "It's obvious she cares about you, man. I didn't want anything to screw that up."

I chug half of my beer, his words prodding at the giant hole in my heart. "That might not be enough, though. How can I compete with her childhood sweetheart?"

Ian's knuckles go white as he grips his beer. "Patrick can never make up for what he did to her. She'll never trust him again."

I scoff and take another swig of my drink. "I wouldn't be so sure of that. Whenever she's talked to me about him, she thinks everything that happened was her fault, and she understands all of his reactions." I finish my beer and wave over my pink-haired friend.

"No way," Ian says, shaking his head. "I know my sister, even though we haven't been as close since our mom died. She would never take Patrick back. Especially not now that she has feelings for you. I mean, come on, man. She freaking showed affection with you in public! She never even did that with Patrick. Beverly's always been a private person."

My breath gets caught in my chest and, for a moment, I forget to exhale. Could Ian be right? Do I actually stand a

chance? But back at her house, she chose him over me; she kicked me out and didn't want me to touch her in front of him.

When my new best friend sets another beer down in front of me, I want to high-five her awesome Mohawk, but I settle for drowning my pain, instead.

Ian shifts in his chair and then fishes his phone from his pocket. "It's her," he says.

— 43 —

Beverly

My stomach clenches as I examine the stranger staring back at me in the mirror. My face is splotchy and red, my eyes puffy and stained with mascara. Unable to look at the mess in front of me any longer, I snatch face wash from the shower and scrub until my cheeks are raw.

Still, my past clings to me like a toddler does to its mom's legs on the first day of preschool. I check the time, Ian and Gavin shouldn't be here for another twenty minutes or so. Stripping off my clothes, I drag myself into the shower and sit on the cold tile, blasting the water temperature as hot as my skin can tolerate.

My mind is trying to sort and file information, but something keeps getting in the way. All the feelings I've kept in check for years are ramming into the walls of my brain like a two hundred-thousand-pound bulldozer. Demanding to be heard.

After letting the water pelt me long enough for my feet, shins, and arms to turn a bright angry red, I'm no closer to planning my next step. I pull myself out of the shower and wish this exhausting day would end. As I slip on my fluffy blue

socks, hoping their softness will comfort my frayed nerves, I hear pounding on my front door, followed by the doorbell.

Normally I'd run down the stairs, not wanting to make anyone wait. But right now, my legs feel weighted, and I'm nervous to see Gavin again. I take it slow, while the pounding on the door continues.

"What the hell, Ian?" I say at the sight of a disheveled and obviously drunk Gavin Reed, his arm slung over Ian's shoulders.

"Don't blame me for this. Your *friend* here can really put it down." He spits out the word "friend" like it should mean something other than it does, but I don't have time to focus on Ian's remark.

Gavin stumbles forward and, with a surprisingly steady hand, caresses my cheek. "You've been crying," he says then slides his thumb over my mouth. "Your lips get puffy when you cry. So soft."

Warmth spreads through my chest, and I gently grab his hand. "Here, let's take you to your room to rest."

Ian follows me, and we usher Gavin into the guest bedroom. "Sit down," I say, pulling back the covers. He plops down on the bed. I kneel down to yank off his shoes, but I make a mistake and look up at his face. His eyes lock onto mine, a sad smile crosses his beautiful lips.

"All right, buddy." Ian's voice pops our bubble. "Get some rest, and I'll see you soon."

I stand up, but Gavin's hands land on my hips.

"Get comfortable. I'm going to walk my brother out. I'll be back soon." I ease away, but Gavin catches my hand and strokes the back of my knuckles, lifting it to his mouth, and planting a gentle kiss.

"I'm not going anywhere," he whispers so only I can hear.

Clicking the bedroom door shut behind me, I stalk over to Ian. "Why'd you let him drink so much?" I slap his arm with the back of my hand.

He rubs his arm and pulls his eyebrows together. *"Let him? Bev, he's a grown man."* Ian points in the direction of the guest bedroom. "A freaking large grown man. Tell me, how was I supposed to stop him from drowning his pain? Hell, I even paid the poor guy's tab. I mean, come on, he just had to leave the woman he loves with a man she loved for most of her life. What'd you expect him to do?"

With a shaking hand, I brush back my wet, knotted hair, and my chin trembles. "I don't know," I say, shaking my head. "I'm just *exhausted.*"

His face softens. "I know, Sis. I know. Do you want me to stay?"

I shake my head. "Gavin's only here a little longer, I need to sort through this mess before he leaves town."

Ian opens his mouth to say something but snaps it shut.

"What?" I ask.

"Nothing . . ." He rubs at the base of his neck. "It's just . . ."

"Tell me."

"It's just . . . you don't have to decide anything right now, B. I mean, Patrick showing up like that, it's all a lot to take in. Give yourself some time. I don't want you to regret anything."

I chew on the inside of my cheek, considering my brother's words.

"Why'd he come, Bev?" Ian's eyes search mine, desperate for me to let him in.

Too exhausted to try and keep my shield up, my shoulders slump forward. "He came to apologize and release himself from the guilt he's been drowning in."

"Does he want to get back together?" His question throws me, and a coldness strikes my core.

"No. He's moving to Puerto Rico with his girlfriend. He's moved on," I explain.

Ian shuffles his feet, unsure what to say next.

"I should go take Gavin some water," I say.

Ian reaches out and stops me. "Wait. Does it bother you that he moved on?"

"Honestly, I don't know what I feel. It's like everything's come crashing down on me within a few days. I know I could never be with him again, not after he broke my heart like that." Although I only just figured that out tonight.

Ian seems satisfied with my response. He nods, then hugs me goodbye.

With Ian gone, I focus on the man at the end of the hall, the one who makes me wish everything could be different. That I could be different. Sucking in a stabilizing breath, I open the door to the guest bedroom one-handed, holding a glass of water in the other.

All the blinds are now open. Gavin's propped up against the headboard, surrounded by pillows, his eyes fixed on the beauty outside.

"Hey," I whisper.

His sleepy blue eyes slide over to me. "Hi."

I hand him the water and then climb onto the middle of the bed, sitting crossed legged. "Drink."

He complies and downs more than half of the glass in a few gulps.

"How you feeling?" I ask, folding my hands in my lap to restrain myself from brushing away the hair that's resting on his forehead.

"Better now that you're here." With his lopsided smile, I know alcohol is still flowing through him.

The growl in my stomach distracts me, and I cover it with my hand. "I'm going to order us food. What are you in the mood for?"

He ignores my question and asks one of his own. "Why are you so far away?" He reaches over and pulls on my leg, his touch igniting little hot tingles to pop off in my belly.

If I open up to love again, I'm opening myself up to possible heartbreak. I would not survive it.

I inch closer to Gavin until my leg rests against his.

"So, Patrick left?" he asks.

I nod, not really wanting to get into this conversation before we eat or before he's sober. "Can we wait to talk about it until after we eat? I'm starving," I say.

Gavin's eyes slide shut. "I'll always wait for you."

After a forty-minute power nap, Gavin strolls out of the guest bedroom and into the kitchen as if he just slept a solid eight hours.

"Are you hungry?" I ask, surveying his wet hair.

He rubs his head. "I took a quick shower. I felt gross. And yes, I'm starving." He lowers himself onto a barstool at my kitchen island.

"I bought you a sandwich." I snag it from the top shelf of the fridge, grabbing chips and water on my way over to him.

"Thank you." He unwraps his food. "Chicken salad?" His eyebrows shoot up in surprise.

I shrug, pushing around a towel on the counter. "Yeah, I wasn't sure what to get you, but I remembered you ate that in your office."

After Gavin eats, I suggest we take a ride to Forest Park.

Surrounded by Western Hemlocks and towering Douglas firs, the birds chirping, we enjoy the last bit of the day before the sun sets.

"Out of everywhere you've taken me, this place is my favorite." Gavin pauses to admire a furry black caterpillar inching up a tree trunk.

We haven't touched the Patrick subject, yet, and I think, like always, he's patiently waiting for me to share. But I gladly stay off the topic, fed up with our time together being tainted by my mistakes.

"I wish we had more time to explore the trails."

Gavin tugs my beanie tighter on my head and then taps his index finger to my nose. "We'll just have to come back."

I watch his mouth as he keeps talking, but nothing processes in my head. Instead, I reach up and run my hands through his hair, then pull him down to me. Our lips collide, and everything except him melts away.

— 44 —

Beverly

Every muscle in my body is squealing as I slip out of my bed and Gavin's arms. Pretending to be asleep for nearly two hours was a grueling task because the damn man wouldn't fall asleep. I blame that stupid nap he took.

Determination can become a perilous trait, especially when used to deceive someone, but I can talk about that with Stan. I'm sure, given my eventful weekend, we'll have enough material to fill months of slots in his appointment book.

Curling up on my unyielding couch with a raggedy blanket from my childhood wrapped around me, my fingers twist in the soft fabric.

Why did you do this? I scold myself.

It's not his fault I almost fell in love with him. It's mine for spurring on his feelings. I say one thing, but do another. Gavin makes all reason vanish. Who I am with him isn't who I've ever been. What will happen when my enthusiasm wears off, when I remember who I am again?

Which will happen, I know it will, the moment he leaves tomorrow. I'll be left with pleasant memories of our time

together, but they'll be tainted with the shame of allowing it to happen.

Even worse, what will become of me if his fervor for me disappears? I'm not strong enough to go through that kind of rejection again.

Sweetheart, open your heart.

The voice sounds so real, and I want her voice in my head to be real, but it can't be. She's dead, and nothing can bring her back.

Fatigue takes over my body as this debate within me continues to rage on. One side of me wants to try and make this work, wants to keep feeling something, anything, even if it means it might lead to heartbreak later on.

The other, more sensible side of me, berates me for permitting those irresponsible thoughts into my head. Arguing that we've done well for ourselves these past three and a half years, and we've managed to keep my dead heart from beating again, escaping any new pain piercing my life. Being alone is safer.

But being with Gavin feels so much better than safe.

Desperate to stop the raging dispute in my head, I bounce up from my pathetic excuse of a couch. For once, I follow Stan's advice to put my thoughts on paper.

Sitting down at my desk, I pull out a pad of paper, two envelopes, one blue and one yellow, and a pen. I start with the easier letter, and it explodes out of me and onto the paper within a matter of minutes. When I reread it, I can't believe those words came from my thoughts. It reads more like a sappy, optimistic teen, who's watched too many romantic movies and still thinks this life ends happily.

The critic who's been in charge since the accident is

ordering me to rip up that bullshit, toss it in a trash can and set flames to it just to be sure it's erased from existence.

She's been around during the dark times, unlike this new bitch who sprouted in my head when I walked into Gavin's office. She doesn't understand yet, life ends in misery. Happy endings are impossible because there's only one way out of this world. Death.

But I follow Stan's instructions and allow the letter to live. I fold it, place it in an envelope, seal it, turn it over and write Reed's name across the front.

The next letter is unbearable, and it takes me minutes to simply scrawl Gavin's name across the top. Since this letter can cause great harm to an extraordinary man, whose heart is wide open and eager to give and receive love, prudence is required in selecting each word.

Three traumatic hours later, with a tear-streaked face, I lick the envelope to the letter that holds the power to hurt the man whom I would love if my life were different, but that will also restore order back into my life.

I hide both letters in the entryway table near my front door, unsure which envelope will make its way into Gavin's luggage.

Blue or yellow?

Knowing I can't climb back into bed with him, I meander into the kitchen, start a pot of coffee at 4:30 in the morning, and wait for my Achilles' heel to wake up.

— 45 —

Gavin

The sound of rain hammering the roof wakes me, and I reach out to Beverly. My hand lands on an empty, cold side of the bed. I scan the room for any signs of her. When I realize she's gone, the disappointment of waking up alone settles in my gut, and I release a heavy sigh.

I don't waste time wallowing, however, because I only have hours left with her before I need to leave for the airport. I hop out of bed and trot downstairs to search for Beverly.

Rounding the corner to the kitchen, I catch a glimpse of her standing outside on the backyard deck. Inching my way to the window, I watch her. She's standing in the rain, gripping the rail of her back deck, her head bowed, and the rain pelting her.

Her hair's drenched and plastered against her back, the pale pink pants and white cotton top she's wearing cling to every inch of her. I can't see her face, but she looks sad, broken almost.

Chills run down my body at the sight of her. Pushing down my fear, I open the door and walk outside. She doesn't seem to

hear me approaching. I wrap my arms around her waist, inhaling the sweet scent of vanilla and Beverly that not even the rain can wash away.

"What are you doing out here?" I ask, nuzzling my nose against her cold neck. She pushes her wet body back against mine, and I hold onto her even tighter.

"I like the rain." Her tone of voice sounds off.

"But it's freezing. You need a jacket, at least. Come on, let's go inside and dry you off."

Beverly turns to face me and a knot forms in my stomach at the sight of her. She has angry, puffy bags under her eyes, and the whites of her eyes are laced with red. It looks like she's been awake and crying all night. But I know that can't be right, because she fell asleep before me.

I clear my throat and do my best to ignore her concerning appearance while I lead her back into her house. Grabbing a dish towel from the kitchen, I place it on her wooded barstool and tell her to sit.

She obeys immediately and folds her hands in her lap, not saying a word. Her disconnected, far-off stare causes a lump to form in my throat. She's mulling something over, and this time I'm terrified to know whatever it is she isn't saying. My windpipe feels like it's being crushed as the ball in my throat constricts tighter and tighter.

"I'll be right back," I say. I sprint upstairs into Beverly's bedroom and to her dresser, ripping open drawers until I find underwear and yellow pajama bottoms with penguins on them, then in her closet I pull down a long sleeve shirt. "This'll do," I mumble to myself.

I rush back downstairs and find Beverly exactly where I left her with a blank stare fixed on the kitchen counter. My

adrenaline spikes at the sight of her, and the desire to take away her pain moves me forward to her side.

"Let's get you out of these." I kiss the nape of her neck.

My hands find the hem of her soaked shirt, and I gently pull upward. The action seems to arouse her from whatever place she's been, and her eyes lift and meet mine.

I kiss her nose and finish pulling off her clothes, careful not to touch her in any sensitive areas.

"Don't do it. Please." The words fall from my mouth, and it's now my voice I don't recognize. I'm not even sure what I'm asking her not to do, but I can feel something has shifted inside of her.

"Gavin…" Her voice cracks, and I know whatever's coming next is going to hurt. "I don't want anyone else to know what happened between us. At least, not yet. I'm not ready." She bites down on her lip.

Oh, thank God.

Gently, I run my fingers down her cheek. "I wouldn't do that to you. I know you're not ready yet. We can wait as long as you need. Just do me a favor."

She offers me a small smile. "What is it?"

"Just try to keep your hands off me when we're working in public in Hawaii," I tease and tap her butt with my hand.

This time I'm rewarded with a real smile.

"That will be a challenge," she says as she reaches up and kisses my cheek. "But that's also something I wanted to talk about."

Okay, so there *is* more. My insides lurch again. Jeez, how does this woman make me so nervous?

"I don't think we should continue this in Hawaii. This time with you has been amazing, and I appreciate your friendship, but

this project is huge for both of our companies, and I think our relationship would be a distraction from completing our job to the best of our abilities."

And there it is.

The swift kick to the gut I knew was coming from the moment I laid eyes on her this morning. At least the hurt on her face matches the pain piercing the deepest parts of my heart.

Stay calm, Gavin.

Don't panic.

She didn't say she wants to end our relationship entirely.

"Are you saying that we shouldn't be together in Hawaii, or that we shouldn't be together at all?" My heart is pounding, the beat almost deafening.

She pulls her hands through her wet hair and lets out a sigh of frustration. "I don't know." She moves away from me and walks to the other side of the kitchen island, beyond my reach. "I'm not good for you. I mean, come on, you're kind, smart, fun, hilarious, and sexy as hell. You're the perfect man, Gavin.

"You deserve to be with a woman who can give you her heart. I was foolish to think we could have a casual relationship, because I'm not blind. I see the way you look at me, and I can tell you already feel too much, more than what I'm ever going to be capable of returning. I don't want to be the one responsible for breaking your heart. And believe me, if I could give my heart to someone, to anyone, it would be you. In another life, I could really love you. But I can't, I just can't." She forces the last bit out, her eyes watering with the tears she's holding back.

My chest burns, my throat closes tight from my anxiety.

Okay, now it's time to panic.

What do I say to change her mind?

I'll take her any way I can have her.

I can't lose her.

I won't lose her.

I refuse to lose her.

She's afraid because she's feeling things she hasn't felt in years, things she promised herself she'd never feel again. I know she's falling in love with me, and I've already fallen for her.

I find the strength to steady my voice, "I'm not asking for your heart, Beverly. I want to take it a day at a time. Honestly, I'm flattered that you're concerned about protecting me, but I'm a big boy, and you don't need to worry about me. I'm okay with casual and just seeing where this takes us."

Wow, that actually sounded convincing.

Beverly shuffles from foot to foot, a restless movement I haven't seen her do. Before she can respond, I kiss her, starting soft and slow. As she relaxes into me, I take it further.

I need to taste her and remind her how good we are together. This kiss feels vital to our survival. She tangles her hands in my hair as I lift her up, and she wraps her legs around my waist.

I carry her into the guest bedroom, where I was supposed to be staying this weekend, and lay her down on the plush bed. I crawl in next to her and whisper in her ear, "You deserve to be happy."

"I want to believe that."

You will. One day, you will, believe me. But my subconscious has doubts . . . is it really true? Will Beverly ever be mine?

— 46 —

Gavin

There isn't any traffic on my way to the airport. Overall, the drive is uneventful. Except for the nagging, sick feeling wedged deep in my gut.

I try to remain confident that my connection with Beverly is too deep for her to toss aside. But the fear that she said goodbye for good when I left this afternoon is burrowing its way into my head.

By the time I check my luggage, crawl through security and make my way to the gate, I'm a ball of anxiety. Each step I take farther away from Beverly makes me feel like I'm walking the plank. Once I plunge forward, going back to the bliss this weekend gifted me will be impossible.

With thirty minutes left to kill before boarding, I spot a bar a couple of gates down.

Perfect.

I stalk my way to the place that will help me forget my worries and hopefully sleep on the plane back to San Diego.

"What can I get for ya?" an attractive blonde, smacking gum, asks from behind the bar.

"Double shot of Jack."

"Coming right up." Blondie bats her fake eyelashes.

While she pours my shot, I check my phone, hoping and praying there's a text from Beverly. There isn't. I fight the urge to be a needy guy who must talk to her after only an hour's separation.

"Here you go, sweetie." She sets the poison in front of me.

"Thanks," I say, less enthused. Anxiety still fires throughout my body.

"Another?" Blondie asks as I set my empty glass back down.

Eh, what the hell. It'll take the edge off. "One more," I respond to the friendly chick behind the counter.

"You flying in or out of town?" Miss Bartender pours more whiskey into my glass.

"Out," I say before I slam back the Jack. "Thank you," I say, setting a fifty on the counter. Then I mope over to the plane that will swoop me hundreds of miles away from the only woman I've ever loved.

Finally, we're up in the air. The whiskey wasn't enough, and I'm still restless. Desperate for a distraction to the swarming doubts in my head, I reach into my carry-on bag to search for my iPad.

Instead of finding my tablet, my fingers connect with paper, and I pull out a soft blue envelope with my name scrawled across the front. My chest and throat tighten, and I instantly know this isn't a good thing.

Ugh. Please not like this, Beverly.

With trembling fingers, I struggle to tear open the envelope. Inhaling to steady myself, I hold the breath for a count of four, then slowly let it seep out of my lungs. Then, I allow my eyes to focus on the paper in front of me.

Gavin,

These are the words I'm too afraid to say face-to-face, and for that I'm sorry.

First, confession time, I know more about you than I should. Between information from Jenny, Aubrey, and even your cousin Trevor, not to mention the internet, my fascination with you started months before we even met.

Then, when you physically walked into my life, or rather I walked into your office, you shined light into my world, which has been bleak for years. This exhilarates and terrifies me. I've truly enjoyed our time together more than I'm capable of articulating in this letter, but I'm going to try anyway.

I need to thank you. Thank you for the comfort you've provided me these past few days, for teaching my heart how to beat, making me forget, and for giving me happiness. Since Patrick left me, I never dreamt it possible to experience passion for life, let alone for another man again.

I did love Patrick, and in a way I still do. He's an amazing person, and he was for the longest time, my very best friend.

But we were young. Back when we were together,

I was more concerned with my running career than being in love. Patrick was okay with that, because he was also busy chasing his dreams. After the accident and my mom's death, Patrick felt like the last good thing I had left of the life I cherished. When I became his painful reminder of his new reality, it destroyed me.

However, I accepted I would spend my future alone, and to my surprise, the revelation brought me a small sense of peace. It seemed fair. More importantly, what I realize now is—it also felt safe.

Falling for you triggered this revelation, because I no longer feel safe or in control. My feelings toward you are so strong, I'm questioning if I've ever really been in love before.

Up until recently, I've been half a woman, living in a hardened shell, avoiding my past and dodging any real emotions. Somehow you were able to see right through my armor and, more than that, you were able to breach it. Your encouragement for me to forgive myself and move on with my life has shaken me to my core.

For so long, I've accepted the sentence life dished out, but you make me want to try.

So, what I'm trying to say is Patrick is my past, and I'd like to try again for something deeper, something more meaningful—with you.

If we do this, I need you to promise me we'll go slow. Have patience with me and please, I beg you, protect both of our hearts.

I'm terrified, but I'd like to try and build a future with you, Gavin. YOU are worth the risk.

– Beverly

Thank you! Thank you!
I have to tell her how I feel, and I can't wait until we land.

I pull my iPad from my bag and hop onto the airline's wifi. When I open my email tab, there's an email that catches my attention with the subject line "Beverly Morgan" from an unknown sender.

The email reads, "You'll never be enough for her."

I discover two attachments. I hover over the first for a moment before clicking on it.

It takes a few moments to download. Once it does, every muscle in my back tenses. I straighten up in my seat, my eyes darting around the plane.

Then, they return to the two images—one from the present, and one from the past. My pulse gallops. I force myself to breathe deeply as I try to calm myself.

Beverly.
Someone poses a threat to her.

About the Author

Ashlynn Cubbison is a goal-oriented, driven woman, who owns and operates four companies with her husband. They have two beautiful sons together, and although her life is chaotic, fun, full of love and never the same each day, somehow she finds room for writing as well.

She hopes to inspire others to find their passion as she has with writing.

Ashlynn lives in Southern California with her husband, two sons, and adorable cat.

Connect with Ashlynn Cubbison at:
WWW.ASHLYNNCUBBISON.COM
Instagram: @ashlynncubbison
Facebook: facebook.com/ashlynncubbison

AVAILABLE FROM ACORN PUBLISHING
WWW.ACORNPUBLISHINGLLC.COM